Daniel Wilson

Reminiscences of Old Edinburgh

Vol. 1

Daniel Wilson

Reminiscences of Old Edinburgh
Vol. 1

ISBN/EAN: 9783337429362

Printed in Europe, USA, Canada, Australia, Japan

Cover: Foto ©Andreas Hilbeck / pixelio.de

More available books at **www.hansebooks.com**

REMINISCENCES

OF

OLD EDINBURGH

By DANIEL WILSON

VOLUME I.

EDINBURGH: DAVID DOUGLAS

1878

TO

David Laing, LL.D.

F.S.A. Scot., Etc.

WHOSE NAME·IS INTIMATELY ASSOCIATED

WITH MUCH THAT IS GREATEST AND BEST IN THE

REMINISCENCES OF OLD EDINBURGH,

THIS LITERARY TRIFLE IS

DEDICATED

IN GRATEFUL MEMORY OF OLD

FRIENDSHIP

CONTENTS OF VOL. I.

CONTENTS.

LIST OF ILLUSTRATIONS TO VOL. I.

[The Vignette is a reduction of a sketch by the late Charles Kirkpatrick
Sharpe. The Views and Tailpieces are Photo-zincographic reproductions of pen-
and-ink sketches by the author.]

CHAPTER I.

Olden Times.

GLIMPSES of olden times have a charm for most of us, and sometimes all the more so if they are not so very old as to lie wholly beyond our own personal sympathies or local associations. Olden times, indeed! what are they, or when were they? The landing of Julius Cæsar is among the oldest of definite events for the British historian, but for Rome it is a recent date, and there are many older things than Rome. Belzoni's mummy "was dead, and buried, and embalmed, ere Romulus or Remus had been suckled." As for us of the New World, anything dating before the landing of Columbus is inconceivably ancient; and yet for England that is the time of the Tudors,—scarcely even medieval. In truth, antiquity is so relative a thing that it becomes doubtful in these modern days of ours if anything is really old. "At Francis Allen's, on the Christmas Eve," the Poet Laureate went to sleep; and before morning there came to him "King Arthur like a modern gentleman of stateliest port." We used to fancy that we were safe at least in pronouncing Father Adam the first of men, and so somewhat respectable in point of antiquity. Not a bit of it. Such old-fashioned notions are quite out of date. There are the Troglodytes, the Palæolithic and Pleistocene Men, the Drift Folk, with probable or possible Pliocene, Miocene, and other older representatives of humanity, compared with whom Father Adam is a very modern gentleman indeed.

As to ourselves, the days and fashions of our grandmothers are quite olden and strange ; and when Scott gave to his *Waverley* its second title of *'Tis Sixty Years Since*, he thereby carried the imaginations of his readers back to a state of society which has already become little less obsolete to the living generation than that of Wamba the Jester and the Holy Clerk of Copmanhurst. The Edinburgh of my youthful remembrance is Scott's "own romantic town ;" that of old High School days before the modern peeler was known, when boys righted their wrongs, and settled their affairs in their own way, without troubling the City Watch. The High School still occupied the ancient site of the Blackfriars' Monastery of King Alexander II.; and a bicker between the Puppies and the Blackguards, *i.e.* the High School boys and the young roughs of the Cowgate, was an ordinary occurrence. The ghost of Major Weir had not wholly deserted " the sanctified bends of the Bow;" nor had Dr. Chalmers yet undertaken to cope with the unexcavated heathenism of the West Port, where Burke and Hare enlisted their services in the advancement of science, and reduced murder to a well-organised trade.

Modern Athens had not even begun her still unfinished Parthenon, much less bethought herself of classic temples wherein to enshrine the memories of her philosophers, when the Calton Hill was my juvenile playground ; though she was fast superseding Auld Reekie. A flavour of the olden time still lingered about the wynds and closes ; and much of the actual material antiquity, in stone and oaken structures, in armorial bearings, carvings, inscriptions, tirling-pins, etc., which has since been swept away, then helped to perpetuate the legends and traditions of the ancient capital of the Stuarts : the city of Dunbar and Douglas, of Mary, Knox, and the good Regent, of Major Weir and Captain Porteous, of Ramsay, Hume, Sharpe, and Scott. It is now upwards of a quarter of a century since I undertook, with pencil and pen, to chronicle such *Memorials of Edinburgh in the Olden Time* as were still recoverable. In those chroniclings, that latest survivor of quaint, obsolete olden times, Charles Kirkpatrick Sharpe, took a special interest. He supplied some curious materials, then turned to account. Still more, he amused himself with more leisurely comment and annotation ; and now that unexpected circumstances have recalled my attention to them, "time, which antiquates antiquities," has added to the flavour of his quaint notes and curious reminiscences, including his own memories of Sir Walter Scott, and his gleanings from those of an elder generation concerning Ramsay, Smollett, Home, Johnson, and less noted celebrities of other days. Those autograph annotations of Scott's friend, his ally in the gathering and manufacture of the *Border Minstrelsy*, the editor of Law and Kirkton, and of much else that is curious and rare, have constituted the nucleus of the following pages. Around this older local associations have shaped themselves into a bit of antiquarian and historical gossip, which may have an interest for some to whom Scotland and its ancient capital retain the charm of olden times.

CHAPTER II.

𝔐𝔬𝔡𝔢𝔯𝔫 𝔄𝔫𝔱𝔦𝔮𝔲𝔢𝔰.

IT is curious to notice, in spite of all the great names and grand associations of Edinburgh, that it is almost as much the city of Scott as the Warwickshire village on the Avon is the shrine of the one great man it has ever known. But it was interesting to note among the reminiscences of Charles Kirkpatrick Sharpe glimpses of the Author of Waverley before he had even begun to be the Great Unknown.

It seems as appropriate that Scott should have been born in an old Edinburgh wynd, among lingering traces of an obsolete medievalism, as that Burns should have first seen the light in a clay-built cottage on the banks of the Doon. The old nook, which would now have such interest for us as his birthplace, vanished long ago ; but happily the house still stands on the west side of George Square (No. 25), with its back windows overlooking the Meadow Walk, where Walter Scott spent under the parental roof those bright young years of which so many pleasant glimpses are preserved.

There the intelligent curious boy grew up under the eye of his good mother. Among his own papers, after death, there was found a piece of verse penned in a boyish hand, and endorsed in that of his mother, "My Walter's first lines."

In that old house all the boy's environments were healthful. His fine genius was allowed to mature without undue stimulus ; and he grew up that strange compound of shrewd, sagacious, worldly common sense, and of romantic longings after a medieval age of his own creating, which wrought for him and for us the heroic tragedy of his life. Here Scott still dwelt, when his true assay-piece as a poet—the spirited rendering of Bürger's weird ballad of *Lenore*,—was produced ; and here it was that, in 1802, immediately after the issue of the first two volumes of *The Minstrelsey of the Scottish Border*, Charles Kirkpatrick Sharpe made his acquaintance. He had known young Scott by sight long before. In one of his notes on my *Memorials*, where reference is made to " that early den " of the young antiquary in his father's house in George Square, Mr. Sharpe writes : "My grandaunt, Mrs. Campbell of Monzie, had the house in George Square that now belongs to Mr. Borthwick. I remember seeing from the window Walter limping home in a cavalry uniform, the most grotesque spectacle that can be conceived. Nobody then cared much about his two German ballads.   This was long before I personally knew him."

Scott, as an Edinburgh citizen and a local lion, was of course familiar to me in early days. I still recall the time and place where my father first pointed him out to me. But it was replete with interest then—and seems still more curious and interesting now,—to glean from the youthful friend of Scott reminiscences of those early days when common sympathies drew them together. It was all the more startling to listen to Mr. Sharpe's comments on his old friend, since it was not in his nature to include a contemporary among the objects of hero-worship; and the cynical humour under which he veiled the promptings of a kindly heart jarred at times on the spirit of veneration with which Scott was already regarded by a younger generation. His feelings towards him were those of a contemporary who had been familiar with him while yet unknown to fame; and even at times were suggestive of a momentary jealousy, as of one who had once contemplated the possibility of competing with him as a rival in the race for fame. He had had a hand in *The Border Minstrelsy*; printed his own choice *Ballad Book* characteristically in an edition of thirty copies in 1823, and inscribed it to Sir Walter Scott; picked up for him, from tradition or otherwise, "The Twa Corbies" and "Lord William;"

furnished the principal materials for the restored version of " The Queen's Marie ;" recovered " Lady Anne " from some obscure and now wholly unknown magazine ; and revised or restored the versions of other and more familiar relics of ballad minstrelsy. Besides all those, he wrote as avowedly modern antiques, " Lord Herries his Complaint," founded on one of the old Hoddam family traditions ; and, from a still older one, commemorated in the historic heraldry of his own crest of the Kirkpatricks' hand with the bloody dagger, " The Murder of Caerlavroc."   Then too, Mr. Sharpe was an old college friend and intimate correspondent of Robert Surtees, Esq., of Mainsforth ; and hinted at doings between him and Scott, since familiar to all readers.

In the year 1807, a letter, professedly written by Sir John Lesley, of the Covenanting Scottish army of 1640, to a loyalist ancestor of the Riddles of Cheeseburn Grange whose fine monument still adorns St. Nicholas' Church, Newcastle, " found its way into a Newcastle newspaper." So says Mr. Surtees in a letter to his friend Mr. C. K. Sharpe, adding, " The original, or what is termed such, but which I suspect to be a waggish imposture, is now in the hands of William Ward Jackson of Normanby, Esq., whose father was once a dealer in corn, hops, etc., and rescued the letter from a parcel of waste paper."   Its humour is of a high order,—in fact, far too good. Nevertheless, Mr. Surtees printed it in his *History of the County Palatine of Durham*, with just a hint that he feared it was not genuine! The whole transaction, with its resuscitation of the old citizen from his tomb in the aisle of St. Nicholas' Church, has a marvellous resemblance to the feats of Chatterton with the Canynges of St. Mary Redcliffe. In the same letter, Mr. Surtees tells his friend, "When *Marmion* is published you'll see, in a note, a very wild Border raid song, or war-whoop, reciting a fray between two Tyndale families, which I procured from recitation. It has a strong dash of coarse humour in it—*e.g.*,

> "' Hoot, hoot, auld Albany's slain outright !
> Whatever come on it,
> I'll lay my best bonnet
> His wife gets a gudeman afore it be night.'"

So wrote Mr. Surtees in July 1807. In the following year *Marmion* issued from the press, duly illustrated with the Border raid song of "The Death of Featherstonhaugh," a valuable gem of antiquity recovered for the author by his friend R. Surtees, Esq., of Mainsforth, from the recitation of an old woman of Alston Moor! Upwards of a quarter of a century later the Rev. James Raine, in a note to one of the Surtees Society volumes, disclosed the secret that this "wild Border raid song" was all a mere figment of his deceased friend's imagination, "originating probably in some whim of ascertaining how far he could identify himself with the stirring times, scenes, and poetical composition, which his fancy delighted to dwell on." It was meant, he surmised, as a mere test of the unbiased verdict of his friend on his own ballad. "The wicked idea of imposing upon Scott one of his most dexterous fabrications," as his brother antiquary, Mr. Raine, infers, entered his head while perusing a genuine will of Albanye Fetherston of Fetherston, dated 1573, in which occur the names of his two sons, the "Nicol and Alick" of the ballad. On the question of Scott's innocent credulity in the acceptance of this fine "antique," Mr. Sharpe only hinted, in general terms, that "Walter knew a hawk from a handsaw!" As to himself, the matter was plain from the beginning; for by the time the ballad appeared in print the fragment forwarded to him as a specimen the year before had expanded into this choice admixture of pathos and sly humour, the genuineness of which it would have been sheer profanity to question :—

> "Hoot, hoot, the auld man's slain outright !
> Lay him now wi' his face down—he's a sorrowful sight.
> Janet, thou donot,
> I'll lay my best bonnet,
> Thou gets a new gudeman afore it be night."

If Surtees did indeed purpose a mere experiment on the acuteness of his friend, the bait took only too well ; and when, too late, repentance came, he did not dare to confess an imposition which Scott would have little thanked any one for unmasking. So there followed by and by " Lord Ewrie," a song with all the requisite antique flavour and minute circumstantial evidence of genuine tradition, for it " was written down by my obliging friend, R. Surtees, Esq., of Mainsforth, from the recitation of Rose Smith of Bishop Middleham, a woman aged upwards of ninety-one, whose husband's father and two brothers were killed in the affair of 1715." Next we have " Bertram's Dirge," a beautiful fragment " taken down by Mr. Surtees from the recitation of Anne Douglas, an old woman who weeded his garden." " It is imperfect, and the words within brackets were inscribed," says Scott, " by my correspondent, to supply such stanzas as the chantress's memory left defective." To those may, with little hesitation, be added, as from the same Surtees mint, " The Fray of Suport, an ancient Border gathering song, from tradition," compiled with the help of four widely differing versions !

The Laird of Mainsforth had found himself, no doubt, in much the same predicament as the Dumfries mason lad, Allan Cunningham, when Cromek made the demand on him for the recovery of the traditional minstrelsy of Nithsdale and Galloway.

Scott had already printed "Johnie of Breadislee, an ancient Nithsdale ballad." Motherwell produced "perhaps a more ancient set" of the same ballad; and no doubt a volume of such gems could be gathered from the old wives on the Nith. The collector was importunate; his humble ally was anxious to gratify him; and so, as genuine antiques were not forthcoming, Allan Cunningham provided for him in due time—"learnt when a boy, from a servant-girl;" "taken from the recitation of a young girl in the Parish of Kirkbean;" "got from Jean Walker, a young girl of Galloway," etc.,—so many fine Jacobite songs and choice ballads, never heard of before, that Cromek was enraptured. "Gad, sir! such a volume!" he exclaimed; and so there did at length appear from the London press, in 1810, the *Remains of Nithsdale and Galloway Song*, with the merest passing allusion in the preface to the unknown mason lad who had played the part of Mr. Surtees to Scott, and found young girls in Galloway with as convenient memories as the old women of Northumberland. Hogg, the Ettrick Shepherd, vowed that he discerned the true authorship from the first. Nevertheless, in his *Jacobite Relics* "The wee, wee German Lairdie" is not only produced as genuine, but it has its variations, "three lines taken from an older collection!" In a footnote to " The Sun rises bright in France "— "a sweet old thing," as Hogg styles it,—he says, " I got some stanzas from Surtees of Mainsforth, but those printed are from Cromek." From Surtees, also, Hogg was supplied with "Lord Derwentwater's Good-night," with an acknowledged stanza of his own to supply "an hiatus at the end of the first twelve lines."

In all this we have a curious commentary on the proofs of authenticity of our historical and romantic songs and ballads; on the value of that conveniently vague and intangible authority styled "tradition;" and on the literary masquerading to which "Hardyknute," "Temora," Rowley's "Ælla," his "Elinoure and Juga," and so many more antique relics, are due. It was a singular confraternity of literary conspirators "deceiving and being deceived:"—Surtees of Mainsforth, young Sharpe of Hoddam, the Dumfriesshire lad Allan Cunningham, the Ettrick Shepherd, and Walter Scott.

Robert Surtees was a gentleman of old family, of refined tastes and sensitive honour. His life was a fine example of scholarly industry and simple kindly benevolence; and he died calmly in the assurance of a well-grounded Christian faith. Yet what are we to make of this systematic manufacture of spurious antiques, palmed off on the Border Minstrel and others, with the most minutely authenticated circumstantial proofs of traditional pedigree? It is a psychological problem for the study of the moralist. Writing to

Mr. Sharpe about a book which he had undertaken to procure for him, he says : " Dear Sharpe, I never was so much concerned in my life before for a Scotch nobleman, as I am for Lord Dundee. To save you a long story, I told you a short one, *Anglicè* A LIE,"—which he accordingly proceeds to correct. The Great Unknown had his own ideas about the legitimate limits of literary mystification, and saving long stories by telling short ones : a process which Mr. C. K. Sharpe did not disguise his belief had been turned to good account in the *Border Minstrelsy*. To this, indeed, he alludes with playful irony in a burlesque essay, quoted in his Memoir, which had gone no farther than this fragmentary scheme : " A specimen of the fourth volume of the *Border Minstrelsy*, shortly to be published. The following ballad was written down from the recitation of a middle-aged woman who resides in a small cottage or hovel near Hoddam (which is spelled in old documents Hoddame) Castle, with no companions to relieve the tedium of solitude but an illegitimate indiscretion of her niece, and a lean tabby cat whose ears have been curtailed to impede her from catching goldfinches and other birds which are wont to render vocal the hedges of Annandale ; etc. etc."

Charles Kirkpatrick Sharpe was himself one of the noted characters of the Edinburgh of his own day ; and not less refined in taste, and sensitive

on all points of honourable bearing, than his old
friend and fellow-student Robert Surtees.   Born
of an ancient Scottish family, and related by col-
lateral descent, not only to some of the oldest
Scottish nobility, but through Lady Marie Stewart,
daughter of Esme, first Duke of Lennox, to the
royal race of the Stuarts: he was a curious
specimen of the high-bred courtesy and old-
fashioned stately reserve which guarded the aris-
tocracy of Edinburgh from undue familiarity in
those good old days when a duchess found genteel
town lodgings up the turnpike stair of the same
wynd in which the plebeian tradesman and the
more humble artizan had their abodes.   Peculiar
in tastes, striking in personal appearance, and with
a curiously-pitched falsetto voice, Mr. Sharpe
would, under any circumstances, have attracted
attention.   But on some particular day, while all
the world was moving along in its wonted way, he
had suddenly paused ; and there he lived on into a
younger generation, with the huge Brutus wig of
light-brown hair, the long blue frock-coat, the silk
stockings and thin dress shoes with large bows of
ribbon, the ample frilled shirt-breast, and plentiful
breadth of linen neckerchief, in strangest antithesis
to the usages of living men.   Nor were his ideas
more modern than his appearance.   His high Cavalier and Jacobite tenets found expression in the
curious annotations with which he enriched Law's

Memorials and Kirkton's *History of the Church of Scotland*, and his antique and grotesque fancies survive for us in his own most curious etchings and drawings. "Charles Kirkpatrick Sharpe," says Scott in his diary, "is a very remarkable man. He has infinite wit, and a great turn for antiquarian lore. His drawings are the most fanciful and droll imaginable—a mixture between Hogarth and some of those foreign masters who painted temptations of St. Anthony and such grotesque subjects. My idea is that Charles Kirkpatrick Sharpe, with his oddities, tastes, satire, and high aristocratic feelings, resembles Horace Walpole." This resemblance was even more strictly true of their mansions ; for his house was not unfitly termed in later years the Scottish Strawberry Hill. It was one of the sights of Edinburgh—if it could only have been seen,—with its antique furniture, paintings, tapestry, and carvings ; its exquisite enamels, bijouterie, bronzes, ivories, old china, old books, and quaint oddities of all sorts: not disposed as in a collection of antiquities ; but scattered about the rooms, or lying in accessible cabinets, as though everything were the most natural complement of time and place.

Mr. Sharpe was also passionately fond of music, and sported at times with its notes, as in this anagram attached to one of his etchings:

i.e. C. sharp. In a letter written in 1812

to " Monk Lewis," he tempts him with a scrap of
verse in his own spectral style, and breaking off
in the middle of a line, he thus banteringly proceeds : " Shall I send you a copy of *Danae*, Mr.
Lewis ? Don't be modest on account of the
trouble, as I never tire of transcribing such pretty
verses ; and in such a solitary, dismal, woebegone
chateau as this, no other task these faded eyes
pursue ; for I see nobody, read little, weep less,
and never draw at all.

" *A propos—*

Shepherds, tell me, tell me, have you seen—

Ha - - - - - ve you se    en De G——

pass this way ? "

The object of his desire was the Count de Gram-
mont, afterwards Duc de Guiche, reputed to have
been the handsomest man of his day, and regarded
with special favour by Mr. Sharpe, as shown in
many early references. Mrs. Cockburn, the poetess,
in one of her letters, so full of incidents of old
Edinburgh society, remarks : " Kelly was at our
Monday's ball, quite melancholy with the death
of ' Bouch,' the celebrated musician." This was
Thomas, sixth Earl of Kelly, a noted character in
the select circles of old Edinburgh ; and related,
through the Erskines of Alva, to Mr. Sharpe.
There was a covert humour, which the modern

reader misses, in the idea of the Earl assuming a melancholy look. In 1836 Mr. Sharpe edited a quarto volume of his noble kinsman's musical compositions, which he limited to sixty copies, and adorned with one of his own spirited etchings representing the Edinburgh Assembly in its bygone glory: as when Goldsmith watched the stately minuet which no Lady Directress invited him to share. "Give my kind love to Charles,"— writes a venerable lady, so entirely of an elder generation as to address him in such style,— "with many thanks for his beautiful book, which brought old times to my mind, when I used to be sometimes in the old Assembly Room, where Mrs. Nicky Murray used to sit in her chair of state at the head of the room as Lady Directress, keeping us all in order, when we had all to dance our minuets before the country dance."

The Lady Directress will come under review again in other company. The Earl of Kelly is ranked by Dr. Burney, in his *General History of Music*, among the most distinguished amateurs of his day. Had not blood, according to the old proverb, been thicker than water, Mr. Sharpe could have narrated some piquant anecdotes of his noble relative. He wrote both ballads and lampoons, by no means devoid of merit. His "Kelso Races," written to the tune of "Logan Water," is a lively satirical description of the beaux and belles assembled òn the occasion, but far too long for singing to any tune ; for it extends to eighteen stanzas. A very brief specimen will suffice to show the nature of its humour. The hero here referred to is Mr. John M'Dowell, a musical friend of the Earl :—

" O' my drunken friend Jock I'll tell you a story O,
  He had of his own a complete oratorio ;
  Three hours after midnight his concert begun,
  When he drank, and he danced, and he had all his fun."

The story which follows amounts to this and little more ; but with its sly allusions to the Elliots of Minto, the Scotts of Gala and Harden, the Kerrs, the Maxwells, and all the other Border families assembled on the occasion, with

" The Great little Percy who came from the Border,
  To keep us poor Scotch a little in order,"

there was, no doubt, more fun in it than is now appreciable. But it was in music that the Earl's chief excellence lay ; though, like his " drunken friend Jock," he was no less famous in Edinburgh circles as a jovial boon companion, given to boisterous mirth and deep play. He led the orchestra in St. Cecilia's Hall, in bag-wig and richly-embroidered suit, with his face rivalling that of Bardolph in its evidences of drinking and jollity. In less formal gatherings he would take for his instrument the Jew's harp, and make it discourse most excellent music. But on state occasions, in

St. Cecilia's Hall, his favourite instrument was the violin.   The Hon. Henry Erskine, when, in his *Musical Instruments, a Fable*, he asserts the pre-eminence of the fiddle, thus associates it with the recognition of the Earl's musical skill :—

> " Twas he that still employed the master's hand,
> Follow'd obsequious by the listening band ;
> Nay, swore that KELLY learnt from him his art
> To rule with magic sounds the human heart."

The concerts in St. Cecilia's Hall, under this noble leader, were of a very select character.   The performers were mostly amateurs like himself ; and inherited this graceful and artistic recreation from elder generations.   In .the first volume of the *Archæologia Scotica*, Mr. William Tytler describes a grand concert performed on St. Cecilia's Day, 1695, with Lord Colvill, Sir John Pringle, and Mr. Seton of Pitmedden, as violinists, and General Middleton with his flute.   Lord Elcho, Sir John Erskine, Sir Alexander Hamilton, and Sir Gilbert Elliot—who first introduced the German flute into Scotland,—are all named among the select amateurs who figured in the orchestra ; along with Mrs. Forbes of Newhall, Mrs. Edgar, and other ladies.   Of the latter, Mr. Tytler adds that he remembered listening to them with rapture in his own younger days ; especially in the genuine performance of Scottish songs, in a style such as only two or three could then equal.

But the elder gatherings in St. Cecilia's Hall had also their humorous interludes to match the musical Earl's performances on the Jew's harp, when General Middleton accompanied his own voice with the key and tongs!

A jest of the comedian Foote is reported in reference to the Earl of Kelly, characteristic of both.   When the latter visited Foote at his country villa, the comedian took him to admire his horticultural arrangements, and as the Earl looked over a terrace-wall at his cucumber beds, he said, with a covert allusion to the beaming face of his visitor, he rejoiced that the cucumbers should have the light of his countenance, for they had not seen the sun that year!   Such a liberty, however, even with the traditions of a noble kinsman, had to be alluded to with caution in the hearing of Mr. Sharpe ; for it was only on rare occasions of unwonted communicativeness that he would condescend to notice a foible relating to any branch of the family pedigree.

The minuets and songs of the Earl of Kelly were dedicated by Mr. Sharpe to his mother very shortly before her death.   The house in Edinburgh which Mrs. Sharpe of Hoddam occupied, and which up to that time had been her son's home, was No. 93 Princes Street.   There he was visited by Walter Scott, Thomas Thomson, and others of his earlier friends and contemporaries ;

and by such men of a younger generation as David Laing, Robert Chambers, Cosmo Innes, and the choicest among the literary antiquaries of his time. There he began the curious collection of old books, pictures, tapestry, and relics of all sorts, which on the death of his mother were transferred for the first time to a house of his own in the vicinity of George Square. From thence he returned ere long to the New Town, and the remainder of his life was passed in No. 28 Drummond Place. One of his etchings representing a lady walking in state under a grand umbrella borne by a female attendant, and receiving the devoirs of a gallant cavalier, while there curls up from beneath her skirts the strange appendage of a crocodile's tail, is believed to have been suggested by an incident in this removal from the Old to the New Town. Jenny, his housekeeper, a trusted abigail, familiar to all privileged visitors in later years, had undertaken to be the bearer of a stuffed crocodile, the safe transport of which was esteemed a matter of special importance. Jenny started accordingly, with the monster wrapped tenderly as a young baby under her cloak, wholly unconscious that its tail dangled from beneath her skirts, to the surprise of all passers-by. It seemed as though some novel variety of scaly mermaid were traversing the streets of Edinburgh in open day, till at length the caudal appendage gave way, and when Jenny reached her destination she was minus her tail ; a terrible catastrophe, over which the lamentation appeared never to be done. For Mr. Sharpe stuck to it from first to last, that no tails suited him so well as his own.   He thus characteristically writes in 1811, of a very intrusive and stupid tail : " O this tiresome comet ! it kills us all. . . . It nightly ruins my temper, for all the people in this mansion have got nothing else of an evening to do but look at it ; so there's a talk about it, too tedious, with every ten minutes a casement cast up, with a current of cold, damp, toothachy air, and a provoking exclamation of ' Dear, how very clear the tail is to-night !   Do come and look at it !' which I never do by any chance.   I see nothing interesting in a comet's tail ; it is the dullest of all possible tails.   I would not give one twinkle of my parrot's for all the comet-tails in the universe."

When I enjoyed free *entré* to the Scottish Strawberry Hill in later years, Mr. Sharpe had made his last move to the north side of Drummond Place.   There a modern dwelling, of most commonplace unpretentious aspect externally, was filled throughout its interior, from attic to cellar, with the oddest and most tempting rarities that antiquary could desire.   A large subterranean apartment had been converted into the receptacle for such bulky relics as would have cumbered hall or parlour ; yet even this in no way resembled an ordinary museum gallery.   Round the walls stood Roman altars from Hoddam and Birrenswark ; sculptured ambries, bosses, and lintels ; carved panels and friezes from the Guise Palace, old St. Giles's, and other historic localities ; a huge Mexican idol : with whatever else was too bulky or incongruous to find a place in the furnished chambers above.

Here the stately recluse welcomed such as he chose to have for visitors, entertaining them with his piquant, caustic reminiscences of elder times, and the illustrations which he produced from odd, out-of-the-way corners, and from unknown or long-forgotten books ; and here those he did not choose to entertain received the most abrupt dismissal consistent with his high-bred courtesy of manners. Here he penned his metrical epistles and verses in various styles ; here he drew felicitously with pencil and crow-quill, etched, coloured, and wrote as it pleased him.   His penmanship was full of character, neat, formal, and withal stately in its peculiar style.   His habit was to enrich with curious marginal notes whatever book specially interested him ; and where an extra margin at the end of a chapter offered a tempting space he indulged at times in a spirited sketch or grotesque caricature.

To the chance comer, and still more to the unwelcome intruder, Mr. Sharpe appeared the

caustic cynic ; but to the favoured visitor admitted
to share the esoteric charms of his family heirlooms, pictures, and miscellaneous articles of vertu,
the running commentary of their owner was charm-
ingly piquant. He dearly loved a bit of scandal,
especially when it had any historical significance,
or was calculated to unmask the pretentious shams
of fashionable society. His *Douglas's Peerage*
was annotated with many a curious memorandum
connected with the celebrities of his own or other
days, such as courtly peerage-writers were little
likely to put on record. He comments thus on a
reference of mine to General Sir John Hope, subsequently fourth Earl of Hopetoun, the friend and
companion of Sir John Moore :—" I cannot remember any *great* Lord Hopetoun. I recollect
one *good* one who had a devil of a drunken wife !"
Again, I find this note to some references to the
titled neighbours of Smollett, when he lodged with
his sister, Mrs. Telfer, of Scotstown, in the Canongate : " Near by, in St. John Street, died the
Countess of Hyndford with the long beard ;
she was exactly the bearded Countess of Don
Quixote." To a notice of the stern old cavalier,
General Dalzell, — who, like Sir Walter Scott's
great-grandfather, " Beardie," allowed his beard
to grow in testimony of his grief at the behead-
ing of Charles I. and the exile of the Stuarts,
—it is added: " His father, or grandfather, was

a gardener.   The late Lady Elizabeth Dalzell
(my dear old friend) told me that the B——
family were descended from a bastard of her
great-grandfather.   She had a portrait of the
General, now in the possession of her nephew,
William Grierson, son of the late Sir Robert
Grierson of Lag."

Reminiscences of this sort were abundant, while
he was no less observant of the assumptions of
spurious gentility.   Woe betide the pretender who
put on airs of birth, or indulged in purse-proud
ostentation.   He drily notes of Sir P——
W——: "An old family?   Well, I suppose so.
We all are.   His grandfather was a cowfeeder."
A wealthy but very vulgar tradesman, who had
attained to the honours of Baron-Bailie of Ports-
burgh, felt so uplifted thereby into a serene aristocratic atmosphere, that he proposed to show his
appreciation of Mr. Sharpe by offering him a foremost place at the grand official entertainment
which celebrated his advent to such civic distinc-
tion.   "Very sorry," was the ambiguous reply,
"but I fear I have no clothes suited to the occasion!"   A tailor named Preston had retired on
the profits of his trade, set up a carriage, and was
rumoured to be in search of the family arms: "O,
nothing easier," said Mr. Sharpe, "a tailor's goose ;
Motto: Press't on!"   A *parvenu* tradesman had
bought some bit of property, sufficient, in Scottish

parlance, to make a cock-laird of him, and so entitle him to dub himself of ——, Esquire. "A goose's grass!" was the summary estimate of the esquire's manor.   In one of his own note-books is a memorandum of "the dead nabob's grave covered with black toad-stools, as I once saw a grave in the Greyfriars' Churchyard."   To pretenders of this class his repulse was given as bluntly as Grandisonian manners rendered possible. Yet rank and title, if at all presuming, had little more guarantee of favour.   He enjoyed nothing better than to ransack his collection of antiquities and works of art for the benefit of an appreciative visitor, especially if some object of research justi-fied the interest manifested in its treasures ; and a rare treat it was to listen to the quaint sallies of wit, and the varied anecdote with which he sea-soned the display.   The whole collections were evidently to him a *memoria technica*, rich with suggestive associations ; and so with a worth of their own to him, which perished with the owner. Transferred as they were, soon after his death, to Messrs. Tait and Nisbet's auction-room, it was hard to believe that the miscellaneous heaps of labelled and catalogued odds and ends bore any relation to the favourite objects of Mr. Sharpe's fastidious care.   His house partook in no degree of the character of a museum ; but was the dwell-ing of a gentleman of refined antiquarian fancies,

retaining the tastes of that elder generation to which
he belonged in spite of all the innovations which
surrounded him. His drawing-room was furnished,
to the minutest ornament .on table or mantle-
piece, according to the peculiar fancy of its owner.
Some of the chairs and cabinets had belonged to
his mother, and been among the heirlooms of
Hoddam Castle. Antique china and choice ma-.
jolica ware mingled with Egyptian and Indian
bronzes. He was particularly curious in musical
instruments. Here stood the long disused spinnet,
such as may be seen engraved in the music for
Allan Ramsay's *Tea-Table Miscellany of* 1724:
near by was a curious old viol de Gamba ; an
oddly-shaped ebony violin, inlaid with silver ; an
ancient lute, with only seven keys ; a still more
ancient Scottish harp ; and, along with sundry
others of different eras, the actual fine-toned old
cremona of his own musical ancestor, the Earl of
Kelly. His bedroom was even more quaintly
antique, hung with tapestry, old paintings, and
armour ; and with a buhl-and-ormolu clock that
had long given up keeping time. Its chairs were
high-backed carved ones, which consorted with
the inlaid cabinets out of which he produced
miniatures, jewels, and endless rarities, fitting in
as though they were part of the current vein of
his discourse. He was curious in matters of
dress ; preserved a complete suit of his own

grandfather, including a waistcoat of gold brocade,
and wondrous amplitude of proportions.   To
young ladies who enjoyed the privilege of his
kindly courtesies, he would produce jewels, point-
lace, high-heeled shoes, and head-dresses, such as
their grandmothers wore ; and illustrate them with
charming anecdotes of the reigning beauties of a
past generation.

It was obvious in all that he said and did that
he had both a will and a taste of his own.   He
bought and collected what pleased himself, without the slightest caring for the opinion of others ;
and his reasons for being pleased often lay far
outside the comprehension of the ordinary dealer
in articles of vertu.   In 1831, a peasant in the
parish of Uig, Isle of Lewis, on looking into a
rude stone-built structure recently exposed by the
waves, was affrighted at the sight of an assembly
of elves or gnomes, and fled in dismay to his
home ; but, urged by the curiosity of his wife, the
superstitious Highlander was induced to return,
and so became the possessor of the famous Lewis
chessmen, subsequently described and illustrated
in the *Archæologia* by Sir Frederick Madden.
They included in all fifty-eight pieces, ingeniously
and elaborately carved from the walrus tooth.
Ultimately the larger number of them were
secured for the British Museum, where they now
are ; but Mr. Sharpe had the first choice of the

whole ; and the eleven pieces selected by him were scarcely those which collectors would have deemed the most covetable.   His own account was that he chose to have those with the most genuine Scotch faces !   It required both tact and caution to attempt to contribute to his treasures. He was sensitively critical, even about his own purchases : with seeming caprice would challenge the genuineness of an object he had paid a good price for ; and invent a pedigree for another that took his fancy.   He had survived those whose goodwill he coveted ; and so lived to please himself.   But it is not therefore to be inferred that he was selfish ; for one of the things that specially pleased him was to gratify others, so long as he was allowed to do it in his own way.   Yet, with the most courteous manners, and with true generosity at times in the favours he conferred, there was something in his mode of receiving, as well as bestowing a kindness, which repelled all undue familiarity.   He could fitly be characterised as one

> " Bless'd with each talent and each art to please,
>   And born to write, converse, and live with ease ;"

but of few men could it less aptly be said, as Pope bitterly wrote of his " Atticus : "—

> " Willing to wound, and yet afraid to strike,
>   Just hint a fault and hesitate dislike ;

> Alike reserved to blame or to commend,
> A timorous foe and a suspicious friend ;
> Dreading e'en fools, by flatterers besieged,
> And so obliging that he ne'er obliged."

That the great master of poetic art in England's Augustan age should rhyme *obliged* with *besieged* seems strange to modern ears. But Charles Kirkpatrick Sharpe had survived into a later age without partaking of any of its novelties ; and when he acknowledged himself "obleeged" it was with the exact pronunciation which Pope has perpetuated in his "Epistle to Dr. Arbuthnot." It struck me curiously,—when, during a visit to Boston in 1863, I enjoyed repeated opportunities of intercourse with the Hon. Josiah Quincy, then in his ninety-second year,—to find the old-world courtesy and stateliness of manners of one who spoke of his interviews with Washington, and his friendship with Benjamin Franklin, accompanied by the same pronunciation of the familiar word. The one perpetuated the usage from times when the Duchesses and Lady Marys of the Cowgate and the High Street Wynds sat in state in the ball-room of the Old Assembly Close ; the other recalled times, also within his own remembrance, when Boston hamlet was still haunted by the Narraganset Indians, and its bay was black with English-taxed tea.

Had Mr. Sharpe not been "born to live with

ease," he possessed all the qualifications for excelling in more than one department of art and letters.   But as the high-born " Horace Walpole " of the northern capital, he shrank with fastidious reserve from exposing himself to the criticism of the vulgar ; and so wrote, etched, collected, and conversed, according to his own whim, in utter indifference to the outer world.   If he printed, it was privately, in editions of twenty, as in *Portraits by an Amateur ;* or of fifty, or, at most, sixty copies, as in his *Surgundo, or the Valiant Christian*, and his musical compositions of the Earl of Kelly. Professed collectors of antiquities he avoided ; the Society of Antiquaries he regarded with contemptuous jealousy, as a rival given to indiscriminate shows of miscellaneous relics, and, at times, to the acquisition of objects on which he had set his heart.   He, himself, resented above all things the remotest approach towards a recognition of himself in the character of " showman " or owner of a private museum.   The slightest hint of such an idea was sufficient to exclude the purposed intruder, no matter what his rank or importance might be ; and as Mr. Sharpe was equally intense in his likings and his dislikes, and made no mystery about either : when he took a prejudice against any one, it was vain for him to covet access either to the mansion or its owner. Jenny thoroughly understood her master's ways ;

and if the intruder, bent on outwitting her, watched, as I on one occasion witnessed, till he saw Mr. Sharpe enter the house, and then, ringing the bell, inquired for him, her cool and persistent assurance that the gentleman she had just admitted was not at home was a repulse not to be misunderstood.

Some of his characteristic comments are in the same vein. In his student-days he writes of Dr. Parr and Queen Caroline: "What a companion for a Princess! I have met him at Oxford—the very worst-bred brute, composed of insolence and tobacco, that I ever saw or heard of." It reads the very counterpart of comments I have heard him utter half a century later; and of others which are pencilled by him on the margins of my own proofs. The *Memorials of Edinburgh in the Olden Time* afforded him abundant opportunity for characteristic annotations. His cavalier and aristocratic leanings were amusingly demonstrative; and his contempt for Knox, Cromwell, the Whigs, and the Covenanters, breaks out on every available occasion. Commenting on the description of the death-bed scene of the Regent, Mary of Guise, in "Knox's loathsome history," quoted on a later page, he characteristically suggests in reference to her daughter, Queen Mary: "You may somewhere remark that Mary's letters to her mother are far from being dutiful, and that very soon after her return to Scotland she annulled her mother's will ;—an ungrateful jade ! In the Privy Seal Register you will find a charge for a green velvet saddle for the Queen Regent's fool ; and again, for yellow satin for my lady the fule's kirtle: for this was a female buffoon. Her daughter, Queen Mary, had a she-fool also, as Mr. Laing tells me. The Regent Murray retained her after her mistress's ruin, for two years, and then sent her back to France : finding, no doubt, among the pack he had in hand that Scotland had fules enough of her own !" Again, commenting on the notice of Queen Mary's reception and entertainment by the citizens of Edinburgh on the 3d of September 1561, when she rode in state through the West Port, " and immediately on her entry a lovely boy descended from a globe, and presented her with the keys of the city and a Bible and psalter, addressing her in congratulatory verses, at which she was seen to smile,"—" probably," Mr. Sharpe adds, " at the bad verses, as she had some taste in poetry, though her own compositions are very poor."

When the queen is described in the *Memorials of Edinburgh* as moved to tears by the vehemence of Knox's exhortations, his comment is : " Mary wept from anger : the sign of a weak woman. She was a bold fool. We have no warrant for believing that Queen Elizabeth ever shed one tear in her long life." Evidently he was not one of the Scotsmen ready to go to the death in cham-

pionship of Mary Stuart.   His biographer refers
to a letter to one who has been studying her
apologists, as "too long and too outspoken" for
quotation.   But when Mr. Sharpe turns from the
queen to "John Knox of stern and pitiless memory,"
he writes with bitterest irony: "He was a man of
great courage, of a haughty and imperious spirit,
and possessed talents which, though neither profound nor brilliant, were admirably adapted to
forward the great aims of his ambition.   He
gloried in extorting tears from a young and disconsolate queen, who was guilty of the heinous
crime of adhering to the religion in which she was
bred ; he instigated the mob to destroy those
beautiful structures erected by Popish devotees or
deluding monks, imagining that God is more properly worshipped in a cow-house than in a cathedral ; and he esteemed the lawless murder of the
Archbishop of St. Andrews so excellent a jest,
that he could not refrain from being facetious on
it even in the history which goes under his name.
He ceased not to arraign with impunity the cor-
ruptions of the Court, the skipping and dancing
and dallying with dames ; while he could wink at,
or overlook the heaviest part of his accusations
in a hater of Popery and the whore of Babylon.
The Regent Morton, by such pretences, managed
to retain his leman Janet Sharp, and his friend
John Knox, at the same time.   Janet did not

meddle with kirk matters, or get drunk with the blood of the saints, and John Knox was content."

There was an amusing indifference to modern opinion in the outspoken sentiments of this antique type of obsolete High Church toryism. He had no wish to indoctrinate you with his opinions, any more than to admit you to a share in his pedigree. He knew they were in conflict with those of the living age. He expected no better from its degenerate sans-cullotism. Some references in the *Memorials* to the associations of the old Parliament Hall of Edinburgh with the meetings of the Covenanting leaders, and "the bold measures which formed the basis of our national liberties," suggest this comment: "Our *slavery* under Cromwell, and the indelible disgrace of having sold our king's blood for a poor sum of money! This the English know, but the *Scotch never will.* In fact, the history of Scotland is, from almost the beginning to the end, a disgrace to human nature. The solution is, that we were always miserably poor, and mean enough to do anything for money!" A reference follows to the still darker scenes even than that of "Scotland's children held captive in her own capital by English jailers," when James, then Duke of York, presided, along with Claverhouse and Dalzell, at the torture of the Covenanters in the same hall ; while the astute lawyer, Sir George Mackenzie, played the part of King's Advocate, and won for himself the popular soubriquet of " bluidy Mackenzie."   " Children indeed ! " is the note of the disgusted commentator ; " Crack-brained fools, anxious to be hanged for what they did not understand !   Scotland is the same still.   The thumbkins were common everywhere, even in coal-pits, then.   Authors now seldom think of the usages of the times they touch on.   Sir G. Mackenzie was no wit, as Dryden calls him.   His *Aretina*, a serious romance, and his poems, prove that ; but he was a clever man, and knew how to put the law in exe-cution against a pack of frantic men and women totally ignorant as to everything but rebellion against kings and the true religion.   His own writings on that head prove it,—but who now reads them ? "   Once more, a reference to General Dal-zell's cruelties provokes this comment : " Sensible men should always consider the notions and man-ners of remote times, and thus make allowance for many horrid things.   I have never found this idea in modern history.   People write as if every-body knew long ago what we know now.   Our great-great-grandfathers were all downright mon-sters.   General Dalzell caused execute a soldier for stealing a pair of pistols out of the magazine. He caused a council of war to condemn another for being found sleeping at the Abbey gate, but the Duke of York obtained his pardon,—equal *justice* to friend and foe."

I had narrated the trial and execution of Richard Rumbold, one of Cromwell's Ironsides, and a daring republican, who was taken at Edinburgh, accused of a share in the Rye House Plot, and suspected of being the actual executioner of Charles I. The latter he denied ; but made no mystery that he was on guard at the scaffold, and craved leave to be excused owning the present king's authority. Fountainhall says he was drawn in a hurdle to the place of execution ; then being hoisted up by a pulley and hanged a while, he was let down, scarce fully dead, his heart pulled out and carried on the point of a bayonet by the hangman, crying, " This is the heart of a bloody traitor and murderer ! " after which it was thrown into a fire. So I ventured to say " he was executed with peculiar barbarity ;" " No !" is Mr. Sharpe's addendum on the margin ; " his head being reserved to grace the West Port of Edinburgh,"—" and I 'll warrant it looked very well there ! " is the finishing comment by this last of the cavaliers.

Again a footnote provokes Mr. Sharpe to a renewal of the defence of the maligned persecutors. Of Claverhouse I had remarked that a sort of compromise seemed to have been tacitly entered into with regard to him. " Dalzell and Mackenzie have been delivered up to unmitigated popular infamy ; while the same censors still speak of *bluidy Clavers* and the *gallant Dundee* as though they had contrived to divorce his evil from his good qualities, in order innocently to indulge their pride in this hero of Scottish song." " *To unmitigated popular infamy*," writes Mr. Sharpe, "by Scotch writers who never read! Sir George Mackenzie was a superior man; Dalzell very well qualified to deal with the idiots who pestered this country; and for Claverhouse, he was one of the few Scotchmen we can boast of. I don't know what is meant by Scottish song. Pitcairn wrote his epitaph in Latin, and Dryden translated it." Mr. Sharpe would have liked nothing better than to have been reminded of " The Bonnets of Bonny Dundee," first produced by Scott in " The Doom of Devorgoil." He knew very well that this was referred to, and had it only been by an older or nameless bard nothing could better have expressed his sentiments; but Scott was a contemporary of his own, and it was not to be tolerated that his songs were to be thrust into an equality with what constituted the national minstrelsy.

A passage in one of Mr. Sharpe's letters to his sister Grace, wife of the rector of Sutton Coldfield, quoted in his *Memoir*, is an apt complement to the sentiments embodied in the above notes of the uncompromising old cavalier. He thus writes to her, giving the soundest advice he can think of in reference to her son's education: "I am glad, my dear, that you have the comfort of a son with a sound literary taste—I judge from his admiration of Spenser. Tell him, with my love, to stick principally to Homer (the *Iliad* I mean), and Virgil's *Æneid*, for the truest beauties of poetry. I think Milton's *Paradise Lost* a heap of blasphemy and obscenity, with certainly numberless poetical beauties. Milton was a Whig, and in my mind an Atheist. I am persuaded his poem was composed to apologise for the Devil, who certainly was the first Whig on record!" The reader will see that Scott had no need to go beyond his own circle for a study of the good old cavalier knight, Sir Henry Lee, who figures in *Woodstock* as the critic of "the blasphemous and bloody-minded author of the *Defensio Populi Anglicani*, John Milton!" The later critic proceeds in his letter to commend Cowley as charming ; Dryden as, for wit, reason, and wonderful strength of expression, deserving to be studied day and night ; but of Pope he says : "I have lost my relish for him in my old age. His poetry runs all in couplets, and it is now to me like a weak cup of tea, with too much sugar in it." Then comes his estimate of his great contemporary : "As to Sir Walter's harmless *romances*—not harmless, however, as to bad English,—they contain *nothing :* pictures of manners that never were, are, or will be ; besides ten thousand blunders as to chronology, costume, etc. etc., which must mislead the million who admire such captivating comfits. The works of Fielding prepare young people for the sad scenes they must bear a part in——the dreary masquerade of knaves and fools. And Richardson's *Clarissa* is a perfect compendium of worldly wisdom, though its greatest beauties can never be relished by a very young person."

Such were the sentiments and opinions expressed in all seriousness, and retained unchanged by a gentleman of refined wit and high-bred courtesy, until the close of life, which was prolonged into the second half of this nineteenth century. Allusion has already been made to his insight into the pedigree of some of the " antiques " enshrined in the *Border Minstrelsy*. On this, and on the general manufactory and patchwork of ballads and antiquities of all sorts, Mr. Sharpe dilated in his most caustic vein. Abbotsford was little better than an old curiosity shop : " a farrago and omnium gatherum of miscellaneous trash. Scott got hold of some things worth having——as what collector does not ? But all geese became swans as soon as they alighted on his midden heap !" Referring to an account, furnished by Mr. Joseph Train, relative to the traditional manufacture of Mons Meg by the MacLellans of Galloway, which I had quoted along with Sir Walter's attestation that the pedigree of the monster cannon was " traced so clearly as henceforth to set all conjecture aside : "——Mr. Sharpe thus notes on the margin, in his most incisive style : " I do not believe one word of this. Mr. Train's authorities I well know. But never mind. Sir Walter knew nothing of antiquity, though he pretended to understand it. In that he was the greatest dunce and liar I ever knew ! " Browning has entitled one of his poems, " How it strikes a contemporary ; " and here we have the very thing,—we who have since seen, and shared in, the world's celebration of a Scott Centenary ! A reference to Scott seemed always to awaken the combative element in his nature ; and a quotation from his novels was sure to provoke a retort. In describing the famous Kirk-of-Field, and the site of its provost's house, blown into the air with gunpowder by Bothwell and his accomplices, I had chanced to quote the exclamation of Roland Græme as he first comes in sight of the ruins, " Blessed Lady, what goodly house is that which is lying all in ruins so close to the city ? Have they been playing at the Abbot of Unreason here, and ended the gambol by burning the church ? " " It is now the fashion," writes Mr. Sharpe, in comment on this : " it is now the fashion to quote *fiction* in historical works, which appears to me very much to lower their dignity,—but I own that I have many old exploded notions."

The specimens thus selected, partly from Mr.

Sharpe's copious marginal comments on a work of
my own, not only illustrate his cynical vein of
humour, and the caustic asides which he indulged
in on the margins of his "Douglas;" and expanded
with more becoming dignity in his curious notes
to " Kirkton" and " Law ;" but they give some idea
of the running comments with which his conversation was spiced.   But a very false impression
would be formed of Charles Kirkpatrick Sharpe,
if he were only to be shown as the cynical censor,
slashing in trenchant fashion at whatever opinions,
prejudices, or shams, excited his antagonism.   He,
at least, was thoroughly truthful ; and lived and
spoke with supremest indifference as to the opinion
of others.   But underneath his caustic satire and
obsolete one-sidedness there lurked a genuine
kindliness and innate courtesy of heart.   I recall
with gratitude many favours, and much wise
counsel given in the half-bantering fashion in
which he was wont to disguise his genuine good
will.   As a rule artists and antiquaries seemed to
excite his peculiar aversion.   He missed, probably,
the deference of an elder generation, when the
very commingling of all ranks in the wynds and
alleys of old Edinburgh demanded a stricter recognition of social distinctions in other ways ; and no
doubt he resented the idea of being in any sense
akin, as a draughtsman and etcher, to the professional " daubers who painted for bread ! "   Wilkie

he remembered as a raw, shy lad ; " the very picture of Fifish stupidity, had it not been for his eyes. They redeemed the face. There was no pretence about him. He spoke with a slow drawl, and seemed to do everything with an effort, like a tame goose getting out of the way of a butcher's cart. But we never had his equal, till he took to travelling and painting what he did not understand." Commenting on a reference to Melville's account of Knox's vehemence in preaching, where he says, " he was like to ding the pulpit in blads, and flee out of it," Mr. Sharpe says, " Wilkie made an excellent picture of this—the principal female figure filched from Sir J. Reynolds' portrait of Poll Kennedy, the noted *dame mercenaire*. See the print of her."

Charles Kirkpatrick Sharpe's own teacher of drawing when a youth was Martin, the fashionable portrait-painter of his day. Dr. Carlyle of Inveresk tells, in 1769, of his good fortune in securing the companionship of Martin on a journey he and Mrs. Carlyle made to Bath and London. " This," he says, " made it very pleasant, as Martin was a man of uncommon talents for conversation." His company seems to have been courted by the wits and men of letters of old Edinburgh one hundred years ago. He instituted a club in that famous haunt of the muses, Johnnie Dowie's Tavern, Libberton's Wynd,—the *Mermaid Tavern* of Edinburgh in the days of Fergusson and Burns,—and quaintly named it, after the host, "Doway College." Thither Kames, Monboddo, Dr. Carlyle, and others of less note, came to join ; and there also his more celebrated pupil, Sir Henry Raeburn, often accompanied him in his younger days. But, as became the courtly portrait-painter of those old aristocratic times, Martin no doubt knew how to comport himself according to the society he was in. Like Counsellor Pleydell, when disposed for "his altitudes," he could play high jinks with the choicest of the company that graduated at Doway College ; but it is another phase of character that Mr. Sharpe notes of him. "Martin lived in a flat in St. James's Square, south side. He was very kind to me when I was a boy. Dr. Bryce was his heir, I think. Martin was a modest man,—not like ·our daubers now, who are all as saucy as the devil."

As to the antiquaries, there was a conflict of feelings in the instinctive antipathy with which Mr. Sharpe regarded a professed collector. The mere curiosity-hunter and accumulator of old nick-nackets was his aversion. It seemed a deliberate parodying of his own doings. Of a fussy investigator of the Dryasdust type he said : "Why can't the goose be a goose, and not din his neighbours, cackling over his mare's nests like a clocking hen ?" I sometimes thought there was a resentment of himself; a little sense of misused talent; a consciousness of powers run to waste, like the ploughshare rusting in the weedy furrow. He had made what should have been a pastime, the business of life. Sir Walter Scott notes in his Diary, in a despondent mood: "I do not know anything which relieves the mind so much from the sullens as trifling discussions about antiquarian *old womanries*. It is like knitting a stocking—diverting the mind without occupying it." But then there is " the gentle dilettanti crew," the sole occupation of whose minds, the very business of their lives, is found in such old womanries; and they were to Mr. Sharpe a standing reflection on himself.   Then, too, he had tastes and ways of his own which they interfered with ; and, like Scott himself, he saw thoroughly the weaknesses of " Jonathan Oldbuck ;" and, as he looked into that mirror, he was well content to laugh, though he resented anybody else doing so.   He had a lynx-eye for the spurious antiques of rival collectors ; delighted to quote his father's dictum, that " that lumber, called Knox's pulpit, in the museum of the Scottish antiquaries, was the old crier's box in the outer Parliament House ; and if ever anybody preached from it, it must have been some sanctified drummer of Old Noll !"   He never wearied of telling how Sir Walter had been hoaxed with the rubbish of Wardour Street ; and stuffed

the nooks and cranies of Abbotsford with " shams
and lies."   But when he chose to have a legend
about some relic of his own, or to identify a
portrait which it pleased him to accept as the
realisation of some noted or favourite character, he
went about it in a thoroughgoing fashion, not to
be trifled with.   He had a portrait of a lank,
gawky youth, which he dubbed " Darnley," and
gravely produced as such to the very historian of
Mary's times ; though it is doubtful if it had any
known pedigree till it took its place on his walls.
Surtees, writing to him in 1808, hints at one of
his appropriations of this sort.   He has just received a copy of Mr. Sharpe's *Metrical Legends
and other Poems*, then fresh from the press ; and is
especially charmed with " An Epistle from the
Shade of the Countess of Roxburgh to the Hon.
. Miss Drummond of Perth," whose picture had only
recently been rescued from the garret at Drummond Castle.   One of Mr. Sharpe's drawings
represents the old countess descending from her
picture frame at the dead of the night, as she has
threatened, and drawing the bed-curtain of Lady
Willoughby d'Eresby—the Miss Jean Drummond
of the epistle.   The shade of the Countess tells—

> " I still was little past my prime,
> So, catching by the pig-tail Time,
> That caused these dire alarms,
> I to a famous limner went,

> Who might on canvas represent
> My sweet but fleeting charms.

> " The picture fairly hung on high,
> Each day, each hour, with gloating eye,
> I at its beauty gazed ;
> Thinking, ' When great-grandnieces see
> This most enchanting map of me,
> They will be so amazed ! ' "

But instead of this, when the time comes round for the admiring wonder of great-grandnieces, Lady Jean is in the garret : a thing which even the gentlest of ancient ghosts could not submit to ; and so her shade thus proceeds :—

> " But, sweet, beware ! you've heard it said,
> That wrongs can rouse the peaceful dead ;
> And nurses hold for certain,
> That ghosts in shrouds of dismal hue,
> Bedecked with poison-dropping yew,
> Can draw the midnight curtain."

It is apropos to this legend that Surtees writes : " The Countess of Roxburgh is most delightfully arch, and reminds me so much of Charles Sharpe that I long for Christ Church again, notwithstanding the appendages of Carey and a long list of frightful spectres that rise in review at the name. It strongly reminds me of a lady whom you were determined to call Lady Southesk, and who, perhaps, now enjoys the title." It required the intimacy of an old college friend to hint even so much, and was a liberty that no man who valued his society would have ventured upon in later days. Certainly when I knew him the visitor who challenged the genuineness of portrait or relic in other than the tenderest and most guarded fashion, would have probably learned from Jenny on his next visit that her master was not at home! Among those who still remember the unique drawing-room in Drummond Place, one of its noticeable features will be recalled as the figure of a strange bronze monstrosity, now in the British Museum, which formed the centre piece of an octagon table bestrewed with kindred oddities and rarities. It was a ewer, fashioned in shape of a tail-less lion, surmounted by a nondescript monster, half greyhound half fish, apparently designed as a handle for the vessel, while a stopcock projected from the breast in form of a stag's head. A similar lion-ewer was dug up, some twenty years ago, on the Pollock estate. Examples of like kind are familiar to antiquaries, and are specially noted among the later Scandinavian relics, not only of Norway and Denmark, but of Iceland. One especially, the principal figure of which is also a lion, was preserved for ages in the church of Vatnsfjord in Iceland, and has since been transferred to the Christiansborg Palace at Copenhagen. A shield on the lion's chest is graven with the inscription in runic characters: "This lion is gifted to God, and to St. Olaf of Vatnsfjord, by Thorvalti and Thordisa."

I made a drawing of the Sharpe lion-ewer, which was ere long reproduced among the woodcuts in the first edition of my *Prehistoric Annals of Scotland*, with its description, which I believed had been correctly noted at the time, as a relic "in the collection of C. K. Sharpe, Esq., found by him among a hoard of long-forgotten family heirlooms, in a vault of his paternal mansion of Hoddam Castle, Dumfriesshire." The "Annals" were not long published when a well-known Edinburgh dealer in articles of vertu put into my hands Mr. Sharpe's receipt for the relic. Shortly after this, a Newcastle antiquary published an account of "a mediæval water-ewer of metal, in the form of a mailed horseman, discovered near Hexham, Northumberland;" and without naming his authority, referred to "a singular variety recently found in an old vault at Hoddam, in Scotland." The word *recently* was an awkward addition; for Mr. Sharpe's connection with his paternal mansion had long been severed, with intermediate litigations of a sufficiently notable kind. The publication seemed to furnish an opportunity for reverting to the reputed Hoddam find, so I ventured to show him the notice. It chanced that the Hexham bronze was described as, like the Hoddam lion, tail-less. Mr. Sharpe returned me the paper with this macaronic comment:—

" Recently found, an English Ass,
Fashioned out of Newcastle brass,
    Noisy with swagger and bray ;
Clad in a recently pilfered hide
Swinging somebody's tale awide ;
    Not the lion's tail, for that was away,
    Recently, so they say,
Whereby hangs a tail,
    A twice-told tale,
      A tedious tale,
A tale told by an idiot, signifying nothing.

" Another lean unwashed artificer cuts off his tail,
    And like a rat without a tail,
      Mars a curious tale in telling it.
But little wist he Maggie's mettle—
Ae spring brought off her master hale,
But left behint her ain metal tail !
    A recent tail, a brazen tale,
      A tithe-pig's tail,
For Don Peter hath borne him beyond the promise
    of his age ;
Doing, in the figure of an ass, the feats of a lion.

He hath indeed better bettered expectation than you must expect of me to tell you how." So I rested contented with the tale " as 'twas told to me." When my " Annals " reached a second edition Charles Kirkpatrick Sharpe was himself among the family heirlooms in the old vault at Hoddam.

There were curious stories told of the rebuffs of would-be visitors at Drummond Place ; and of the irrevocable doom of expulsion pronounced on offenders, alike for obtrusive lack of faith and intrusive proffers of service : in all which artists, somehow, bore an undue share. One of them chanced to be his rival at an auction, and to carry off a picture which he had coveted. Learning of Mr. Sharpe's disappointment, he volunteered shortly afterwards to let him have it, as he set no store by it ; though, as he added, he had touched it up and greatly improved it. "Oh! you've improved it, have you?" was the caustic answer of the touchy dilettante; "then you had better keep it!" But when Mr. Sharpe did make an exception from among the distasteful fraternity of artists or antiquaries, it was done in a thorough-going.fashion. "You will always find me at home," and the *open sesame* might even be extended to a judiciously selected friend.

Alike in art and vertu, Mr. Sharpe was a law unto himself. His collected drawings and etch-ings, in the memorial volume published by Messrs. Blackwood, are unique, and suggestive of a power as original as that of Hogarth himself. But they are the mere fruits of occasional pastime, or of friendly goodwill ; and cannot but be regarded as mortifying glimpses of a genius which, under other circumstances, might have enriched the world with choice treasures of art. But art and authorship had alike been degraded into mere professional and money-making crafts, and so Mr. Sharpe would as soon have turned tailor or cobbler. "Artists !" he writes, in one of his own note-books, "everybody artists now—fiddlers, players, John Ketch, Esq., artist." In the same humour he comments on a chance reference of mine to "Mr. Alexander Kincaid, bookseller, a gentleman of a highly cultivated mind," who died in 1777, while Lord Provost of Edinburgh : "Everybody is a *gentleman* now in print ; I shall soon see the hangman termed a gentleman and artist."

But tender traits must not be overlooked. His memories of old friends were frequently recalled with an evidence of feeling all the more striking from the cynical disguise in which it was apt to be veiled. He had many curious reminiscences, derived from his mother, of her intercourse with Smollett, Johnson, and Burns ; of her recollections of Home, and his " Douglas ;" of Ramsay the painter, and other notabilities of last century, several of which are noted hereafter. But he rarely named his mother without some betrayal of affectionate tenderness, as if the best of life for this lonely recluse had gone down to the grave with her. One or two characteristic marginal notes will help to unveil this phase of his character ; and illustrate, at the same time, the abrupt intercalation of genial thought amid his most satirical comments. A reference to the death of a once distinguished judge, Lord Stonefield, in the Mint Close, led to this note : " Lord Stonefield died in George Square, in the house which once belonged to my great-grand-mother—whom I well knew and loved!—Lady Alva, grandmother of the late Dowager Countess of Sutherland. The Lady Glenorchy, of pious memory, Lady Alva's second daughter, died there ; her memoirs, written by a rascal, are replete with lies." He adds, "I well remember Lord Stone-field's widow residing in said house, her own property."

Referring to the fine octagonal crypt attached to the ancient church at Restalrig, he writes : " I believe it belongs to Lord Bute ; and that applica-tion was made to him to allow Miss Hay, whom I well knew,—daughter of Hay of Restalrig, Prince Charles's forfeited secretary,—to be buried in the vault. This was refused ; and she lies outside the door. May the earth lie light on her ! old lady, kind and venerable." An account is given in the *Memorials* of the trial of Katharine, the daughter of Sir Thomas Nairn, Bart., of Dunsi-nane, for poisoning her husband. She and her paramour, an officer in the army, were condemned ; but she escaped from the Tolbooth. This Mr. Sharpe supplements with curious reminiscences de-rived from his mother. His aunt, Lady Murray of Clermont, lodged then near the Bowhead ; and she and his mother went to Goodtrees at the time of the execution, to escape the horror of even hearing the noise attendant on such a tragedy. " But,"

THE COLLEGIATE CHURCH, RESTALRIG.

VOL I.

P. 54.

he adds : "a near relation of mine, a lady I paid five shillings for a window in the Grassmarket, to see this execution.   But she always chose to *forget* it when I talked about it, and I wish to forget it too, as she was the kindest of relations to me."

There was, in truth, an innate kindliness, and a manifest pleasure in gratifying, obliging, and aiding, in which the high-bred gentleness of his nature triumphed over the sarcastic habit of the amiable cynic.   Had a Scottish Chatterton dealt with him, as did the boy of Bristol with Horace Walpole, and sought to beguile him with such wondrous " antiques " as those of " the good priest Rowley," I can fancy the kindly irony with which he would have unmasked the disguise ; and then, with true-hearted liberality and wise monition, have put him on the road to honest fame and fortune.   He is laid with his forefathers in the family vault at Hoddam.   May the earth lie light on him ; and no plebeian dust invade the last resting-place of a thorough gentleman of the antique type, now wholly gone with other good things of the olden time !

CHAPTER III.

The Wynd of the Blessed Virgin Mary-in-the-Field.

THE literary and the personal associations of
Charles Kirkpatrick Sharpe alike recall those of
the Minstrel of the Scottish Border. They were
both representatives of ancient Border races ; and
both claim a place among the " bright particular
stars" of Auld Reekie and of Modern Athens.
But with Scott the associations connected with old
Edinburgh are manifold as its own historic memories. Knox and Queen Mary, the good Regent,
the Bothwells, the Setons, the Hamiltons, and the
Douglases, the Castle and its Regalia, the City
Cross, the Flodden Wall, the Heart of Midlothian,
Holyrood, St. Anthony's Well, and all else, are his
own. He was born in one of its old closes, lived
in a stately old-fashioned square, was educated in
its old College, did daily duty in its old Parliament
House, and in all ways made of it his "own
romantic town." We may expect, therefore, to
come across his path in many a nook of its bygone places and times ; and need not specially

appropriate a chapter to him, as might fitly enough be done to lesser men.   But one among the vanished nooks of old Edinburgh, which had its peculiar associations not only with Walter Scott, but with other literary and local celebrities, was THE WYND OF THE BLESSED VIRGIN MARY-IN-THE-FIELD ; and a little antiquarian rummaging among its dusty parchments may be excusable in view of all that has pertained to it and its surroundings, from its days of ancient sanctity and later gentility, on to the event in which its glories culminated ; and so permitted it forthwith to hasten to decay and extinction as a purlieu of Auld Reekie which had well and worthily done its appointed task.

The stately quadrangle of the University of Edinburgh occupies the site of the Collegiate Church of St. Mary-in-the-Fields, or as it was familiarly called, the Kirk of Field.   It included prebendal buildings of some extent, in addition to the Provost's lodging.   David Vocat, one of its prebendaries, and a liberal benefactor, was master of the Grammar School of Edinburgh ; and Richard Bothwell, its second Provost, was also one of the Lords Spiritual of the College of Justice, and Director of Chancery to James V.   He was, moreover, the uncle of Adam Bothwell, Bishop of Orkney, whose family history has yet to be noted. The old Provost of the Kirk of Field appears to have been a scholarly man, of good repute, a graduate of the University of Paris, and one whom the king delighted to honour.   He died at a venerable age in the Provost's lodging in 1547.   Twenty years thereafter, on the night of the 9th of February 1566-7, Queen Mary, for the last time, parted from Lord Darnley, in that same Provost's lodging. Before dawn it was heaved into a pile of ruins by the gunpowder which the Earl of Bothwell and his accomplices had fired ; and the mangled corpse of Lord Darnley showed that the chief impediment had been removed to the fatal marriage of Bothwell and Mary Stuart.

Kirk and provostry having gone to ruin, the city of Edinburgh acquired the site, with sundry prebendal and other buildings, including the old lodging of the Duke of Chatelherault ; and there started the college on which King James afterwards conferred the royal name.   In Gordon's view, of 1647, the antique quadrangles of the " Academia " are seen, bounded on the south by the town wall ; and with the " Vicus Academiæ " leading from the Cowgate to its main entrance on the north.   This is what is styled in the descriptive inventories of the seventeenth century " The Wynd of the Blessed Virgin Mary-in-the-Field, now the College Wynd." In our younger days a portion of the old college buildings continued to occupy the site of the present quadrangle, and of the library which now forms its south side.   Down to a more recent period the neighbouring thoroughfare retained some of the mediæval features which best comported with its earlier title, and mingled the half-obliterated traces of the Wynd of the Blessed Virgin Mary-in-the-Field with the later associations of the College Wynd.   For here, if tradition is to be trusted, was the fitting lodging of Oliver Goldsmith, in his brief term of student life in Edinburgh.   Here too, beyond question, was the residence of the great chemist, Dr. Joseph Black, "the illustrious Nestor of the chemical revolution," as he is aptly termed by Lavoisier ; and the intimate personal friend of Adam Smith, Hume, Carlyle, Home, and Hutton. But all other such associations assume a secondary place, alongside of the fact that here, in a little court at the head of the Wynd, and close by the residence of Dr. Black, Sir Walter Scott, as he himself records, was born on the 15th of August 1771.

It is in full accord with such associations that we now recall the lingering traces of elder times which preserved even to our own day somewhat of the flavour of romance about the curious old thoroughfare which had been the birthplace of "the Ariosto of the North."   It was, indeed, a place where sober matter-of-fact realities came into collision with the mediæval elements which still struggled for perpetuity in an age for which they had grown obsolete, even as romance and reality conflicted in the life of Scott himself. A quadrangular building about the middle of the wynd, on its east side, enclosing its little court, in the Parisian fashion common enough in the Edinburgh of Queen Mary's days, had obviously been the lodging of one of the prebendaries, or chaplains, of the neighbouring Kirk-of-Field ; but its transformation into a brewer's granary had wrought woful havoc with its antique features. When Arnot wrote in 1779 the archway into the quadrangle stood intact, and over it the fine sculptured lintel, inscribed in decorated characters of the fifteenth century with the salutation of the Virgin:—

AVE . MARIA . GRATIA . PLENA . DOMINUS . TECUM .

Above this stood a beautiful Gothic niche, vacant of course,—like that of our Lady of St. Giles, which lingered at the Lady Steps, by the Luckenbooths, till the restorers of 1829 swept it away,—but which the inscription leaves no room to doubt had been filled of old with the statue of our Lady, the Blessed Virgin of the Kirk-of-Field. In later days the old archway had been enlarged for modern uses ; and though both niche and inscription remained, they were displaced from their original site, and the old lintel stood over a window on the upper floor. But the windows, in spite of modern mutilations, retained the mouldings, and some of the stone mullions and transoms

of the old casements ; and to complete the ecclesiastical aspect of the brewer's granary, a boldly cut
shield under the crow-stepped gable bore the
sacred monogram, **iḥs.** The interior preserved
some faded traces of later secular honours.   In the
troublous times of Charles I. it had been the town
mansion of the Douglases,—if we mistake not, of
William Douglas, Viscount Drumlanrig, created
Earl of Queensberry by the King during his
memorable visit to Scotland in. 1633 ;—and accordingly the fine stuccoed ceiling had as the
most prominent of its devices the crowned heart
and other heraldic cognisances of the Douglases.

Had Sir Walter Scott noted the significance of
those features of his old neighbourhood, he would
doubtless have had our Lady's niche and salutation
transported to Abbotsford, and so given them a
longer lease of life.   In our younger days the old
wynd had still its overhanging timber fronts and
picturesque turret-stairs, breaking the line of the
narrow thoroughfare, to the delight of the artist
and the disgust of the civic reformer, who has, at
last, carried the day, and swept wynd and all out
of existence.   Inscribed lintel, croqueted niche,
sculptured shields, shot windows, the antique oaken
transom and shutters of the sixteenth century, and
even the old-fashioned risp, or tirling-pin, so frequently alluded to in Scottish song, all lingered
appropriately about the old wynd to the last.

The tradition which professes to identify the College Wynd as the locality where one famous Edinburgh student, Oliver Goldsmith, lodged, has now been so long accepted that it would be hypercritical to reject such an association with the unheeded Oliver of 1752. It is, in truth, surprising to find that so much information is still recoverable about those student days. We know that the young Irishman found at once a hearty welcome among the undergraduates of Edinburgh, as an inimitable narrator of humorous stories and singer of Irish songs. We know, too, that he frequented the Assemblies, then and long afterwards held in the Old Assembly Close; for we have his own account of the solemnities of an Edinburgh ball a century and a quarter ago. He is writing to his friend, Bob Bryanton, at Balymahon; and thus the light-hearted young Irishman describes the astonishment with which, on entering "the dancing-hall, he sees one end of the room taken up with the ladies, who sit dismally in a group by themselves. At the other end stand their pensive partners that are to be; but no more intercourse between the sexes than there is between two countries at war. The ladies, indeed, may ogle, and the gentlemen sigh, but an embargo is laid on any closer commerce. At length, to interrupt hostilities, the Lady-Directress pitches on a gentleman and lady to walk a minuet, which they perform with a formality that approaches to despondence. After five or six couples have thus walked the gauntlet, all stand up to country dances, each gentleman furnished with a partner from the aforesaid Lady-Directress; so they dance much and say nothing, and thus concluded the Assembly. I told a Scotch gentleman that such profound silence resembled the ancient procession of the Roman matrons in honour of Ceres; and the Scotch gentleman told me—and faith, I believe he was right,—that I was a very great pedant for my pains." It is certain, at any rate, that the Edinburgh ladies regarded their Assemblies as no such lugubrious gatherings. The vivacious Mrs. Cockburn found them delightful, even in old age; and, not very much later, writes of one of them: "Never was so handsome an Assembly. There were seven sets—one all quality ladies, and all handsome; one called the maiden set, for they admitted no married women; one called the heartsome set, which was led off by Lady Christian Erskine," and included, amongst others, a rollicking, eccentric Scotch lass, Miss Soph Johnston, who shod a horse better than a farrier, played the fiddle, and in other ways encroached on the rights of the rougher sex; but yet had such attractive elements, commingled with those of the Amazon, as made her a favourite with Mrs. Cockburn and her sister-poet the Lady Anne Barnard. Had

Goldsmith got into "the heartsome set," instead of being merely ogled by them outside of the charmed circle, he would have made a less dismal report of an Edinburgh Assembly.   But, in truth, the chances of young Oliver being pitched upon by the Lady-Directress as partner either in minuet or country dance were remote enough ; for, as he says, somewhat plaintively, to his friend Bob, "an ugly and a poor man is society for himself ; and such society the world lets me enjoy in great abundance."

Pre-eminent among those fair potentates to whom the direction of the old Edinburgh Assemblies was confided, or who by effective *coup d'etat* had assumed the supremacy over its sacred mysteries, was one whom Goldsmith must have eyed with envious reproach.   The Honourable Miss Nicholas Murray,—or, as she was more generally designated in the days of her supremacy, with a becoming respect for her years, Mrs. Nicky Murray,—was a daughter of Viscount Stormont, and a sister of the illustrious Lord Mansfield. She was a Lady-Paramount of the true old feudal type ; and as such took little pains to disguise her favour for the exiled Stuarts, her dislike to the "unkos" who had "sat doun in our gude lord's chair ; " and her belief that, somehow or other, "the king shall enjoy his own again ! "   Her right to such obsolete loyalty rested on grounds even more indisputable than those of Lady Margaret Bellenden, at whose poor Tower of Tillietudlem, his sacred Majesty Charles II. condescended to partake of a disjune on his way to the rout of Worcester : for when Prince Charles Edward reached Perth, on his way to the more fatal field of Culloden, he had been hospitably welcomed by Lord Stormont ; and it was whispered that Miss Nicky made the Prince's bed with her own fair hands.   Certainly no Stuart could wield a sceptre with more arbitrary authority.   She is described as more polite than good-natured.   But that was inevitable, since she must needs disappoint many, and offend still more.   She must have had no little tact and affability to maintain her rule among rival beauties, ambitious chaperones, and touchy spinsters of high degree, jealous for their own rights, or those of some country niece or other debutante whose cause they had espoused ; not to speak of gallants, lovers, and ambitious claimants for *entrè* into the exclusive circles of the little world over which she ruled.   Sir Alexander Boswell thus describes the scene in his poem of " Edinburgh :"—

" Then the Assembly Close received the fair ;
   Order and elegance presided there ;
   Each gay Right Honourable had her place,
   To walk a minuet with becoming grace.
   No racing to the dance, with rival hurry ;
   Such was thy sway, O famed Miss Nicky Murray !

> Each lady's fan a chosen Damon bore,
> With care selected many a day before;
> For unprovided with a favourite beau,
> The nymph, chagrined, the ball must needs forego;
> But, previous matters to her taste arranged,
> Certes, the constant couple never changed;
> Through a long night to watch fair Delia's will,
> The same dull swain was at her elbow still."

It requires no great stretch of fancy to picture poor Oliver Goldsmith, (to whom, by his own confession, "fortune had denied circumstances, and nature a person to look charming in the eyes of the fair world,") in very disconsolate mood, eyeing such dull, yet fortunate swains, from his place among the sighing aspirants of the outer circle. But to do justice to the picture, we have to realise him for ourselves in his new-bought finery of sky-blue satin and Geneva velvet, with his silver-laced three-cocked hat below his arm,—so far as dress could make him, a match for the best of them.

On the death of this model Lady-Directress no one was found fit to fill her place. The Edinburgh Assemblies lost their charm, and survivors sighed in vain for a return to "the old Saturnian reign." When they were at length transferred from the cozy quarters in the Old Assembly Close to the modern rooms in George Street, the ancient despotic monarchy was put into commission; and a female oligarchy has since controlled, with such diplomacy as it could muster, the select assemblies over which Miss Nicky Murray ruled of old with supreme and undisputed will. The Honourable Miss Murray resided, with her sister Margaret, in the third flat of a large tenement styled " Smith's Land," at the head of Bailie Fyfe's Close. It had its sculptured armorial bearings of the Trotters, with the date 1612 ; and of the Parleys, with the inscription in Roman characters: BE . PASIENT . IN . THE . LORD ; and on a panel over a window in the rear: THE . LORD . KNOWETH . WHO . ARE . HIS.   It was an aristocratic quarter of the town in that eighteenth century, as such denizens proved.   From the evidence in the famous Douglas cause, it appears that Lady Jane Douglas resided in the adjoining building,—styled " Bishop's Land," from its olden owner and occupant, John Spottiswood, Archbishop of St. Andrews,—and was visited there by Lord Prestongrange, then Lord Advocate, in the very year of Goldsmith's experiences of Edinburgh student life.

As " an ugly and a poor man," according to Oliver's own description of himself, and a youthful stranger in the northern capital, the wonder rather is that he obtained the *entré* to the Assembly, than that he had there to sigh in vain, in its outer circle, like a forlorn Peri at the gate of Paradise.   But, as a graduate of Trinity College, Dublin, he had recommendations of another kind, and as such he obtained an engagement, apparently as tutor, in

the Duke of Hamilton's family. But the odd
figure and droll simplicity which marred his reception even in the more appreciative London
circles of later days, cut short this chance of ekeing out his slender finances. His visits to Holyrood Palace—of which the Duke was hereditary
keeper,—did not last out three weeks. " It seems,"
he writes to his uncle Contarine, " they like me
more as a jester than as a companion, so I dis-
dained so servile an employment." To jest, with
all the vivacity of unrestrained mirth, among his
fellow-students in the College Wynd, or the Old
Fleshmarket Close, was one thing ; but to be the
butt of ducal jesters was more than even their pay
could reconcile him to. So Bob Bryanton has
this somewhat overdrawn sketch furnished to him :
" Some days ago I walked into my Lord Kilcoubry's—don't be surprised, my lord is but a
glover,—when the Duchess of Hamilton (that
fair who sacrificed her beauty to ambition, and
her inward peace to a title and gilt equipage,)
passed by in her chariot ; her battered husband, or
more properly the guardian of her charms, sat by
her side." Straightway, as he describes, envy, in
the shape of three ladies present, began challenging
her form, complexion, and all else. " ' And let me
tell you,' adds the third lady, whose mouth was
puckered up to the size of an issue, 'that the Duchess
has fine lips, but she wants a mouth.' At this

every lady drew up her mouth as if going to pronounce the letter P."

As to my Lord Kilcoubry, the Edinburgh glover, there is more of truth in the incident than might be anticipated in Oliver's epistolary romancings to Bob Bryanton. The MacLellans of Kirkcudbright possessed lands in Galloway so early as the reign of Alexander II., and they figure repeatedly in the wild romance of Scottish story. The Earl of Douglas, who lorded it over Scotland in the minority of James II., in high-handed fashion, reunited the dominions of his house by divorcing his wife, and marrying his cousin, the Fair Maid of Galloway, while still a child. A few years later he seized MacLellan, the tutor of Bomby, as a contumacious vassal ; and on his uncle, Sir Patrick Grey, arriving at Thrieve Castle with a royal warrant for his release, the knight was hospitably entertained, while a whisper to an attendant provided for the *dénoûment*. When at length a pause in the feasting permitted the reading of the royal warrant, the Douglas was prompt to comply with its requirements ; only, unfortunately, the offending vassal was, by this time, headless. When Oliver Goldsmith came to Edinburgh as a student, the old lords of Kirkcudbright had once more fallen on evil days ; their misplaced devotion to the cause of the Stuarts had wrought their ruin ; and the sixth Baron Kirkcudbright, — whom Goldsmith styles " my Lord Kilcoubry,"—was so reduced in circumstances that he did actually support his family by keeping a glover's shop. He was wont to ply his trade in the lobby of the Assembly Room, while the Honourable Miss Nicky Murray presided within : attending there to supply gloves to the gentlemen who were fortunate enough to be furnished by her ladyship with partners. But when an election of peers occurred my lord asserted his claim to vote ; and at the ball with which it was the custom to close that important ceremonial the noble glover laid aside his apron and took his full place among his brother peers. The title was legally confirmed to his son John, who became seventh Lord Kirkcudbright in 1773 ; and exactly a century thereafter, in the month of July 1873, the noble line came to an end by the death of the Honourable Camden MacLellan, daughter and only child of the last Lord Kirkcudbright.

We have Goldsmith's authority for the fact that some of his slender funds went to sustain the honours of the noble glover, who, like Davy Ramsay, the king's horologer in *The Fortunes of Nigel*, came of an auld and honoured stock ; and, as King Jamie says, " Ye see that a man of right gentle blood may, for a season, lay by his gentry, and yet ken whaur to find it when he has occasion for it. It would be as unseemly for a packman, or pedlar, to be blazing his genealogy in the face of those to whom he sells a bawbee's worth of ribbon, as it would be for him to have a beaver on his head and a rapier by his side when the pack was on his shoulders. Na, na—he hings his sword on the cleek, lays his beaver on the shelf, puts his pedigree in his pocket, and gangs as doucely and cannily about his peddling craft as if his blood was nae better than ditch-water ; but let our pedlar be transformed, as I have ken'd it happen mair than ance : out he pulls his pedigree, on he buckles his sword, gives his beaver a brush, and cocks it in the face of all creation." Scott had " my Lord Kilcoubry" in his eye when he thus pictured the packman of right gentle blood. But Oliver's dealings were of a less satisfactory kind when brought, as already noted, into more intimate relations with Scottish nobility—not under a cloud. The Duke of Hamilton had engaged the services of the young Irishman, with an eye, no doubt, to his reputed scholarship as an alumnus of Trinity College, Dublin ; and whether in view of his anticipated visits to the ducal lodging at Holyrood Palace, or to those other temptations which kept him fluttering, like a moth round a candle, in the outer circle of Assembly Close, a curious old document has come to light to help us to rehabilitate Oliver Goldsmith " in his habit as he lived," and call him up before the eye of fancy radiant with the tailorings of those student days.   An old ledger was being torn up for waste paper, when happily one of its leaves attracted the observant eye of Mr. David Laing ; and there he found, preserved for us, the veritable account, in that year, 1753, between "Mr. Oliver Goldsmith, Student," and some Edinburgh Mr. Filby, of tailoring celebrity, whose name is now unhappily beyond recall.   Goldsmith had a passion for fine clothes ; missed his chance of ordination, according to Dr. Strean, by presenting himself before the Bishop of Elphin in scarlet breeches ; and lives in the fancy of all readers arrayed in Mr. Filby's famous bloom-coloured coat.   The fragment of the Edinburgh tailor's ledger, thus snatched from oblivion, illustrates the marvellous change since that olden time when a medical student's wardrobe shone resplendent in " sky-blew sattin, rich black Genoa velvett, fine sky-blew shalloon, and best superfine high clarett-coloured cloth ; " to which has to be added, " a s'fine small hatt," laced with eight shillings' worth of " silver hatt-lace," duly charged by its weight of precious metal, in ounces and drachms.   The first bill was paid " by cash in full " before the end of the year.   The second is carried over " to folio 424," which unfortunately has vanished, along with the superfine high claret-coloured suit, which there stands charged against Oliver for £3 : 6 : 6, like later unsettled accounts of the poet's wardrobe.

Mr. Foster tells us, in his life of Goldsmith, that "he was really fond of chemistry, and was remembered favourably by the celebrated Black." It would be pleasant to think of the great chemist, himself rigidly decorous, and never known to have uttered a joke in his life, taking kindly notice of the dressy, witty, amusingly simple young Irishman, quartered in some humble attic down the same old wynd in which the Professor had his abode. But facts and dates alike contradict the biographer, wherever he may have got his information. In his first letter to his uncle Contarine, Oliver sketches the professors : Munro, by his eloquence and varied learning, attracting students "from all parts of the world, even from Russia ;" Alston speaking much, "but little to the purpose ;" and "Plume,"—a misprint no doubt, for Dr. Andrew Plummer,—whom Goldsmith names as the professor of chemistry, adding, he "understands his business well, but delivers himself so ill that he is little regarded."   Dr. Cullen succeeded him in the chair ; and Dr. Black did not enter on his duties, or take up his quarters in the College Wynd of Edinburgh, till thirteen years after Goldsmith had bidden it a final adieu.   By that time, indeed, his *Traveller* had reached its fourth edition, and Newberry was bringing out his *Vicar of Wakefield ;* and so possibly Goldsmith did win the favour of Dr. Black, though neither as student nor chemist. But we are free to fancy young Goldsmith finding his way down a narrow turnpike in the College Wynd, and so round the corner into the Cowgate, on his road to the Old Assembly Close, where, by some means or other, he had got the *entré* to the assemblies. There he flaunted, as gay as the best of them, in sky-blue satin and Geneva velvet; and played off the brogue of Balymahonc, against what he ironically describes to his friend Bob, as the broad Scotch which "so becomes a pretty mouth. For instance, teach one of your young ladies to pronounce, 'Whoar wull I gong?' with a becoming wideness of mouth, and, I'll lay my life, they will wound every hearer!"

The college in Oliver Goldsmith's student days was the old group of quadrangles that had grown up, and displaced the collegiate buildings of the Kirk of Field. Facing the head of the College Wynd, in Maitland's time, was a lofty bell-tower which must have been one of the latest features of the old building, as it does not appear in Gordon's view of 1647. Maitland speaks of three courts, of which the upper quadrangle to the south was occupied on two sides by the schools and professors' houses, and on the others by the College Hall, the principal's lodging, and the quarters of some of the graduates in residence. From this a flight of steps led down to the Western Court, a picturesque quadrangle, with turret-stairs, crow-

stepped gables, and dormer windows.   Here were
the students' quarters.   The remaining quadrangle
to the east contained the library and convocation
hall ; and portions of its buildings long survived
the demolition of other parts of the old college.
The South Bridge had as yet no existence ; the
College Gardens, on the site of the ancient Church
of the Blessed Virgin, and the house of its provost,
—so memorable for the event in which its own ruin
was involved,—stretched eastward over what is
now one of the main avenues of the city ; and the
gateway at the head of College Wynd, opening
through the great bell-tower, seemed to our forefathers a very dignified and fitting approach to their
principal seat of learning.   Dr. Robert Chambers
describes it as having a richly ornamented architrave, and an inscription.

It was in the same old halls that Walter Scott
completed his education, in so far as that was due
to masters and professors ; and directly opposite
the great gateway stood the house which would
possess such a world-wide interest now as the
place of his birth.   The elder Scott, the lineal
descendant of Auld Watt of Harden and Mary
Scott, the Flower of Yarrow, was a gentleman by
birth and professional status ; but he lived, according to the simple habits of our fathers, in a flat of
the old tenement, approached by a turnpike stair
within a little court at the head of the College

Wynd.   The different floors opening on the common stair were tenanted by equally reputable neighbours.   The father of Sir Alexander Keith of Ravelston, Knight Marischal of Scotland, occupied the first floor ; in another corner of the little court resided Mr. Alexander Murray, the future solicitor-general, who ultimately took his seat on the bench as Lord Henderland ; professors of the University made choice of the same eligible neighbourhood ; and advocates and writers to the signet shared with them its flats and common stairs. Nor did there seem any incongruity in the close vicinity of plebeian neighbours.   The age had not yet grown so picked that the toe of the peasant, or of the artizan, though it did come so near the heel of the courtier, was felt to " gall his kibe."

Here, within the compass of the wynd memorable as Scott's own birthplace, were representatives of nearly every order and rank of society, sufficient to have furnished him with characters to people a whole series of Waverley Novels.   It was therefore in no degree more out of the ordinary experiences of old Edinburgh, that " Daft Bailie Duff," one of the noted city characters of that eighteenth century, should dwell at the foot of the same wynd, than that the poor student, Oliver Goldsmith, should have found in this aristocratic alley an attic suited to his slender purse.   The titular Bailie, a poor widow's idiot boy who in those olden times had

VOL. I.   WYND OF THE BLESSED VIRGIN MARY-IN-THE-FIELD.   P. 76.

come to be regarded as one of the indispensable accompaniments of an Edinburgh funeral, survives for us still among the minor characters introduced into " Guy Mannering," attendant on the funeral pomp in honour of the well-preserved maiden fame of Mrs. Margaret Bertram of Singleside. But though unobjectionable in the quality of good neighbourhood, the wynd shared with other courts and closes of old Edinburgh the inevitable results of such a congregation of human dwellings " piled deep and massy, close and high."

In Sir Walter Scott's desk, after his death, among other sacred family relics, was found a little packet containing six locks of hair, and inscribed with the same number of names of little brothers and sisters, including another Walter, all of whom died in infancy. A suspicion at length dawned on the minds of the older folk that the little court in College Wynd was unfavourable to the health of the family ; and the poet was still in his infancy when his father removed to the house in George Square, where he grew up to manhood under the genial influences of a kindly home. Early memories, however, carried him back to neither of those homes of his infancy ; but to Sandyknowe and Smailholm Tower, where " the young ewe-milkers delighted to carry him about on their backs among the crags ; and he proved very gleg at the uptake, and soon kenned every sheep and lamb by head mark." It was the true school for the Border Minstrel ; and when in later days he penned the romantic epic of "Marmion," the memories of childhood revived, and he wrote :—

> " Thus, while I ape the measure wild
>   Of tales that charm'd me yet a child,
>   Rude though they be, still with the chime
>   Return the thoughts of early time ;
>   And feelings, roused in life's first day,
>   Glow in the line, and prompt the lay.
>   Then rise those crags, that mountain tower,
>   Which charm'd my fancy's wakening hour."

The time came, while Scott was yet a youth, when Edinburgh could no longer endure to be "within its steepy limits pent." It had crowded dwellings into every unoccupied nook, piled storey on storey, reaching skyward from its lofty crags, and striven to be contented with the ancient limits of its Flodden wall ; but all would not do. It burst the old swaddling bands at length, and by the time that Scott recalled "life's first days" at Sandyknowe, he could also reflect on the changes his own romantic town had undergone :—

> " Dun-Edin ! O, how altered now,
>   Where, safe amid thy mountain court
>   Thou sit'st, like Empress at her sport,
>   And liberal, unconfined, and free,
>   Flinging thy white arms to the sea."

In the revolutionary process which wrought such changes, the Cowgate was spanned by the South Bridge, a broad thoroughfare was carried from ridge to ridge over the ancient street, and through the gardens of the college. The academic cloisters, thrown open to the light of day, seemed no longer suited for the requirements of the University, already famous in the reputation of illustrious teachers and students. So a new edifice was planned ; and the enlarged area, and widened thoroughfares thereby rendered necessary, led to a wholesale demolition of the buildings occupying the site, and in some cases including remains of the collegiate buildings of the Church of the Blessed Virgin Mary-in-the-fields. Among the rest, the little court at the head of the College Wynd, so interesting as the birthplace of the great novelist and poet, was involved in the common destruction ; and more recent civic improvements have swept away the wynd itself, with all its ancient and modern associations.

CHAPTER IV.

Palaces of the Cowgate.

'Twas within a mile of Edinburgh town,
   In the rosy time of the year ;
Sweet flowers bloom'd, and the grass was down,
   And each shepherd woo'd his dear ;
     Bonnie Jockey, blithe and gay,
     Kiss'd sweet Jenny, making hay,
The lassie blushed, and frowning cried, Na, na, it wunna do;
I canna, canna, wunna, wunna, mauna buckle to.

So sang some old minstrel prior to 1698, when this fine song made its appearance in print. The English muse will have the credit of the dainty pastoral by hook or by crook ; for the words are assigned to Tom D'Urfey, the author of a multitude of dramas in all respects unlike the simple naturalness of this song ; and as for the air, it is claimed for James Hook, a brother of the witty Theodore. Probably enough the songster fashioned the lyric on some old Scottish model : though later recensions of Scottish songs have originated most frequently in the effort to divorce their airs from association with words partaking of characteristics only too noticeable in the witty productions of D'Urfey's licentious muse.

It would be a curious pastoral ramble if we were now to go in search of that Arcadian hay-field within a mile of Edinburgh town, where the shepherd swain wooed and won his Jenny while the sweet flowers bloomed and the grass was down, till

> " She gave him her hand and a kiss beside,
> And vow'd she'd for ever be true."

A mile from the Edinburgh of 1698, however we may now measure it, will surely land us in paved streets or crowded alleys in the old new town which stretches its " white arms to the sea," or the newer new town that reaches southward to Blackford Hill ; or in the still later western city, now fairly across the Water of Leith, on its way to Corstorphine and Royston, and busy with its own St. Mary's Cathedral.

But in this respect the old lovers' hayfield has many a fellow. One might be tempted to think of the Molendinar Burn in those olden times when St. Kentigern had his pool, and bed, and chair, all clustered together in the romantic glen, where now an unsavoury Glasgow sewer represents the stream which replenished the saint's bath when he bore his part in the romantic legend of the lost ring, and saved a noble lady from the wrath of her jealous lord. The fish which then played the counterpart to that of St. Peter with the tribute money, still bears aloft the trophy in the quaint device of the city arms.   But a fitter analogy may be traced where Kelvin Water finds its way to the Clyde.   The winding streamlet is not wholly effaced, but the lover of the muses' haunts asks in vain for the Old Pear Tree Well, or the wooded dingle, where, when western grandsires were in their teens, the fond youths could say to our blooming grandames :

> " O Kelvin's banks are fair, bonnie lassie, O,
>   When in summer we are there, bonnie lassie, O ;
>   There the May-pink's crimson plume
>   Throws a soft but sweet perfume
>   Round the yellow banks o' broom, bonnie lassie, O."

Through the mazes of Kelvin Grove, according to another version of the old song, the western lads and lasses were wont to rove, but now they would vainly search for the wooded glen

> " Where the rose in all its pride
>   Decks the hollow dingle side,
>   And the midnight fairies glide."

Yet, not wholly to desecrate this haunt of lovers and fairies, the encroaching crescents, streets, and squares, have spared a patch of the grove as a parterre, in which the city nursery-maid may follow Jenny's time-honoured example, if only some bonny Jockie will give her the chance.

But, in spite of all the accumulated labours of
' Time's effacing fingers," the eye can readily
detect the lines of the ancient watercourses buried
under Edinburgh thoroughfares.   The gardens
below the castle rock occupy the bed of the Nor'
Loch, replenished of old from St. Margaret's Well,
which still gushes forth from its renovated fountain
amid the ruins of the Well-house Tower.   After
filling the shallow bed of the loch, the streamlet
found its way, between the Calton and the Canongate ridges, past Holyrood and Restalrig, to the
sea.   But before it reached the shrine of St.
Triduana at Restalrig, it was joined by another
stream which flowed from the south side of the
castle rock, along the low ground now occupied
by the Grassmarket, and so through the Cowgate
valley, to the skirts of Salisbury Crags, where
it was covered over only in recent years.   Pleasant
glimpses of the old fountain-head survive to connect it with historic times.   In deeds of the reigns
of James IV. and V. the ground to the west of
the Grassmarket is called " The Barras," or tilting-
ground, whereon, in the tournaments of the earlier
reign, knights from every court of Europe displayed
their skill with horse and lance.   So late as 1571,
in the challenge between Alexander Stewart,
younger of Garlies, and Sir William Kirkcaldy of
Grange, the place of combat proposed is " upon
the ground, the Baresse, bewest the West Port of

Edinburgh, the place accustomed and of old appointed for triele of suche maters." When Maitland wrote, nearly two centuries later, he could still speak of the King's Stables on the southern side of the way leading to St. Cuthbert's, and of the chapel dedicated to the Virgin Mary, "the vestigia of which" the old topographer speaks of as still to be seen at the foot of the Chapel Wynd ; and then he adds : "Adjoining to this chapel, on the west, is a pleasant green of the length of about fifty yards.   This is the remaining part of the royal tilting or tournament ground, whereon feats of arms or martial exercises were performed by the brave, whose exploits might be seen by royal and other spectators from the walls and windows of the castle."   The pleasant green underwent one more transformation, as indicated in its designation in an old title transferred with it to the City Improvement Commissioners of 1829, wherein it is styled "the Yards of Orchard-field, commonly called Livingstone's Yards, comprehending therein that piece of ground called the Barras."   But ere that final transfer was effected, the pleasant green and orchard of other days had reached their lowest stage of degradation.   Mean dwellings, tan-pits, and slaughter-houses contended for mastery ; and among the wretched hovels of the West Port, Burke and his accomplice Hare had made their den, and degraded an illustrious name into the epithet for novel and hideous crimes.

Dank and foul ran the stream which still in our younger days coursed its way along the open gutters of the Cowgate, and at times converted the narrow thoroughfare into a torrent. In olden times it had been a pellucid stream, with the green bank above, along the slope of which, in the fifteenth century, the first city wall extended from the line of the Nether Bow to the fortified gate at the angle of the old West Bow, where Free St. John's Church now stands. Traces of diverse kinds preserved the memory of the ancient town wall. A tall land erected in Liberton's Wynd in 1728, and occupied a little later by that famed patron of Bacchus and Apollo, Johnnie Dowie, was defined in its title-deeds as bounded on the south " by the auld king's wall." In clearing away the old Parliament stairs, on the site of the Lower St. Giles's Churchyard, in 1844, a considerable fragment of this substantial bit of masonry was laid bare ; and thus its line is indicated half-way up the ridge, on the summit of which stood St. Giles's Church, the Tolbooth, and the City Cross.

With such guides, fancy readily fills up the outline, and pictures the lower slope as a grassy bank, broken with jutting rock, and variegated with gorse and broom. Below this, in the marshy hollow in which the Cowgate rears its antique tenements, the streamlet wended its way eastward to St. Margaret's Loch, and so, by the low grounds of Restalrig and the Figgate Whins, to the sea.

The rivulet and the leafy grove seem fittest haunts for muse and lover. Yet, when the old ravines and grassy slopes were converted into the streets and alleys both of the Old and New Town, they became more than ever the haunts of the muses ; and still retain many a pleasant association with them, in spite of changes wrought by time and civic reformers. Around old Holyrood linger memories of Dunbar and Lindsay, and associations with more than one poet-king : with Mary Stuart, poor Rizzio, and the not less hapless Chastelar, grandnephew of Bayard, a high-bred courtly gallant who chaunted his own verses to his lute— "usant dune poesie fort douce et gentile en cavalier."

Dunbar's strong attachment to the old Scottish metropolis may be noted in more than one of his poems. But Gawin Douglas, in his official relations as provost of St. Giles's, is *par excellence* the Edinburgh laureate :—

> "More pleased that, in a barbarous age,
> He gave rude Scotland Virgil's page,
> Than that beneath his rule he held
> The bishopric of fair Dunkeld ;"

or that, as a younger son of Archibald, fifth Earl of Angus, he ranked with the noblest of the land.

He had already written his fine allegory of "The Palace of Honour," before he was advanced by James IV. to the provostship of St. Giles; and it was not till after his royal patron had fallen on Flodden Hill that the poet obtained precarious tenure of his northern bishopric. It is, therefore, as the provost of the collegiate church of St. Giles, and a residenter in the adjacent parsonage-house, that we may most fitly recall the scholarly translator of Virgil into the Scottish vernacular.

The *Ecclesia parochialis Beati Ægidii* of earlier charters, appears for the first time in 1475, as "the College Kirk of St. Geill of Edinburgh." The chapter consisted of a provost, curate, sixteen prebendaries, a minister of the choir, four choristers, a sacristan, and a beadle; and, doubtless, before the close of the century, the Prebend's Close formed a fitting enclosure to St. Giles's cemetery. Beneath this, on a terrace of the sloping bank behind the later Parliament House, was the Lower Churchyard, with its Chapel of the Holy Rood, in which a famous contemporary of the poet and provost of St. Giles, Walter Chepman, the introducer of the printing-press into Scotland, founded and endowed a chaplainry at the altar of Jesus Crucified, specially requiring the chaplain to offer up continually prayers for the souls of the king, the nobles, and others slain at Flodden.

The vicissitudes of the ancient cemetery of St.

Giles have been great and manifold.   The Chapel
of the Holy Rood, in the Nether Kirkyard, appears
to have been demolished in 1559, and in 1562 its
materials were appropriated to the building of the
New Tolbooth, or Heart of Midlothian.   In 1566
Queen Mary granted the gardens of the Greyfriars'
Monastery to the citizens, to be used as a cemetery;
but thirty years later, when a memorable tumult
occurred, in 1596, "the noblemen, barons, and
gentlemen, with the ministrie," are described by
Calderwood as convened in the kirkyard of St.
Giles, where "some hote speeches passt betwixt
the Erle of Mar and the Lord Lindesay, so that
they could not be pacified for a long tyme."   But
before that occurred the quiet Prebendal Close had
been occupied by the Tolbooth ; and the readiest
access to the New Parliament House was through
the open churchyard.   Instead of some old Prebendary or Sacristan quietly pacing among its grassy
hillocks, it had become the lounge of grooms and
lackeys in attendance on their masters during the sit-
tings of Parliament, or of quarrelsome litigants, and
the usual retainers of the law, when the College of
Justice was in Session.   Nothing but the lingering
attachment to an old family burial-place could any
longer induce a preference for St. Giles's cemetery
over the quiet garden of the Greyfriars' Monastery ;
and so that last resting-place of Edinburgh's forefathers from the time when the little hamlet

clustered round the mother church of St. Giles, the
spot in which the dust of John Knox had been
reverently laid to rest, was forsaken, neglected,
and at length paved over and converted into the
Parliament Close.

When Gordon of Rothiemay executed his bird's-
eye view of Edinburgh, in 1647, the ground was
still open on the east side of the Parliament House ;
and the green slope behind, where the Laigh Kirkyard and its Chapel of the Holy Rood had been of
old, remained unoccupied.   In Edgar's map of a
century later is shown a small open court, about
the middle of Forrester's Wynd, which retained
traces of the entrance to the lower churchyard of
St. Giles within memory of the elder generation, from whom I have gathered reminiscences of
Edinburgh in the eighteenth century.   It was
pointed out as such to the Rev. John Sime by
another zealous gleaner of the relics of the past,
Mr. Alexander Cunningham, who built into Porto-
bello Tower a curious collection of the ancient
sculptured stones of Edinburgh.   The elaborate
device which adorned the gateway of the Nether
Kirkyard is referred to in the *Edinburgh Magazine*
for July 1800.   It was "a long stone, on which
was curiously sculptured a group resembling
Holbein's Dance of Death.   It was a curious piece.
Amid other musicians who brought up the rear,
was an angel playing on the Highland bagpipe,

a national conceit which appears also on the entablature of one of the pillars of the supremely elegant Gothic chapel at Roslin." It had also, according to the notes of Mr. C. K. Sharpe, a group consisting of a very grotesque devil, with his attendant imps, in conflict with the archangel Michael, who was busily weighing the good and evil deeds of those who had just passed the dread portal. A similar scene forms the subject of one of the bas-reliefs on the capital of a column in the cathedral of Iona. Unfortunately the curious bas-reliefs from Forrester's Wynd were defaced and broken by careless workmen in their removal, and have not been preserved. The extension of the Court-Houses, in 1844, to the south of the Parliament Hall, led to the discovery of sundry oaken coffins of antique form: straight at the sides, and with the lids rising into a ridge in the centre, like the stone coffins of still earlier centuries. An Act of the Town-Council of September 30, 1618, "discharges Oak Kists to be made for the burial of the deceased persons within the Brough ;" and a later record refers to the evil resulting from the use of " Wainscott Kists " in the Greyfriars' Cemetery.

The old Parliament House of Scotland, with its historical associations, and its later use as the supreme seat of Scottish jurisprudence, is no unworthy supplanter of the parsonage of the Provost of St. Giles.   Above all, no more appropriate site could have been found for the Advocates' Library, with its precious relics of Chepman and Miller's press, than the spot where Gawin Douglas rendered the Æneid of Virgil into Scottish verse ; and where our Scottish Caxton founded his chaplainry for perpetual masses for the soul of James IV., the royal patron of the first printing-press introduced into Scotland.

As a satirist, Gawin Douglas is at times as pungent as Dunbar ; but his picturings have less of local character.   The prologue to the eighth book of the Æneid, for example, is his Lenten reflections embodied in a general " satire on the manners of the times."   Gallant and fair lady, priest, laird, servitor, and thrall, come under review ; the drouthy and thieving miller, the knavish shepherd, the greedy burgher, the sailor, brewer, fiddler, and the wives that " wald haif al thare wyl," are all in turn referred to ; until he escapes from the unpromising picture of his own times ; and reclining at the root of a tree,—in the provost's garden that overlooked the Cowgate, with the Pentland Hills beyond, as we may be allowed to surmise,—he begins the eighth book of his Virgil. Any reference to the characteristics of the locality so pleasantly associated with his name would have been singularly welcome.   Here and there, how- ever, a stray allusion does help us to realise the

local aspect; as where, in the prologue to the
seventh book, he pictures a Scottish winter, with its

> "Sharp soppis of sleit and of the snyppand snaw,
>   The plane stretis and every hie way
>   Full of fluschis, dubbis, myre, and clay;"

and again, warned that "the day is dawing" by
the whistling of a sorry gled fast by his chamber
window, glancing through:—

> "Ane shot window unshut, a little ajar,
>   Perseived the morning blae, wan, and har, . . .
>   And as I bounit to the fire me by,
>   Baith up and doun the hous I did espy;
>   And seeing Virgil on ane letteron stand
>   To write anon I hynt my pen in hand!"

The shot window of the poet's prologue continued,
with the timber fronts, oaken galleries, and fore-
stairs pictured by Dunbar, down to our own day;
nor have they even now wholly disappeared.
Sometimes they are no more than little unglazed
openings with sliding shutters. In other cases the
lower half of the casement window is divided by
a carved oaken mullion and transom, and closed
with hinged shutters decorated with carved panels.

The death of James IV. apparently put an end
to Dunbar's hopes of a bishopric. To Douglas,
on the contrary, it secured its more rapid acquisition, though with neither peace nor permanency
of tenure. The marriage of Queen Margaret to
his nephew the young Earl of Angus brought the

Douglases for a time into supreme power. The poet was nominated to the primacy on the death of Archbishop Elphinston ; but faction cared little for either the virtues or the learning of the Queen's nominee. The canons of St. Andrews elected their own prior to the see ; and Pope Leo X., taking advantage of the collision, set both aside in favour of Andrew Forman, Bishop of Moray, who chanced then to be at Rome. But the opportune death of the Bishop of Dunkeld helped the Queen out of her difficulty ; and the poet was presented to the vacant see.

This promotion would lead, among other changes, to the desertion of the provost's lodging in St. Giles's Churchyard, for the episcopal residence in the Cowgate. Bishop Lawder, the preceptor of James II., had provided a fitting mansion for the Bishops of Dunkeld within easy distance of the palace of Holyrood ; and to this George Brown, the poet's immediate predecessor, added a south wing. This episcopal dwelling stood a little to the west of the old High School Wynd ; and its gardens extended southward to " the gait that leads to the Kirk-of-Field," the Infirmary Street of later times. Robertson's Close now marks the eastern boundary of the Bishop's grounds ; and itself occupies the site of a tenement which in 1498 was bequeathed by Thomas Cameron to the chaplain of St. Catharine's Altar in St. Giles's

Church.   But palace and pleasure-grounds have long since vanished.   A modern building occupies the site of the lodging ; and the southern slope, once laid out as the " garden of plesaunce," wherein the poet found retirement from the broils of the turbulent capital, has long been crowded with meanest structures of plebeian resort.

An interesting notice of only half a century later, while it illustrates the revolutions which that brief interval had witnessed, also furnishes evidence of the magnificence of the old episcopal residence. We learn from Knox's history that when the Reformer was summoned to appear in the Blackfriars' Church, on the 15th of May 1556, and his opponents abandoned their intended attack through fear, " The said Johne, the same day of the summondis, tawght in Edinburgh in a greattar audience than ever befoir he had done in that toune.   The place was the Bischope of Dunkellis, his great loodgeing, whare he continewed in doctrin ten dayis, boyth befoir and after nune."

This " Palace of Honour," once rich with memories of the poet, and of the historian and reformer of that sixteenth century, has vanished, with many another edifice striking in aspect and interesting for its old associations.   Yet the ancient thoroughfare must not be robbed of its historic memories, though time and rude hands have made such havoc as to render the very allusion to the palaces of the Cowgate a seeming jest. Right opposite the lodging of the Bishops of Dunkeld there stood within very recent years the most famous of all the Cowgate palaces, built by James Beaton, Lord High Treasurer of Scotland in 1505, and in later years Archbishop of Glasgow. He, too, was a great builder; enlarged and beautified the archiepiscopal palace which stood .of old in front of Glasgow Cathedral, and on that and all his other works the Beaton arms were conspicuously displayed. The archiepiscopal lodging in the Cowgate inclosed a court or quadrangle entered by an archway from Blackfriars' Wynd. Over this was a panel with deep mouldings, sculptured with the arms of the archbishop, supported by two angels in dalmatic habits, and surmounted by a crest, scarcely less obscure latterly than the Trotcosey mitre over the Monkbarns doorway. The arms were undoubtedly those of the Beatons, and the crest was most probably their otter's head, though sharp eyes contrived to recognise in it both the archiepiscopal mitre and the cardinal's hat. The armorial stone was transferred latterly to Mr. Sharpe's collection, and he chose to believe in the insignia of the Cardinal, so there was an end of all question on that matter. The sympathetic onlooker could only respond in the words of the Laird of Monkbarns,—with a difference,—"I protest you are right! you are right! it never struck me before. See what it is to have older eyes. A cardinal's hat—it corresponds in every respect;"—for the ancient edifice had undoubtedly gone by the name of "The Cardinal's Lodging," or Cardinal Beaton's House, from the days of Queen Mary to our own.

There is no room for doubt that this old Cowgate palace was possessed and occupied both by the archbishop and his more celebrated nephew, the cardinal. It is described, in a deed of the year 1639, as "that great lodging, or tenement, sometime pertaining to the Archbishop of St. Andrews, thereafter to umqle John Beaton of Capeldraw;" and the same deed shows that even at that date open pleasure-grounds were attached to it, extending over the whole space between Blackfriars' and Toddrick's Wynd. The exterior angle of the building towards the Cowgate, with its hexagonal turret rising from an ornamental stone pillar,—as shown in the accompanying view from the Old High School Wynd,—formed a singularly picturesque feature in the old thoroughfare, but the upper part of the main building had been greatly modernised. Beyond it is seen the ancient Vennel of the preaching friars, with its timber-fronted tenements projecting storey above storey till their carved eaves nodded greetings to the crow-stepped gables on the other side of the way. Rich in antique memories and associations, it seemed to the last a living remnant of the olden time. Everywhere it appeared as though the builders had laid their foundations in the clouds, in those elder days when apples still hung in the gardens behind Blackfriars' Wynd, and nobody in the Cowgate, or out of it, dreamt that it needed a philosopher to tell them why they fell. But Newton's law of gravitation has proved inimical to timber-fronted lands and much else that was equally picturesque and lawless.

The close vicinity of the Bishop of Dunkeld's lodging to the old archiepiscopal palace at the foot of Blackfriars' Wynd helps to illustrate a familiar scene in a burgher story connected with the famous faction fight styled " Cleanse the Causeway." The Earl of Arran and the chief adherents of the Hamilton faction assembled secretly in the neighbouring monastery of the Blackfriars, on the 30th of April 1520, to mature a hastily-concerted scheme for the capture of the Earl of Angus and the overthrow of the Douglases. Gawin Douglas learned of their proceedings, and, alike as a minister of peace and a member of the house of Douglas, he desired to avert the threatened conflict. He accordingly repaired to the neighbouring palace, where the archbishop was already in armour, though under cover of his rocket ; and urged him by every pure and generous motive to use his influence to stay the purposed strife.   Beaton excused himself on various grounds, protesting on his conscience that he could not help it.   Thereupon striking his breast in the heat of his asseveration, he betrayed the presence of the concealed coat of mail ; on which Douglas retorted in good Scottish equivoke: "How now, my Lord ? methinks your conscience clatters !"

The good bishop had his revenge.   A furious battle of the barricades ensued on the neighbouring High Street, between the Arrans and the Anguses, much after the fashion of later Parisian civic warfare.   William Douglas, the brother of the Earl, stormed the Netherbow Port at the head of a band of Humes and Douglases, and turned the scale against the aggressors.   Beaton and the Hamiltons were utterly routed.   The Master of Montgomery, heir to the earldom of Eglinton, Sir Patrick Hamilton, the Earl of Angus's brother, with nearly eighty of their followers, were left dead on the street.   The Earl himself narrowly escaped through the marshes of the Nor' Loch ; while the archbishop, who, according to Buchanan's description, while the fray lasted "flew about in armour like a firebrand of sedition," in vain took sanctuary in the church of the Dominicans, near by.   "Bishop James Beatoun," says Pitscottie, "fled to the Black Freir Kirk, and thair was takin 'out behind the alter, and his rockit riven aff him, and had beine slaine, had not beine Mr. Gawin Dowglas requeisted for him, saying it was shame to put hand on ane consecrat bischop."

James V. appears to have taken up his abode in the ancient lodging at the foot of Blackfriars' Wynd on his arrival in Edinburgh some eight years later, when he was liberated from the Douglas faction ; and the archbishop, who had once more been active in the matter, became his entertainer and host. Here, also, was the scene of some of the first festivities of his daughter, Queen Mary, soon after her arrival from France. She was accompanied by the Grand Prior, her two uncles, the Duke d'Aumale, and the Marquis d'Elboeuf, the Marshal d'Amville, and other French nobles ; and on the 24th of August following, as the old diarist, in his *Diurnal of Occurrents*, records, they were entertained, on the eve of their departure, at a banquet provided by "the toun of Edinburgh, in ane honourable maner, within the lugeing sumtyme pertenying to the Cardinal." It was evidently the most sumptuous private mansion in the town, with a magnificent banquet hall, where the primate had practised the hospitalities of a churchman and political leader on a grand scale. Here, accordingly, as the diarist narrates, the Queen herself was entertained by the citizens. " Upoun the nynt day of Februar at evin, the Queenis grace, and the remanent lordis come up in ane honourabill maner fra the palice of Halyrudhous, to the Cardinallis ludging in the Blakfreir Wynd, quhilk wes preparit and hung maist honourable ; and there her Hienes sowpit, and the rest with her ; and efter supper the honest young men in the toun come with ane convoy to hir," and so escorted her back to the palace.

It is curious thus to recall the Cowgate as it existed in those olden times, with episcopal palaces, and royal and noble guests resorting thither as to their fittest haunt. Difficult as it may be for us to realise it now, this was doubtless an attractive district of the old capital. The monastery and church of the Blackfriars, on the neighbouring slope to the south, continued to be surrounded with gardens in the sixteenth century ; and immediately to the west were the lodging and pleasure grounds of the provost of the Kirk-of-Field, so tragically associated with the fate of Darnley and of Mary Stuart. Civic revolutions have done their utmost to efface the old traces ; but the contour of Edinburgh, with its ridges and dividing valleys, defies the erasures of time. Nor need such historical associations wholly fade away because garden and pleasure grounds have been appropriated for more needful uses, and builders of modern centuries have wrought up the old materials of their palaces, for the most part, into very plebeian structures.

The arms of the Beatons have vanished with their palace. The lodging of the poet Bishop of

Dunkeld has long been among the things of the past. But the arms of Queen Mary's mother, the Regent, Mary of Guise, have survived in more fragile form, and are still blazoned, within a laurel wreath, on a window of the neighbouring chapel of St. Mary Magdalen. Along with them is a Saint Bartholomew, sole survivor of all the apostles, spared as fitting consort of the Scottish representative of the Guises, at the general massacre of Edinburgh saints in 1599. The old century, and much that pertained to it, were coming to an end together. But it is far from improbable that the Scottish iconoclasts, when winding up the strange doings of that century with a general clearance of the much-abused saints, indulged in a characteristic touch of grim humour in sparing the patron saint of the Guises of Paris, and of the pious work wrought by them on St. Bartholomew's Eve, 1572. The Chapel of St. Mary Magdalen was founded in 1503, " to the praise and honour of Almighty God, and of His Mother the Blessed Virgin Mary, and of Mary Magdalen, and of the hail celestial court ; " and there the chaplain and seven poor bedemen were " to give forth their continual prayers for the salvation of the soul of our most illustrious Mary Queen of Scots," as well as for those of the founder and foundress. The bedemen survived as pensioners of " The Hammermen of Magdalene Chapel," but their perpetual prayers soon came to an end, and their oratory was diverted to purposes very different from the praise and honour of the Blessed Virgin.

John Craig, the Scottish Dominican, had been condemned to the stake by the Roman Inquisition as an incorrigible heretic, when, in the tumults which followed on the death of Paul IV., the dungeons of the Inquisition were broken into, and, escaping thence, after many strange vicissitudes he made his way back to Scotland in 1560. He had then been absent from his native country for twenty-four years, and had nearly forgotten his mother tongue. Nevertheless he met with a hearty welcome at Edinburgh from his brethren of the reformed faith. The Chapel of St. Mary Magdalene was set apart for his use, and there he preached in Latin to such scholars as his learning and abilities attracted to hear him. After a time he recovered the mastery of his native tongue, and was appointed colleague of John Knox in the parish church of St. Giles. To him, accordingly, in 1567, Queen Mary sent her mandate, requiring him to publish the banns of marriage betwixt her and Bothwell. The sturdy reformer did not indeed refuse, but on the contrary performed the double function of proclaimer and protester, "taking heaven and earth to witness that he detested that scandalous and infamous marriage," which the more pliant Adam Bothwell, Bishop of Orkney, performed in the chapel of Holyrood.

To follow out in detail all the associations of the Cowgate of Edinburgh would lead us through that antique thoroughfare in company with nobles, ecclesiastics, statesmen, and scholars of successive centuries, and link its old denizens with some of very modern times. Near by the Magdalene Chapel, on the opposite side of the way, stands the house where Henry Brougham the elder, of Brougham Hall,—then heart-broken at the death of his betrothed,—fell in love with the daughter of his Scottish landlady; and so the future Lord Chancellor of England became grandnephew of Principal Robertson, and grew up an Edinburgh boy, with Scottish training and associations which left their impress on him to the last.

Not far from the once genteel and eligible lodgings of Widow Syme is the spacious mansion of Sir Thomas Hope, the Lord Advocate of Charles I., with its quaint punning legends and other characteristic devices, referred to in a subsequent chapter. To the east of the Magdalene Chapel, on the site of George IV. Bridge, stood another of the civic mansions of the Cowgate's old palatial days, with enclosed quadrangle and great hall, the lodging of Thomas Hamilton, Earl of Haddington, the favourite of James VI., facetiously styled by him Tam o' the Cowgate.

Thomas Hamilton, President of the Court of Session, and Secretary of State for Scotland, was held in equal repute for his legal astuteness, and his canny prudence in the amassing of wealth ; so that when his royal master returned to Edinburgh in 1617, he found his old favourite currently credited with the discovery of the philosopher's stone. James, who was credulous enough to be quite capable of putting faith in this popular solution of the Earl's source of wealth, gave him a hint of the rumour that had reached him. The Earl responded by asking the King to honour him with his company at dinner ; and, extending the invitation to the courtiers in attendance, he promised that they should be regaled with the choicest feast the Cowgate could furnish, and ere they left he would disclose the secret of his philosopher's stone. The King and courtiers duly arrived, the banquet was discussed, and the wine freely pledged, till at length the royal Solomon grew impatient, and reminded their host of his promise. Doubtless "Tam o' the Cowgate" knew by long experience how far he might safely venture with his royal guest. Nevertheless some of the expectant courtiers must have felt themselves outwitted when told that the whole secret of the wondrous talisman was embodied in this aphorism :—

> Ne'er put off to the morn what can be done to-day,
> Ne'er send anither whar yoursel' can gae,
> Ne'er trust to ither what yoursel' can dae !

Some obscure tradition assigned to a picturesque old fabric on the north side of the street the name of the French Ambassador's Chapel. Its western wing was surmounted with a pediment, sculptured with the twelve apostles along the gable-cornice, and crowned with a figure astride on the apex, which was supposed to represent the Saviour. Over the entrance was the motto :—

SPERAVI . ET . INVENI,

surmounted by a shield cut in bold relief with armorial bearings, the singular character of which had attracted the attention of the old Scottish Herald, Alexander Nesbit, and puzzled a later antiquary, Robert Chambers, when time and dirt had added to their obscurity. Ending the section of his heraldic blazonry which dealt with " four-footed beasts," Nesbit describes " one of a monstrous form " to be found in Scottish armorial bearings. " Its body is like a wolf, having four feet, with long toes and a tail ; it is headed like a man, called in our books a *warwolf*-passant, and three stars in chief argent ; which are also to be seen cut upon a stone above an old entry of a house in the Cowgate in Edinburgh, above the foot of Libberton's Wynd, which belonged formerly to the name of Dickison, which name seems to be from the Dicksons by the stars which they carry." In reality, however, the actual bearing of the shield was a crescent between two stars in chief. The hideous bugbear of medieval superstition which thus frowned over the portal of the old Cowgate mansion is still an object of superstitious dread among the French habitans of Lower Canada.

Behind the French Ambassador's lodging there led up to the High Street the ancient alley styled Libberton's Wynd, of which all that now remains is the lane at the back of the County Hall. It is mentioned by this name in a charter granted by James III. in 1474; and the old protocol books of the city include repeated references to it during the twelve years immediately preceding Flodden. William Libberton's heirs are mentioned as residents in 1501; and the Forresters of Corstorphine, whose ancestors were famous for centuries before, had the great mansion at the head of the wynd, on the site of the present County Hall, extending eastward to Forrester's Wynd. It appears to have enclosed a quadrangular court, as was usual with city mansions of the first class. A covered archway formed the entry from the main street into the quadrangle. Here the grand staircase led to the great hall, and stone turnpikes gave access to the different floors; while the ground floor was doubtless arched with stone, as was the case with that of the Cardinal's Lodging in Blackfriars' Wynd, and other lodgings of this class. In this way the old civic mansion formed a secure shelter on occasion of such brawls and emeutes as Edinburgh was notorious for throughout the sixteenth and seventeenth centuries.

It was by Forrester's Wynd that the Earl of Mar made his way, at the head of a band of hackbutters, to the rescue of King James, when the faithful, after listening to a sermon in St. Giles's, withdrew to one of the aisles, and amid cries of " The sword of the Lord and of Gideon !" proceeded to the Laigh Tolbooth to demand redress in matters of religion from " God's silly vassal."   On such occasions the foregate of the Forresters' lodging was closed against all comers ; and the old Scottish burgher appreciated the maxim that every man's house is his castle only so long as he is able to hold it.

The Forresters and Libbertons were, without exception, the most ancient representatives of burgher nobility in the Scottish capital : not unlike the citizen nobles of Florence and other medieval republics.   Their ancestors figure together in the oldest surviving rolls of Edinburgh's magnates.   In 1373, before the office of provost was known, Adam Forrester appears under the ancient Anglo-Saxon title of alderman; and in 1425, when James I. had just brought with him to Scotland the Lady Jane Beaufort, for love of whom the " King's Quair " was penned by the royal prisoner at Windsor, William Libberton was provost of Edinburgh. He is succeeded, in 1434, by Sir Henry Preston of

Craigmillar; and then come Cranstouns, Cock-
burns, Napiers, and other well-known names, till
we find Archibald Douglas, Earl of Angus, as
provost, appointing his deputy before marching to
Flodden; and when the fatal results left the civic
chair as well as the throne vacant, his successor is
Alexander, Lord Home, Great Chamberlain of
Scotland.

The Forresters have left their memorial in the
venerable church which still shelters the dust of the
old burgher line. They were lords of the manor
of Corstorphine, situated immediately to the west
of Edinburgh, between the Pentlands and Corstorphine Hill. Torphin's Cross, from whence its name
is derived, doubtless stood there in some old century
to mark the last resting-place of a rough son of
Thor. There was a chapel there before the time of
David I., who conferred on his newly-erected abbey
of Holyrood the church of St. Cuthbert and its
dependencies, including the chapels of Corstorphine
and Libberton. In 1376, Adam Forrester, the
alderman of previous years, acquired the manor of
Corstorphine from the Mores of Abercorn. In
1402 he followed the Douglas in the famous English
raid which ended with the battle of Homildon Hill,
and fell a prisoner into Hotspur's hands, but was
ransomed in due course, and ere long received the
honour of knighthood. Sir Adam Forrester's
memorial tablet may still be read. He died at

Corstorphine on the 13th October 1405, and is believed to have been interred in the chapel of St. John the Baptist, which he had founded beside the parish church. His son, Sir John Forrester, Master of the Household of King James I., and Great Chamberlain of Scotland, endowed a chaplainry, in 1425, at St. Ninian's altar in St. Giles's church, Edinburgh, requiring the chaplain to offer up perpetual prayers for the welfare of his sovereign James I. and Queen Jane, "the fairest and the freshest young flower," that ever the poet of "the Quair" saw, whom he had brought with him on his return from his long exile the previous year. Along with them, Sir John commends to the prayers of his chaplain the souls of Sir Adam and Margaret Forrester, his father and mother, and of Dame Margaret his deceased spouse.

Four years later the church at Corstorphine became a collegiate foundation, with a provost, four prebendaries, and two singing boys ; and when the poet Dunbar wrote his beautiful "Lament of the Makaris," he embalmed among the lost poets of his time "gentle Rowell of Corstorphine," one of its first provosts, as is inferred. Beginning with his master in the divine art, "the noble Chaucer, of makaris the flower," Dunbar goes on to enumerate those whom "that strang unmerciful tyrant" Death "has ta'en out of this countrie." Along with such familiar names as Barbour,

Wyntoun, and Blind Harry, he refers to a list of fully a dozen poetical contemporaries, of most of whom no specimen of their art survives; and among the latter are the pair of good fellows thus commemorated :—

> " He has tane Roull of Aberdeen,
>   And gentle Roull of Corstorphine ;
>   Two better fallowis did na man see :
>   Timor mortis conturbat me."

The poet's requiem would not ill consort with the assignment to the old Makar of Corstorphine, a humorous contemporary allusion to be found in the *Select Remains of the Ancient Popular Poetry of Scotland*, printed by Dr. David Laing in 1822 :—

> " The cursing of Sir John Rowlis,
>   Upoun the steilars of his fowlis !"

The fine old church in which "gentle Roull" officiated in the days of James IV. and Dunbar retained within my own memory much of its pristine character, before ruthless restorers took in hand to remodel it. A summer's holidays spent in a Corstorphine farm-house, fully half a century ago, come back on me now with all the vividness with which such golden days in a town boy's life impress themselves on the memory. I still remember the awe with which I followed the old village sexton, and had pointed out to me the reputed crusader, lying there, a mailed knight, on his altar-

VOL. I.

CORSTORPHINE CHURCH.

P. 110.

tomb praying in stone. It was a curious sombre old parish church, with its little windows, dark double aisle, and cumbering galleries, offering irresistible temptations to the tasteless restorers, who wrought such havoc on it ere long. But mutilated though it be, the old church still retains much of the same picturesque quaintness with which the English tourist is familiar in his antique parish churches. The chancel has indeed been debased to a porch, but they have spared the altar-tombs with their recumbent effigies ; and so the knights still perpetuate such chantry services as they did of old. Two of the altar-tombs occupy arched recesses in the chancel, one of them being the monument of Sir John Forrester, the founder of the collegiate church, and his lady, apparently a St. Clair of Orkney, judging from the arms impaled with the Forresters' on one of the sculptured shields. The knight and lady are in armour and dress of the fifteenth century, and the latter clasps her breviary in her hands. In the other monument, supposed to represent the son of the founder and his wife, the lady's hands are meekly crossed over her breast. The supposed crusader lies apart, on his altar-tomb in the south transept, with his dog at his feet. He is traditionally affirmed to be Bernard, Lord of Aubigny, who died in the castle of Corstorphine, while on an embassy to the court of James IV. in 1508 ; but the monument is of older date, and the shield bears the Forresters' own heraldic hunting-horns, stringed.

> " The knights are dust,
>   Their good swords are rust.
>   Their souls are with the saints we trust."

Certainly their earthly tenure, outside of their old collegiate foundation, has long been at an end. Of their castle under Corstorphine Hill, and their town mansion in the High Street of Edinburgh, not one stone remains upon another.   The very wynd that long preserved their name, where once they flourished among the civic magnates, has itself vanished; but here is a Corstorphine ballad, indubitably of unknown antiquity, since it was never printed before :—

MAYE MARION.

O mikle turns up atween lip and caup,
    'Tween the lyk-wake and nurse's croon ;
The bride that leugh when the sun rase up
    Grat sair or that sun gaed doun ;
An' sae it befell on ae lang summer-day
    To Lord James and Maye Marion.

Lang, lang had he courted Maye Marion,
    He lo'ed her better nor life ;
But she has spoken a word in jest
    Has bred them bitter strife ;
An' he's vowed proud Marjory Forrester
    Shall be his wedded wife.

" Gae bring to me my siller kaim ;
    Kaim out my yellow hair,
  An' busk me in my best attire
    Or I to kirk repair.
  Mak haste, bower-maid, or my fause love
    Will wed or I win there.

" Now wons he at the haly altar
    O' our mother-kirk Sanct Geile?
  Or wons he at the Holyrood,
    Or St. Anton's on the hill,
  Or at our Lady Kirk-o'-Field?
    Gude yeoman, to me tell ;

" Or at St. Roque's, in the Boroughmuir Wood,
    Or St. Ringan's in the hollow? "—
" O, he is gane to Corstorphine kirk,
    Whar eident you maun follow ;
  For it is na ae hour, but only three,
    Sin' I heard Lord Forrester's hollo.

" His four bauld sons rade him beside,
    His daughter them between ;
  The siller that hung at her bridle-reins
    Wad been ransom for a queen ;
  But I'd ware ae glint o' your flashin' ee
    For a' her siller shene."

  The wedding wons at Corstorphine kirk ;
    The cleadin the bride had on
  Shimmered wi' pearls to her waist sae jimp,
    And jewells that on her shon ;—
  Lord James wad gien a' for ae kindly look
    Fra' the ee o' Maye Marion.

Proud Marjory looked to her brithers four,
  They were stalwart knights to see ;
But the bridegroom was a comelier knight
  Than a' that companie,
Had it no been for his wae wan look
  And the sault tear in his ee.

Proud Marjory knelt in the sculptured quire,
  Her forebears' banners aboon ;
Frae each shafted window their scutcheons bright
  On the auld-wed Forresters shon,
Each knight and dame 'neath their arch o' stane,
  But the bridegroom looked mair wan.

The priest has chaunted the holy mass,
  He has join'd their hands as ane ;
Proud Marjory's taen the wedding vows
  Tho' the bridegroom answers nane ;
The fingers that held her lily hand
  Were cauld as the dead's through stane.

" Now wha are ye would glamour our bride
  Wi' sic wae and tearless een ?
And what would ye at the Forresters' kirk
  Or the wedding guests hae gaen ? "—
" O wae betide the ill-waled words
  That cam true love between !

" I cam na to glamour your braw wed bride
  Wi' my wae and tearless ee ;
Nor to ware ae word on an eident guest
  O' your wedding companie ;
But I cam, Lord James, to gie you back
  Love-tokens ance dear to me :

" To gie ye back the gowden ring
    We broke in the Roslin wood,
And the bonnet-piece o' siller fine
    We dipp'd in the warslin flood,
And the troth, wi' ae kiss o' your faithless mou,
    Ance plighted by a' maist good.

" 'Twas a lightsome word fra a mirthfu' heart
    That bred sae mickle pain ;
'Twas a fickle troth sae soon forgat
    For ae proud word come and gane :—
Bird Marjory, ill was't a woman's part
    To come true love atween.

" But walth gang wi' ye, my false, fain love,
    And mirth wi' your bride sae slee ;
Weel marrow false friend and lover fain
    Ilk other's companie ;
Yet I wad na ware on warst waled fae
    What either has done to me."

She 's mounted her eident dapple steed
    And aff wi' the tear in her ee ;
The drumly Leith was rowing deep,
    And the kelpie's shriek was hie ;—
O wae betide the frusch sauch wand
    Sae fecklessly gied way.

Maye Marion was dround or the laverock left
    The sun in the lift o'er head,
And lang or it sank in a cloudy west
    Her fause lover shared her bed ;
They 've laid them thegither in haly earth
    E'en as though they had been wed.

> There's preaching for fausehood and pride, Marjory,
>   Mang the mouls where thae twa are lain ;
> But soundly asleep in the auld kirk's shade,
>   As nae ill them cam atween,
> Baith kindly byde, happ'd by ae gowand sod,
>   For ilk spring to renew its green.

Latest among the noble occupants of Forrester's Wynd was the Earl of Dunmore ; and the destruction of the old thoroughfare early in the present century rescued it from the degradation that has since befallen other aristocratic haunts of elder times. In a little court at the foot of the wynd, with its southern windows looking into the Cowgate, lived and died the last lineal representative of the elder branch of the St. Clairs of Roslin, who, as such, claimed and executed the office of Hereditary Grand Master of the Scottish Free Masons ; and now lies in the collegiate church of Roslin, where Father Hay assures us, when the vault of Sir William St. Clair, who fell at the battle of Dunbar, was opened, he saw him lying in his armour, as all his ancestors had been buried before him. The last of the old race was not allowed to pass away without the popular assignment of exceptional attributes to the representative in whom the ancient line of St. Clair came to an end. Constable, writing to Sir Walter Scott in 1822, refers to the destruction of the old mansion-house of Carnbee in Fifeshire, near to the spot where the bibliopole himself was born, and he adds—"I saw the last Sinclair of Roslin here when I was quite a youth He was pointed out to me by the children as the man without a shadow, from a supposed connection with the devil." The entrance to the aristocratic little quadrangle, where this last scion of the old Roslin tree withered away, was from Libberton's Wynd, the early associations with which have already been noted. It has others of still greater interest when it became a favourite haunt of the Muses, where Bacchus and Apollo held their shrine in common, and Johnnie Dowie long ministered as high priest. But meanwhile let us turn back once more to older times, and, emerging from the head of Forrester's Wynd, in its palmy days, seek to recover some traces of its aristocratic vicinage, when the neighbouring closes of the Lawnmarket and the Castle Hill were the abodes of civic gentry, Scottish nobles, and for a time of royalty itself.

CHAPTER V.

A Queen Dowager's Neighbours.

THERE stood within our recollection, on the north side of the Castle Hill of Edinburgh, an antique timber-fronted land two stories high. The ground-floor was substantially arched in stone, and from this rose the walls of the main floor, which appeared to have originally formed a single apartment, with its open timber gallery projecting into the street. The west wall, towards the castle, was occupied by a huge stone fireplace, with overhanging chimney, supported by grotesque corbel figures ; and its hearthstone was raised above the floor, and guarded with a stone ledge or fender somewhat resembling the arrangements of an ancient fireplace still existing at St. Mary's Abbey, York. The open timbers of the roof were exposed up to the collar-beam, and a large dormer window gave the main light to the hall, while small shot windows opened on the gallery. In the front stone wall were, two ornamented ambries with sculptured sills, one of them still closed by an antique oak door, rudely carved with two dolphins and other ornamentation. The timber front, though seamed and patched like a beggar's coat, had a look of faded gentility, as of one that has seen better days; and the entire building was singularly quaint and picturesque. Yet not even the most enthusiastic of antiquaries could honestly protest against its demolition, for it was one of those old-world relics, which having wholly outlived their time, can by no conceivable ingenuity be made to adapt themselves to the wants of our nineteenth century. Its title-deeds confirmed the fact that it belonged to a bygone state of things, for it was there set forth as "the tenement of land belonging to the chaplain of the chaplainry of St. Nicholas's Altar, founded within the College Church of St. Giles, within the burgh of Edinburgh."

Of the chaplains of St. Nicholas, confessor, sundry notices can still be gleaned from old charters. In 1426 Sir John Bridin served at the altar; in 1467 he was succeeded by Sir John Skynnar, another Pope's knight, and not improbably an occupant of the old house which survived to our day. By a later council record of 1506, we learn that Sir Alexander Panter having resigned his prebend of St. Nicholas, the same was given to Mr. Patrick Clerk; while another which he had held at the altar of St. Michael was transferred to Sir John Thomson, chaplain, so that the chaplainry of St. Nicholas seems to have been one of the church prizes, in fact St. Giles's golden stall. It further appears that, in 1532, the lands of Petravy, in Fife,—famous in later days by reason of Elizabeth, Lady Wardlaw of Pitreavie's labours as a masquerader in antique poetic guisings,—were granted in feu to his successor, Sir Gilbert Lauder, who thereupon " resigned the altarage and service of St. Nycholace altar, which same was granted to Sir David Purdome be the deliveryng of ane bonet as use is efter the fundatioun."

But such antique usages were already on the wane. Only four years before, Patrick Hamilton, titular Abbot of Fern,—who, as Knox says, had sat at the feet both of Luther and Melancthon,—lighted up the darkest recesses of medieval conservatism with the first martyr-fire of the Reformation dawn. He was burnt at the stake in front of the old college of St. Andrews, for protesting against pilgrimages, purgatory, prayers for the dead, " and such trifles," as in bitter irony Knox adds. It was, in truth, a time when many old-world beliefs and prejudices were coming into harshest collision with the earnest thought of a new era. We learn, for example, from the Register for 1535, that in the month of May of that same year " the prebend of St. Androis altar in the collegiate church of St. Giles was given to Sir William Cady, the same being vacant, because Mr. Andro Johnestoun, last prebendary, had left the land for heresy." By this time Henry VIII. of England, though holding stoutly to his title of Defender of the Faith, had come to open rupture with the papal court; and was beset with anxiety on behalf of his royal nephew, James V., and the allegiance still maintained by him to the old church and faith. Scottish heretics therefore, who were willing to forfeit prebendal and other church revenues, had not far to go in search of a foreign asylum.

Only a very few years later there was erected close by the quaint old lodging of the chaplain of St. Nicholas, on the Castle Hill, a palatial mansion for Mary of Guise, the Queen of James V., which also survived to our day: a curious memorial of times and habits of life so strangely diverse from our own. Tradition had perpetuated the memory of the Queen's city residence, for Maitland, writing in 1753, says—" In Blyth's Close, in the Castle Hill Street, is an ancient chapel, said to have been a private oratory belonging to Mary of Lorain, Dowager to King James V., and mother to Mary Queen of Scots." In later days it was a curious maze of turnpike stairs, halls, and passages, leading up and down in the most intricate fashion. Modern partitions subdividing the old chambers of royalty helped to fit the whole for a rookery of such denizens as now monopolise the closes of

Edinburgh, and added to the intricacy of the labyrinth through which the curious visitor had to grope his way. Traces of faded grandeur peeped out here and there from amid the gloom and squallor of its long-deserted halls, and helped to confirm tradition by undoubted evidence of their royal lodger. Over the main entrance a sculptured lintel bore the royal initials, along with the monogram of the Virgin, and the legend: LAUS . HONOR . DEO . Sculptured Gothic ambries, and fireplaces elaborately decorated with moulded ledges and carved pillars, looked strangely out of place with their dingy modern accompaniments; and, peering through the dirt and whitewash of centuries, were heraldic devices which chronicled beyond dispute the history of the antique dwelling. They looked indeed under their obscuring whitewash like poor stucco work; nor was it till, by the zealous acquisitiveness of Charles Kirkpatrick Sharpe, they had been transferred from a place where they were subject to such renewed indignities, that their true character and significance became known as fine specimens of oak carving heraldically blazoning the history of the place. They included the armorial bearings of the Duke of Chatelherault, with his initials I. H.; those of Henry II. King of France, with the royal initials H. R.; and those of the Queen Regent impaling the Scottish Lion in the double tressure, with her initials, M. R.

Those heraldic bearings not only confirm the tradition of the old presence of royalty, but they afford a satisfactory clue to the period of Mary of Guise's abode there. James Hamilton, Earl of Arran, was created Duke of Chatelherault in the year 1548, but not fully confirmed in the title till 1551, when it was made part of the reward bestowed on him for resigning the regency to the Queen Dowager, who thereupon returned from France to assume the government on behalf of her daughter. The death of Henry II., in 1559, marks a memorable date in more ways than one. In France it was a startling crisis. In a tournament with the Sieur de Montgomery the King received a wound in the face which proved mortal ; and the young beauty, Mary Queen of Scots, stepped into the place of Catherine de Medici, as the consort of her son Francis II. But it was just about the time when the Dauphin thus unexpectedly succeeded to the French throne, that the Queen Regent and the Lords of the Congregation came to open rupture at the Scottish court ; and from that date she resided chiefly in Leith, until her last illness. The city and palace had been burnt by the English in 1544 ; Holyrood, if then restored from their ravages, offered inadequate protection for the court in a period of factious strife and revolt ; and hence, as we may assume, the choice of a lodging within the city walls and in close vicinity to the castle.   The tradition of Maitland's time was genuine and undoubted ; as to those of later date, Mr. Sharpe remarks in trenchant fashion in one of his marginal notes to my " Memorials," where the account of the discovery of an iron casket or reliquary in the supposed chapel of the Queen Regent is quoted in detail :—" There was no chapel there, and the Gothic niche was only a cupboard, with a shield of arms to be painted on it.   The iron casket is all a lie.   It was *found* after I had *found* the queen's house,— forgotten by all.   I read Arnot over again after I resided in Edinburgh, and till I made a noise about the close nobody knew anything about it."

Whatever be the truth about the casket, its history was fully credited by Dr. Robert Chambers, who recovered it from a relative of the reputed finder, and presented it to Sir Walter Scott to add to his Abbotsford treasures.   Moreover, when at length this ancient civic abode of royalty was demolished in 1845, there is no question that some highly curious revelations were made in the process of removing plaster ceilings and partitions. Two arched or waggon-shaped roofs were disclosed, panelled in wood, and elaborately decorated with painted devices and inscriptions.   One of the halls or chambers of dais was so lofty, that the modern ceiling cut off a range of dormer windows rising on either side, with round-headed recesses, into the arched roof. The panelled ceiling was painted in rich arabesques and graceful designs of flowers, fruit, leaves, etc., with appropriate legends. On one portion all that remained decipherable was—YE TRVBILIS OF YE RIGHTIOUS. On another this metrical legend remained entire:—

> Gif yow wt. syn afflcitit be,
> Och yan say Chryst com yow to me.
> Swith ye way, walk yow thairin,
> Embrace ye truth, abandoun ——

The last word, obviously SIN, had been purposely omitted, and a dash substituted, as though for an enigma, or puzzle. In the centre of the roof was a ring, for suspending a chandelier; and one of the walls was pierced with a trefoil-headed niche. The appearance of the walls and large but inornate fireplace suggested that the chamber had originally been finished with a carved oaken mantelpiece. The hooks remained at the spring of the arched ceiling from which the royal tapestry had hung; and some of the items mentioned in the " Collection of Inventories " may help us still to realise the original decorations of the walls. Among " the Queene Regentis movables " are specified " ane tapestric maid of worsett mixt with threid of gold, of the historie of the judgment of Salamon, the deid barne, and the twa wiffis. Item ane tapestrie of the historie of the creatioun, contening nyne peces; ane of the King Roboam, contening foure peaces; ane other of little Salamon;" besides which are mentioned "two paintit broddis, the ane of the muses, and the uther of crotesque or conceptis."

Such grotesques and conceits as are here referred to remained in abundance on the other arched ceiling, brought to light in 1845. Some of them are to be found in "Paradin's Emblems," published at Lyons in 1557; and others in the "Traicte des Devises Royales." But such conceits were in vogue at the time, and the artist probably mingled with borrowed devices some of his own invention, such as a hand amid flames, holding up a dagger, with the motto: AGERE ET PATI FORTIA; a branch hanging with apples: AB IN-SOMNI NON CUSTODITA DRAGONI; two hands emerging from a cloud, one holding a sword, the other a trowel: IN UTRUMQUE PARATUS; a royal orb, surmounted by the cross, and entwined with snakes: IN CRUCE TUTA QUIES; and a hand out of a cloud, holding a pair of balances on the point of a sword: QUIS LEVIOR? CUI PLUS PONDERI ADDIT SOLUM. Among devices ascertained to have been in vogue elsewhere, were an ape crushing her offspring in the fervour of her embrace, with the motto: CÆCUS AMOR PROLIS; a serpent among strawberry plants: LATET ANGUIS IN HERBA; and a porcupine with apples on its quills:

MAGNUM VECTIGAL PARSIMONIA. Those emblematic devices were united by ornamental borders ; and when the colours were fresh, and the chamber walls decorated with tapestry, the whole effect must have been harmonious and striking.

The Guise Palace stood on the west side of Blyth's Close, on the site now occupied by the eastern side of the quadrangle of New College. On the opposite side of the same narrow thoroughfare was the supposed " chapel, or private oratory" of the Queen Regent, in a building notable for various features suggestive of ecclesiastical uses. Its stone fireplaces with clustered Gothic pillars, and sculptured ambries alongside of them, corresponded in style with those of the royal lodging ; but a large elaborately sculptured niche in the east wall of the great chamber,—the same which Mr. Sharpe contemptuously designated a cupboard,—stood apart from any fireplace. In the centre of the florid tracery with which its arch was filled, there was sculptured an angel holding a shield, as on the beautiful corporate seal of Mary of Gueldres ; and an elaborately carved hood-mould and sill completed the ornamentation of this unique ambry. Here, if anywhere, had been the altar and credence table of the reputed oratory. The hall or chapel, of which it formed so remarkable a feature, was lighted by tall narrow windows, originally divided by stone mullions and transoms, and splayed externally on the north side so as to catch every ray of light that entered the narrow close. But in later times its true dimensions were concealed by partitions subdividing it into apartments suited to the wants of its humble tenants. Before it reached this latest stage of degradation, it was occupied about the middle of last century by Mr. John Johnston, a teacher of note in his day. In the niche there then stood an urn, in front of a square stone, which, according to the account derived from his family, excited his curiosity, and so induced him to force the latter from its place, when he found that it concealed a recess, within which lay the reliquary, or iron casket, already referred to, long after recovered by Dr. Robert Chambers from the widow of his son. This may still be seen at Abbotsford. Had its lot been to pass, with other undoubted de Guise relics, into the hands of Charles Kirkpatrick Sharpe, there would probably have been no challenge of its genuineness; for it is a curious, antique casket; and in the Abbotsford Edition of " The Monastery," is unhesitatingly produced as " a jewel-box that belonged to Mary of Guise." It is figured at the end of this chapter, with its arched lid, and wrought iron bands, two of which terminate in clasps falling over holes in the front, and originally securing it by means of intricate lock-work within;

while the handle is attached to the central band of the lid. No doubt was ever hinted as to the genuineness of a gold ring of antique workmanship, which was found during the demolition of the building, and passed into Mr. Sharpe's own hands. It is greatly worn. Around the hoop is an inscription in fifteenth century characters, of which no more could be deciphered than the sacred monogram. The stone setting is gone; but a sharp gold wire projecting from the socket illustrates the process of ancient jewellery, and probably shows that its setting had been a pearl.

So long as Blyth's Close remained, no more curious historic nook was to be found in the old town of Edinburgh. As the abode of the widowed Queen of James V., and the daughter of the Duke of Guise, who played so prominent a part in one of the most critical eras of Scottish History, the ancient lodging was worthy of notice, apart from its curious details. Here, doubtless, the leading churchmen and nobles who adhered to her party met in secret deliberation, to resist the early movements which led to the Scottish Reformation; through the mean and obscure alley, as it latterly seemed, ambassadors and statesmen of England and France, and the messengers of the Scottish Queen, were wont to find their way to the presence of the Regent, where they were received in halls not unsuited to the dignity of such a presence.

In the little oratory too we may picture to ourselves royal and noble worshippers kneeling before its altar, amid the fragrance of incense, and the gorgeous ceremonial of a church so soon to be proscribed. It is a dream of times so different from our own, that it is difficult to believe that even such traces of them survived to our own day.

The old stone land fronting the street at the head of Blyth's Close bore the inscription on its front in curiously wrought iron letters : LAUS DEO M. R. 1591. Its oldest title-deeds show it to have been occupied, like other dwellings on the main street, by wealthy burgesses. But it, too, had its hall of dais, with painted ceiling not less curious than that of the neighbouring royal abode. In the centre a large circular compartment contained the figure of our Saviour, with a gilded nimbus round his head, and his left hand resting on the royal orb. Around this ran the legend, in gilded Roman characters on a blue ground : EGO SUM VIA, VERITAS, ET VITA. 14 JOHNE. The paintings in the large compartments into which the ceiling was divided represented Jacob's dream, Christ asleep in the storm, the Baptism of Christ, and the vision of Death from the Apocalypse, surmounted by the symbols of the Evangelists. The series of sacred subjects thus combined formed a singularly effective pictorial decoration ; but an amusing anachronism gave special local interest to the second-named picture. The distant landscape of the Sea of Galilee consisted of a view of Edinburgh from the north, terminating with the Castle on the right, and Salisbury Crags on the left. The details of the civic landscape afford some clue to the date of the work. The steeple of the Netherbow, erected in 1606, and that of the old Weigh House on the Castle Hill, taken down in 1660, both appear in the view; and the whole pictorial decoration may be ascribed to a period little later than the former date.

The Apocalyptic vision, which constituted the fourth of the series, was the most curious of all, affording full play for the allegorical fancies so familiar to the men of that seventeenth century, with their frequent masques, pageants, and symbolical interludes. It presented the Christian church in allegory. A ship of antique form, in full sail, bore on its pennon and stern the sacred symbol IHS. A crowned figure standing on the deck looked forth on a burning city in the distance, and overhead the word VÆ may be presumed to have combined, along with the general allegory of escape from the City of Destruction, its special allusion to the triumphant cry heard by St. John in vision: "Babylon the great is fallen, and is become the habitation of devils." Death appeared as a skeleton armed with bow and arrow, riding on a dark horse amid the waves in front of the ship. Behind it came a draped figure, similarly armed, and mounted on a dragon, entitled PERSECUTIO ; and overhead was the winged demon DIABOLUS. The ship rode safely onward in the midst of those perils, for in the sky a heavenly radiance surrounding the Hebrew word יהוה indicated the over-ruling presence of God : and from this symbol of Deity a hand issued holding a line, by which the vessel was being guided through the tempest. The painting was a singularly interesting specimen of Scottish art, executed at a period in the national history which gave it peculiar significance and value. Broad borders dividing the compartments of the ceiling were decorated with flowers, fruit, birds, harpies, and grotesque fancy devices ; and at each intersecting point was a raised and gilded star. The paintings were executed in tempera on wood ; time and damp had wrought great havoc. Possibly, however, the paintings still exist. It is upwards of thirty years since, in the obscurity and straitened limits between its arched roof and the modern flat ceiling, I noted the details above described, and sketched the quaint anachronism which transplanted the crags and steeples of old Edinburgh to the shores of the Galilean lake.

The initials R. M. accompanying the inscription in ornamental iron letters on the front of the ancient civic mansion, so singularly decorated within, were popularly assigned to royalty, in spite of the conflicting date of 1591, and the notorious appropriation of the houses in the main street as the dwellings and booths of the merchant burgesses. The house itself was of older date; but as appears from the earliest titles now existing, bearing date in the previous year, it was then acquired in part by Robert M'Naught, merchant burgess. The timber galleries of its antique front were replaced by a handsome façade of polished ashlar, in the style of that sixteenth century, and the good burgess supplemented the pious motto with which he adorned it with his own initials. By a happy coincidence they fitted in to the revived traditions of a later age; and so the R. M. of Robert M'Naught, familiar enough to his fellow citizens in his own day, became for us moderns the REGINA MARIA, and an indisputable memorial of the royal denizen once familiar to the neighbourhood!

Immediately adjoining the Guise palace, in the close behind, the mansion of another old citizen of the sixteenth century retained to the last its traces of adornments nearly coeval with those of the neighbouring royal apartments, and perpetuated other associations with the connubial ties which linked France and Scotland together. In the year 1537 there came to Scotland the Princess

Magdalen, daughter of Francis I., the fair but frail lily brought by James V. from among the sunny vines of France, in all the hectic beauty of consumption, only to droop and die; and in her retinue John de Hope, the founder of a family of note in later times. The substantial, though now sorely dilapidated mansion built for himself near the Netherbow, still stands, I believe, in Bailie Fyfe's Close, bearing his name in antique characters over its main entrance. His son Edward, ancestor of Sir Thomas Hope, famous in the era of the great rebellion, and of the later Earls of Hopetoun, was probably driven out of the paternal mansion by the sack and burning of the English, under the Earl of Hertford, in 1544; and so built his new lodging alongside of that of the Queen Regent on the Castle Hill. The alley adjoining Blyth's Close, and latterly bearing the name of Todd's Close, is styled in all the older deeds "Edward Hope's Close." The sons of the French emigrant flourished in the land of his adoption, and accepted the popular elements of Scottish life in that stirring era. Edward became one of the magistrates of Edinburgh, incurred the wrath of Queen Mary for his reforming zeal in enforcing "the statuts of the toun" against any "masse-moonger, or obstinat papist that corrupted the people, suche as preests, friers, and others of that sort, that sould be found within the toun." The

Queen caused Archibald Douglas of Kilspindie, the provost, with Edward Hope and Adam Fullerton, " to be charged to waird in the Castel, and commanded a new electioun to be made of proveist and bailliffes ;" but the citizens sympathised with their leaders, and so civic matters had to be left to their wonted course.

The demolition of Edward Hope's mansion, in 1845, brought to light a small secret chamber on the first floor, lighted by a narrow slit looking into Nairn's Close.   The entrance to it had been by a movable panel in the wainscoting of the larger room, from which Mr. C. K. Sharpe rescued some fine carved oaken arabesque work, divided into compartments by terminal figures in high relief. The sliding panel gave access to a narrow flight of steps ingeniously wound round the wall of a turnpike stair, and thereby effectually precluding suspicion.   The existence of this mysterious chamber was wholly unknown to its later occupants.   When its builder dwelt there, such hiding-places were in frequent requisition ; while the wainscoted hall with which it communicated must have often been used in the deliberations of the Reforming party with which he was identified. Here, we can scarcely doubt, the Earls of Murray, Morton, and Glencairn, John Knox, Erskine of Dun, the Lords Boyd, Lindsay, and other leaders of the popular cause, have assembled to mature plans pregnant with results of lasting importance to the nation.

The house of Edward Hope's brother magistrate, Adam Fullerton, still stands in the Fountain Close, near the Netherbow, with curious sculptured architrave over its twin doorways. The two are linked, as it were, with the date and characteristic motto: VINCIT VERITAS 1573. Over the one lintel the bailie's name and confession of faith are thus set forth: ONLY . BE . CRYST * ADAM FULLERTON : and on the other the equally devout prayer of his wife: ARYIS . O . LORD * MARIORIE . ROGER . Four years before the date thus inscribed on his house, Adam Fullerton was chosen captain of a burgess force raised by the citizens who favoured the Regent Mar, when he laid siege to Edinburgh in the name of the infant King. He was consequently denounced as "our souerane ladie's rebell, and put to the horne," and along with the Earl of Mar and other nobles, knights, and burgesses, was "outlawed and foirfalted" by the parliament of the Queen. His house at the Netherbow, close by the city wall, was thereupon seized and converted into a fort and battery; a platform was constructed on its summit, wherefrom to assail the besiegers, who had erected a battery on the neighbouring height of St. John's Hill. Thus the outlawed bailie's dwelling became a special target for the "nyne pece of ordonance great and small" brought by the Regent Mar for the purpose of besieging the queen's men within the walls. The contemporary author of the "History of James the Sext," tells us that "the gunnis war transportit to a fauxburg of the toun, callit Pleasands; and thairfra they laid to thair batterie aganis the toun walls, and shot at a platforme whilk was erectit upon a housheid perteining to Adame Fullertoun;" but, as we learn from the same authority at a later date, "thai did litill or no skaith to the said hous and platforme." When, accordingly, Adam and his friends got the mastery, he returned to town; and in this very year, 1573, in which he repaired his house, and decorated its lintels with his triumphant VINCIT VERITAS, Sir William Durie laid siege to the castle on behalf of the young king; and Adam Fullerton was chosen a burgess of the Parliament which assembled at the Tolbooth on the 26th of April following.

The title-deeds of the old mansion in Todd's Close record the fortunes of one line of descent from John de Hope, the attendant of Queen Magdalen. He was himself probably of Huguenot leanings, and we trace the mansion in succession from the sturdy king's man and reformer, Edward, to his grandson, Henry; and then to "Sir Thomas Hope of Craighall, knight baronet, his majesty's advocate," who makes it over to his niece, Christian Hope, a daughter of Henry, the progenitor of the Hopes of Amsterdam, merchant princes of their day. It passed thereafter, by marriage and succession, through several hands, until in 1641 it lapsed to James, Viscount Stair, in settlement of a bond for the sum of "three thousand guilders, according to the value of Dutch money,"—probably some transaction with the great house at Amsterdam. Sir David Dalrymple, a younger son of the Viscount, occupied the house till 1702, when he sold it to John Wightman of Mauldie, afterwards Lord Provost, and founder of the school which bears his name.

The house of Sir Thomas Hope, famous for his doings as king's advocate of Charles I., has been already noted among the Cowgate palaces. It stands nearly opposite to St. Magdalen's chapel, in the midst of modern degradation and decay; yet with unmistakable traces of the patrician occupants for whom it was erected. A broad archway leads through the plain, substantial front facing the street, into an enclosed quadrangle, with two doorways, each surmounted by a carved lintel with its anagrammatic legend. Over the main entrance, the anagram of the builder is thus rendered: AT HOSPES HUMO, according to the old spelling of the family name, as noted in the Coltness Collections of the Maitland Club; "for the anagram is *At hospes*

Humo, and has all the letters of Thomas Houpe."
Over the other doorway are the motto and date :
TECUM HABITA, 1616,—a memorable year in far
other ways ; for in this same year, as the stone
in the chancel at Stratford-on-Avon testifies,
Shakespeare died ; and on the very same day
and year Oliver Cromwell was admitted an
undergraduate of the University of Cambridge.
The latter coincidence has a certain aptness,
when we remember that the crafty statesman, at
the very time that he filled the office of King's
Advocate, was foremost among those who organ-
ised the opposition which not only effectually
defeated the schemes of Charles and Laud for
remodelling the Scottish church, but which led
to the great civil war. The philosophy of the
founder's quaint motto *At hospes humo,*—which
may be rendered : "But a sojourner in the land,"—
seems to find a realisation in his mansion as it
now stands. Within the entrance which it
decorates, a handsome but woefully dilapidated
oaken staircase leads to the main floor, where the
old hall still exhibits traces of bygone splendour,
amid the tatters with which poverty's palaces are
chiefly tapestried. Here not a few of the bold
councils were held which gave the first check to
the despotic schemes of Charles I. Here too,
we may presume the national league and cove-
nant to have been debated, and the line of policy

matured by which the unhappy monarch found himself foiled alike in Parliament and on the battlefield. No wonder that the Cavaliers held Hope's memory in special abhorrence. Mr. C. K. Sharpe characteristically writes on the margin of one of my old proofs : " The King's Advocate proved his honesty as a confidential servant, as Arnot justly says, by assisting at every cabal, and suggesting every device for his master's ruin. Had the d——d old rogue survived the Restoration he would certainly have been hanged. My grandfather's grandfather, Sir Charles Erskine of Alva, disgraced himself by marrying his daughter ; an ugly slut !"

The Hope lodging was not only a first-class civic mansion of that seventeenth century ; but even now, in a fitter locality, might be renovated into a dwelling not unsuited for modern require- ments. There Mary, Countess of Mar, the daughter of Esme, Duke of Lennox, resided for a time. The countess's household book has been preserved ; and helps us to realise the doings of one of the aristocratic denizens of the Cowgate in that seventeenth century. On 17th January 1639, a dole of six shillings is noted as " given to the poor at Nidries Wynd head, as my lady cam from the treasurer deputes," where we may fancy her to have been drawing some pension, or other perquisite, that stimulated her to such liberality. She pays the moderate custom dues of tenpence at the Water Gate for the horses that entered with my lady's carriage ; and then we seem to trace her on Sundays and week days traversing with becoming dignity the aristocratic thoroughfare of the Cowgate ; or threading one or other of the Wynds by which its denizens made their way to the burgher world above. Six shillings is noted as paid "to ye Abay Kirk broad, as my Laidy went to the sermon." A similar sum is given "to the gardener in ye Abay yard who presentit to my Laidy an flour ;" and then we catch a glimpse of the Cowgate lighted up with the countess's flambeaux, as on the 16th of September 1641 she goes to Holyrood in state, to pay due honour to his Majesty, Charles I., who set out for his ancient kingdom on the 10th of the previous month, to compose matters there at least, as he vainly trusted. Poor Queen Henrietta flattered the hopes of her friends with the best of news. The king writes her "word he has been very well received in Scotland ; and that both the army and the people have showed a great joy to see the king : pray God it may continue !"—a very needful, though unavailing prayer, as it proved. Of the heartiness of the Countess of Mar, however, in the Holyrood reception, there need be no doubt. Her household book preserves the note of twenty-four

shillings "payit for torches to lighten on my
Laidy to the court with my Laidy Marquesse
of Huntlie." Within less than three years thereafter the Countess died, in the Hope mansion, in
the Cowgate, on the 11th of May 1644, while
Leslie, Earl of Leven, was already across the
Tweed with twenty-one thousand Scots; and
things were rapidly tending to their worst for
Charles and his Cavaliers.

Thus the Huguenot proclivities of the old De
Hopes of Francis I. seem to have cropped out anew
in the descendants of the Edinburgh burgher of
Queen Mary's reign. In later generations they
have come to greater honour in the service of kings,
and still take their place among Scottish nobility
as the Earls of Hopetoun.

Adjoining the Hope lodging on the Castle Hill,
stood another mansion of some importance in its day.
The heraldic and other decorations over its entrance,
with the quaint flourishes of its inscribed lintel:
A 1557 A. NOSCE TEIPSUM, made it one of the
most characteristic door-heads of Old Edinburgh.
When the traditions of Blyth's Close were revived,
they gave a royal flavour to the whole neighbourhood. In the popular topography of the locality
accordingly this and all the antique buildings in
the vicinity, from the foreland with its misleading
M.R. and date of 1591, to the most northerly of
them overlooking the Nor' Loch and the distant

Fifeshire hills, were all assigned to the Queen Regent.

In one of his most characteristic commentaries, Mr. Sharpe thus reverts to the spurious traditions of the place :—" The chapel was unheard of when I first came to Edinburgh. Arnot has described what he calls the private oratory of Mary of Lorraine, but nobody cared about such things then ; and it was only after I resided here that I found it out. It was as little known then as St. Margaret's Chapel in the castle,—that is not at all. As to the Queen Regent's Oratory, that is all stuff ! I doubt if there was anything of the sort. Chambers has a grand story in his *Traditions* of a font, and a pillar at its side, on top of which, *within these few years*, stood the statue of a saint presiding over the font ! I should certainly have seen it in that case. But John Knox and the Edinburgh rabble had a keen eye to saints before my day. He was right to make a good story when he was at it. But the niche, or credence, or whatever be the fine new name for such things, was only a cupboard. Arnot calls it a baptismal font. Just as likely I daresay ! More's the pity that Knox should have missed the scandal of a Dowager Queen in need of so many baptismal fonts. He would have contrived some more bruit about lusty Mary Livingstone, and the rest of the dancing hussies. See his account when the

Queen Dowager lay dying in the castle, etc., as recorded in Knox's loathsome history. As to your other story of her tears and humility, asking forgiveness of Argyle, Lord James, and all the rest of it ; I do not wish you to alter this, but I must remark that I do not believe one word of it. It is an historical lie. After all, what is history but a mass of lies ; a dull romance with only a glimpse of truth now and then ?"

The arms and initials on the sculptured lintel, of 1557, equally suffice to show that the mansion which they adorned was no part of the Guise palace. They marked the lodging of Archibald Achison, an influential burgess, who only four years subsequent to the date carved over its doorway, acquired by a charter of Queen Mary the estate of Gosford, in East Lothian, from which his descendants took the title of Vicounts Gosford. One of them, Sir Arthur Acheson, has his picture thus drawn for him by Dean Swift, in 1730 :—

> " What, if for nothing once you kiss't
> Against the grain, a monarch's fist ?
> What, if among the courtly tribe
> You lost a place and sav'd a bribe ;
> And then in surly mood came here
> To fifteen hundred pounds a year,
> And fierce against the Whigs harangued :
> You never ventur'd to be hanged."

Sir Arthur gave the name of Gosford to his Irish

estate ; and there, in spite of his bantering irony, the Dean of St. Patrick's found congenial society. Sir Arthur was a good classical scholar, and his lady a woman of superior intelligence, whom the Dean undertook to instruct in various abstruse subjects when the weather excluded them from the garden and the farm. He resided for years at Market Hill, near Sir Arthur's house, and under his roof for months. Lady Anne, as he styles her, was a special favourite ; and it was professedly as her production that he wrote his humorous " Panegyric on the Dean." In his lines " On cutting down the Old Thorn at Market Hill," he refers to a more famous offshoot of the old stock, Sir Archibald Acheson of Glencairney, the friend of Drummond of Hawthornden, and of Sir William Alexander, Earl of Stirling. He was one of the Scottish Judges promoted to the bench by Charles I. ; and whether by favour of royalty, or through the direct intervention of his friend the earl, he was advanced to the honours of a baronetcy, by a novel process then recently brought into operation. The rank of baronet originated in a scheme of James I. for raising money and promoting the settlement of the province of Ulster. Charles I. revived the scheme for the purpose of planting and settling his New World province of Nova Scotia, which his father had granted by royal deed, in 1621, to the Earl of Stirling. The profitable traffic in honours was entrusted to the earl, and the object is thus set forth by Sir Thomas Urquhart of Cromarty, in his " Discovery of a most exquisite Jewel, found in the kennel of Worcester streets the day after the Fight!" It did not satisfy the earl, he says, " to have a laurel from the muses, and be esteemed a king among poets, but he must also be king of some new-found-land ; and like another Alexander, indeed, searching after new worlds, have the sovereignity of Nova Scotia. He was born a poet, and aimed to be a king ; therefore he would have his royal title from King James, who was born a king, and aimed to be a poet. Had he stopped there it had been well, but the flame of his honour must have some oil where-with to nourish it ; like another Arthur, he must have his knights, though nothing limited to so small a number!" and so Sir Thomas proceeds with his ironical narration of this new mode, " whereby to ascend unto the platforms of virtue, and to take possession of the temple of honour." The earl had authority to sell to two hundred imaginary colonists of his new-world kingdom deeds of conveyance of manors therein, which entitled their owners to the territorial rank and title of knight baronets. The difficulty of enfeof-ing the baronets in their remote signiories was overcome by a royal mandate which converted the Castle Hill of Edinburgh for the time being into the soil of Nova Scotia ; and made the earth and stones thereof, by a legal fiction, the veritable elements of the manors acquired on Acadian territory beyond the Atlantic.   There, accordingly, Sir Archibald Acheson and his brother knights were duly invested with their lordships and honours, including the right to add to their coat-armour the arms of Nova Scotia.   As to the planting and settling of the colony, that seems to have been included in the ceremonial, doubtless gone through with becoming gravity, under my Lord Lyon and his pursuivants, on the Castle Hill.

The favour in which Sir Archibald Acheson was held by Charles I. was further proved by his being made one of the King's Secretaries of State for Scotland.   The mansion which he built and occupied still stands on the east side of the Hammermen's Close in the Canongate.   An ornamental archway, with a pendent key-stone, and other characteristic details in the style of the age, gives access to a quadrangle enclosed on the other three sides by the baronet's residence.   It is built of polished ashlar, with sculptured dormer windows, mouldings, and architectural devices of the period, among which his initials, and those of his wife, Dame Margaret Hamilton, are prominent.   The date of 1633, carved on the front, assigns its completion to the memorable year in which Charles I. paid his first visit to his native capital; and Dr. Laud—then on the eve of his archbishopric,—performed service in the renovated chapel of Holyrood, in a style of ritualistic development which he fondly trusted was ere long to come into universal use in Scotland. An elaborately decorated pediment over the main entrance to the mansion of Sir Archibald bears in bold relief the family crest. A cock stands on a trumpet, the emblem and embodiment of boastful vigilance; and below are the baronet's and his lady's initials interlaced in elaborate monogram, with the motto: VIGILANTIBUS. The whole style and arrangements of the Canongate mansion serve to illustrate the change in fashions and in taste in the interval between the building of the town lodging on the Castle Hill in Queen Mary's reign, and that of the courtier of Holyrood in the days of Charles I.

In point of site and outlook the older mansion was greatly to be preferred. The approach was indeed by a steep and narrow close; but its northern windows overlooked the Nor' Loch, and the wooded heights where the new town now stands, with the Forth and the Fifeshire hills beyond. In lieu of those the dwellers in the Canongate enjoyed the gay cavalcades that were wont to enliven that aristocratic approach to the palace of Holyrood; and could felicitate themselves moreover on being at the court end of the town, the Belgravia of Auld Reekie in its palmy days of revived royalty. In the older mansion there lingered nearly to the last sundry curious relics of its original possession. A large oaken front of an ambry or wardrobe, with elaborately carved panels, was rescued from it shortly before its demolition, and formed one of the prized treasures of Mr. Sharpe's collection. A more valuable relic of the same class, now in the museum of the Scottish Antiquaries, is a doorway with richly carved panels, which long constituted one of the chief lions to the antiquarian explorer of the locality, associated in all its intricate recesses with the memory of Mary of Guise.

The account furnished of this piece of carving in the *Traditions of Edinburgh* amusingly illustrates the co-operation of fancy and tradition in identifying the assumed memorials of royalty. One of the most remarkable curiosities, writes Dr. Robert Chambers, "is a door of black oak, carved in the style of the celebrated Stirling heads, and containing, among other beautiful devices, portraits of the king and queen, the whole in excellent preservation. There are four panels in this exquisite piece of workmanship, on each of which is a circular entablature." He then describes the heraldic devices on two of those, and thus proceeds: "The lower departments contain the portraits, which form by far the most interesting part of the curiosity. That of the king, which is under the deer's head, bears a strong resemblance to the common portraits of James V., and has all that free carriage of the head, and elegant slouch of the bonnet, together with the great degree of manly beauty, with which this monarch is usually represented. He wears moustaches as usual, but in other respects it may be said that he is here drawn rather later in life than in most other portraits, which is implied by a comparative grossness of features, indicative of middle age. In the queen's portrait we have the head and bust of a female about forty years of age, dressed in a coif or antique head-dress, and without any other remarkable ornament." The narrator concludes his description with a declaration that the ancient door is a very flattering specimen of the arts of Scotland at the period when it was executed.

In reality the fine old piece of carving, though an undoubted relic of the building in which it was found, and where it had survived the vicissitudes of three centuries, had no more to do with Mary of Guise or the palace of Lorraine than the R. M. of Robert M'Naught, merchant burgess, at the head of the close, had to do with " the cipher of *Maria Regina*." The armorial bearings on two of the panels repeat the arms impaled on one shield on the sculptured lintel of Archibald

Acheson's lodging. It is not absolutely impossible that the carved basso-relievos might be designed to represent James V. and his queen. But at the date sculptured on the old lintel James V. had been dead for fifteen years ; and his dowager was exercising the regency in name of their daughter Mary. It is not therefore likely that the old citizen, if he bethought himself of doing honour to his royal neighbour in the carvings of his mansion, would have ignored the reigning sovereign ; and it is still more improbable that he would have surmounted the heads of royalty with the arms of himself and his wife. In truth the "free carriage, elegant slouch of the bonnet," and still more the "manly beauty" of the supposed monarch, are mainly due to the narrator's fancy ; and this flattering specimen of early Scottish art was more probably designed to show off the old burgess and Dame Acheson at their best.

CHAPTER VI.

The Queen's Marys.

WHEN the youthful Queen, Mary Stuart,—then a beautiful child in her sixth year,—set sail for France in 1543, she was escorted by her governors, the Lords Erskine and Livingstone, and accompanied by her natural brother the Lord James, then a youth in his seventeenth year, though to be known in due time as "The good Regent." Along with the Scottish Queen there went also the "Queen's Maries," four noble maidens selected as her playmates and future maids of honour, from the families of Seatoun, Beatoun, Livingstone, and Fleming. They returned to Scotland along with their royal mistress, with all the charms of youthful beauty refined by the courtly graces of France; and in the "Pomp of the Gods," a masque originally composed by Buchanan in Latin, and enacted at Holyrood on the marriage of the Queen to Darnley, on the 29th of July 1565, Diana thus addressed the Father of Olympus:—

> " Great father, Maries five late served me,
> Were of my quire the glorious dignitie ;

> With these dear five the heaven I'd regain,
> The happiness of other gods to stain ;
> At my lot Juno, Venus, were in ire,
> And stole away one :"—

The Queen herself, as one of the five Marys, is now being stolen away ; and indeed ere this the vacancies which wedlock had caused in their ranks had probably more than once needed to be filled up. Mary Fleming is referred to in one of Buchanan's epigrams as " the King's valentyn ;" but in the ballad of the Queen's Marie, as it has come down to us, both she and Mary Livingstone disappear, and are replaced by Mary Hamilton and Mary Carmichael. In the course of the Holyrood masque it appears that three of the maids of honour had preceded their royal mistress: stolen away by Juno's wiles, from Diana's service, in spite of the virgin goddess's remonstrance ; and the remaining one was about to follow their example. Jupiter exclaims :—

> " One Marie now remains of Delia's five,
> And she at wedlock o'er shortly will arrive."

This no doubt alludes to the expected marriage of Mary Livingstone, which provoked John Knox into the indulgence of his most censorious vein ; for, says he, " it was weill knawin that schame haistit mariage betwix Johne Sempill, callit the Danser, and Marie Levingstoune, surnamet the Lustie." He then adds : " What bruit the Maries and the rest of the danseris of the Courte had, the ballatis of that aige did witnes, quhilk we for modesteis sake omit." To the stern reformer the pastimes of the court, its music, dancing, and all else, seemed abundant confirmation of the most censorious gossip. The revellers were the vain sons and daughters of pleasure ; "and giff thai luikit for no uther lyffe to cum, thay wald haif wissit thair soneis and dochteris rather to have bene exerceit in flinging upone ane flure, and in the rest that thair of followis, than to haif bene nurisched in the companie of the godlie, and exerceissit in vertew, quhilk in that Courte wes haittit ; and fylthines not onlie maintenit, but also rewairded. Witness the lordschip of Abercorne, the baronie of Authormortie, and diverse utheris pertenyng to the patrimonie of the Crowne, gyffin in heritage to scouparis (*i.e.* skippers), dansaris, and dalliaris with damis."

But in all ages there have been two ways of telling the same story. So far is there from being any confirmatory evidence of this marriage having been "haistit," that letters from Randolph, the English ambassador, both to Cecil and the Earl of Bedford, and from the French ambassador, Paul de Foix, to Catherine de Medicis, speak of preparations for the marriage months before. Queen Mary named the marriage day, and gave a liberal dowry. The marriage-contract, dated at

Edinburgh on the 3d of March 1564-5, is subscribed by the Queen, and witnessed by Lord Erskine, Lord Ruthven, and Maitland of Lethington. Mary Livingstone had been the intimate companion of the Queen from that year, 1548, when they sailed together on their way to France, as young children, "in the King's own galley," there to spend what, to the poor Queen at least, were undoubtedly the happiest days of her life. No wonder then that she treated the lovely Mary Livingstone as a sister, gave the bride her wedding dress, furnished the bridal masque, and a dowry of £500 a year in land. This was the barony of Auchtermuchty, to which Knox alludes when he selects this wedding for his most censorious comments on the Court of Holyrood. Yet it is to this same marriage that Queen Mary thus refers in the royal charter bestowing her gift of lands on the newly-wedded pair: "In consideration that it had pleisit God to move their hartes to joyne togidder in the stait of matrimonye :"—so differently does the same act appear according to the sympathies or prejudices of the observer. When James VI., in 1581, revoked numerous grants of the previous reign, the charter of infeftment in the lands of Auchtermuchty to the Queen's Marie and her husband is specially "reservit and exceptit" from revocation ; and he is there styled by his territorial designation of Butress, or Beltrees, in Renfrewshire. By this title the name Sempill became associated in various ways with the national literature and history, but especially with Scottish song. Whether from honest indignation or politic time-serving, Robert Sempill deserted the cause of Queen Mary after the death of Darnley; and the "Sempill Ballates" assailed her as a Delilah, a Jezebel, a Clytemnestra, and Semiramis, until her flight to England. Then his humour changed, and the Regent brother was produced as the real author of crimes, by which he sought to play anew the part of Crookback Richard.

The descendants of Mary Livingstone are an interesting example of hereditary genius. Her son, Sir James Sempill, a man of ability and great influence in his day,—the ambassador to Queen Elizabeth in 1599,—was the author of the clever satire entitled "The Packman's Paternoster." His son manifested the same literary tastes in his "Elegy on Habbie Simson, the Piper of Kilbarchan," whose loss is recalled in the "Maggie Lauder" of his grandson Francis. By him the name of Sempill of Beltrees has been made famous by more than one popular lyric. He is the reputed author of the fine song, written to what appears to have been the still older tune of "She rose and let me in." It has been pruned and remodelled by Ramsay, Tannahill, Chambers, and others, to fit it to the severer taste of modern times. Burns wrote on the margin of his copy of Johnstone's *Musical Museum*, " The old set of this song is much prettier than this, but somebody—I believe it was Ramsay, —took it into his head to clear it of some seeming indelicacies, and made it at once more chaste and more dull."   More than one claimant disputes with Sempill of Beltrees the authorship of the original song.   Tom d'Urfey appears to have the right to at least one early version, while another has been claimed for Sir William Scott of Thirlstain, the ancestor of the Lords Napiers, who also disputed Sempill's title to "The Blythsome Bridal," which reproduces, in the humble life of a later age, the skipping, dancing, and feasting, which the stern Reformer denounced, with an appeal to what "the ballatis of that aige did witness : "—

> "Fy, let us a' to the bridal,
>   For there'll be liltin' there ;
> For Jock's to be married to Maggie,
>   The lass wi' the gowden hair."

The characteristic old Edinburgh mansion in which the Sempills resided still stands in Sempill's Close on the Castle Hill, with its octagonal turret staircase and inscribed lintels.   Over the main entrance is the device of an S. entwining an anchor, with the inscription and date : PRAISED BE THE LORD MY GOD MY STRENGTH AND MY REDEEMER. ANNO DOM. 1638.   The date and device are repeated on another doorway, with the legend :

SEDES MANET OPTIMA CŒLO. Those, however, are the pious inscriptions of the original builder, whose arms accompany them : party per fesse, in chief three crescents, a mullet in base. The house was purchased in 1743 by Hugh, twelfth Lord Sempill, and enlarged, somewhat to the damage of its antique picturesqueness, as appears from the dormer windows now built up in its west wall. Lord Sempill, who had seen considerable military service, commanded the left wing of the royal army at the battle of Culloden.

His Lordship was succeeded in the old mansion on the Castle Hill by Sir James Clerk of Penicuik, the representative of another Scottish family associated in more than one way with letters. Sir John— or Baron Clerk, as he is more generally styled, the friend of Sandie Gordon of the *Itinerarium*,—was a poet before he became an antiquary, and, like the Laird of Monkbarns, had reasons of his own for regarding somewhat cynically even the best of womankind. The verses which he sent to Miss Susanna Kennedy, the reigning beauty of the days of our great-great-grandmothers, were communicated by Mr. C. K. Sharpe to Dr. Robert Chambers. They are printed in his *Traditions of Edinburgh* along with an account, not wholly correct, of the wooing of the fickle beauty by the Earl of Eglintoune, and her consequent jilting of the Laird of Penicuik. Miss Kennedy being fond of music, he sent her a flute as his love-gift, with a copy of verses enclosed in the instrument, ending with these lines :—

> " Go, happy pipe, and ever mindful be
>   To court bewitching Silvia for me ;
>   Tell all I feel,—you cannot tell too much,—
>   Repeat my love at each soft melting touch ;
>   Since I to her my liberty resign,
>   Take thou the care to tune her heart to mine."

The earl is described in the *Traditions* as an amorous Bluebeard of patriarchal years, who was watching with ill-concealed disgust the valetudinarian longevity of his second countess, when the beautiful Miss Kennedy made her *debut* in Edinburgh circles. " I believe," writes Mr. Sharpe, in one of his marginal notes, " that I unwittingly misled Mr. Chambers about Lord Eglintoune's age. There were, as I remember, some rhymes on the occasion about ' Susanna and the elders,' which I daresay misled me. When he married Miss Kennedy he could not be much turned forty ;"—old enough, however, for the jest, when the opportunely widowed earl cut out the laird of Penicuik, and carried of the reigning toast and beauty, in spite of his amorous muse. Sir John Clerk was the author of the fine song,

> " O merry may the maid be
>   That marries the miller."

It appeared anonymously in " The Charmer," in 1751, when its author was far advanced in years ;

but like so many other current songs of Scotland, it is wrought upon an older model, and fitted to an ancient tune. The first verse must be accredited to some elder minstrel: but the newer stanzas are replete with homely vigour. Even they, however, mingle traces of older song: for Mr. Stenhouse claims that "the thought expressed in the last two lines appears to be borrowed from a similar idea in the old ballad of Tarry Woo." The homely joys of the miller's hearth are thus graphically pictured :—

> " In winter time, when wind and rain
>   Blow o'er the house and byre,
> He sits beside a clean hearthstane,
>   Before a rousing fire ;
> O'er foaming ale he tells his tale ;
>   Which rows him o'er fu' nappy ;
> Wha'd be a king, a petty thing,
>   When a miller lives sae happy ? "

But it was a younger generation that succeeded to the lodging of Lord Sempill ; for the muse of Penicuik belongs to recent times, and sports with fancies differing widely from those of the ballads challenged by Knox to witness against the frail beauties of Mary Stuart's court.

The Guise palace has vanished from among the historical dwellings of the Castle Hill ; but still among the old mansions of the Canongate, though "fallen on evil days," there survive some relics of that olden time to perpetuate genuine associations with Queen Mary. Oliver's land, to the east of Morocco Close, is a good specimen of the old stone land of that sixteenth century, with timber gallery, crow-stepped gables, a finely moulded doorway on the first floor, and within the gallery and fore-stair inscribed: SOLI · DEO · HONOR · ET · GLORIA. The area of its floor is limited enough according to modern ideas. Nevertheless it is described in the old titles as having "a fore chamber and gallery, a chamber of dais," and the like patrician requisites. Here resided Lawrence, fourth Lord Oliphant, an active adherent of Queen Mary. His elder brother, the Master of Oliphant, joined the Ruthven conspirators in 1582, and perished in the wreck of the vessel in which he was escaping to France. An equally antique mansion alongside of it was occupied in the following century by Lord David Hay of Belton, a son of the Earl of Tweeddale; and, according to its title-deeds, is bounded on the north, in the close behind, "by the stone tenement of land some time belonging to the Earl of Angus."

Time and the changing requirements of modern centuries have wrought sad havoc with the old scenes. But wherever the local antiquary extends his researches, he finds the antique thoroughfares of the Canongate haunted with memories of Holy-

rood. The name of Kinloch's Close, which still
pertains to the alley that led of old to the Earl
of Angus's lodging, is the memorial of a civic
mansion where the beauties of Holyrood held
some of their gayest masqueradings. The un-
picturesque Chapel of Ease in New Street occupies, in part, the site of the lodging of Henry
Kinloch, a wealthy burgess of the burgh, to
whose hospitable care Queen Mary consigned the
Seigneur de Rambouillet, ambassador from France,
when he arrived at Edinburgh in 1565.   His
mission was to invest Henry Lord Darnley with
the Order of St. Michael ; and therefore it is not
to be doubted that her Majesty designed to entertain him with all honour when she consigned him
to the hospitalities of Kinloch's Close.   The
gossiping diarist to whom we owe the " Diurnal
of Occurrents," relates that " Vpoun Monunday the
ferd day of Februar, thair come ane ambassatour
out of the realm of France, callit Monsieur
Rambollat, with xxxvj horse in tryne, gentilmen,
throw Ingland, to Halyrudhous, quhair the King
and Queenis Majesties wes for the tyme, accom-
panyit with their nobillis.   And incontinent efter
his lychting, the said ambassatour gat presens of
thair graces, and thairefter depairtit to Henrie
Kynloches lugeing in the Cannogait besyid
Edinburgh."   A few days after, " the Kingis
Majestie," as Darnley is styled, " in Halyrudhous

ressavit the ordour of knychtheid of the cokill fra the said Rambollat, with great magnificence." The same evening there was a grand "maskery" following the banquet given in honour of the occasion, when "the auld chappell of Halyrudhous wes reapparrellit with fyne tapestrie, and hung magnificentlie." Another entertainment of feasting and masquerade followed on the eleventh of the same month, on which occasion the old diarist gives us some insight into the skippings, dancings, and dallyings, which so roused the ire of John Knox. "The King and Quene in lyik manner bankettit the samin ambassatour; and at evin our soueranis maid the maskrie and mumschance, in the quhilk the Queenis grace, and all her Maries and ladies wer all cled in men's apperrell; and everie ane of thame presentit ane quhingar, bravelie and maist artificiallie made and embroiderit with gold, to the said ambassatour and his gentlemen." When it is remembered that down to a much later date the female characters on the English stage were personated by boys; and the Puritans, so soon as they got the ascendant, put an effectual stop to all stage playing; it is easy to conceive what prejudice would be excited by rumours of the Queen and her maids of honour, bringing the free fashions of the French court to the Canongate, and carrying on such "maskrie and mumschance " in male attire.   Yet it is to the approving pen of a scholar, more dignified, and little less rigid in Puritan strictness of morality, that we owe some of the choicest illustrations of Holyrood masqueradings.

The Twelfth Night pastimes appear to have been in special favour with the Queen's Marys. On that holiday the Queen of the Revels was selected by means of a bean hidden in the cake ; and so was known as " The Queen of the Bean." In one of his fine Latin epigrams, Buchanan, commemorates the choice of Mary Beatoun as Queen of the Twelfth Tide revels at Holyrood, and renders justice alike to her beauty and to the charms of her mind.   A portrait of her, preserved at Balfour House, in Fife, shows her very fair, with golden hair and dark eyes.   She appears to have been of a happy disposition, and the most gifted among the beauties of Queen Mary's Court.   Sir Thomas Randolph, even in writing to Queen Elizabeth, alludes to the enjoyment he had derived from her society ; while he tells more freely to the Earl of Bedford how greatly he was fascinated by her wit and beauty. Queen Mary recognised the fine qualities of her mind in the bequest to her of all her English, French, and Italian books ; while those in Latin and Greek were left to the University of St. Andrews.   By her marriage she is curiously associated with the fate of her royal mistress. She became the wife of Alexander Ogilvy of Boyne, who survived her, and in his old age married Lady Jane Gordon,—then the venerable Countess Dowager of Sutherland,—whom Bothwell divorced to make way for his fatal marriage with the Queen.

Twelfth Night, or the Eve of the Epiphany, "on whilk the starre guydit the thre kingis to Bethlem," was called in Scotland "Uphalieday," because with it the Christmas holidays came to an end ; and so there was the greater reason to make the most of it in merriment. Mary Fleming, already mentioned as another of the Queen's Marys, figures in 1563 as Queen of the Revels at Holyrood at this merry season ; and Randolph once more helps us to realise the scene. Writing to Lord Robert Dudley, he describes her appearance as " Queen of the Bean, in a gown of cloth of silver," and so bedecked with jewels, that, he says, " more in our whole jewell-house were not to be found." Queen Mary herself, entering into the full spirit of the pastime, appears to have abdicated for the night in favour of the mimic sovereign ; and is described by Randolph as dressed in simple black and white apparel. " No other jewells or gold had she about her, but the ring which he brought her from the Queen's Majesty,— Queen Elizabeth,— hanging at her breast." It was in this same year that the strange outrage of Chastillard disturbed the Queen's equanimity ; and then for her protection she selected Mary Fleming to share her chamber, and be her bedfellow. She was betrothed soon after to Maitland of Lethington. The murder of Rizzio separated the lovers for a time ; but they were married at length in 1566.

Mary Seyton, the fourth of the Queen's Marys, is extolled by the Queen for the matchless art with which she could dress her royal mistress's hair. She alone of the fair sisterhood never married. She had vowed herself to a life of celibacy, when Andrew Beatoun, master of the Queen's household, and brother to the Archbishop, —then ambassador at Paris,—induced her reluctantly to seek release from her vow. But his sudden death seemed to pledge her anew to the vows she had abjured. She lived to share her mistress's prison life for upwards of fifteen years, and then retiring to the convent of St. Peter's at Reims, of which the abbess was an aunt of Queen Mary, she there ended her days. She had a half-sister, Marion, who became Countess of Menteith, while another of her sisters helps to awaken still more romantic though fictitious associations with the Canongate in the passages of love between Catherine Seyton and Roland Græme. Time has long since dealt with the Canongate mansion

of the Seytons.   In Edgar's map of 1742 the
ruins still constituted a prominent feature there;
but before the century closed they had been displaced by Whitefoord House, a fitting memorial
of the latest generation of Canongate gentry.

Rambling as we are, with the help of fact and
fancy, through deserted scenes of old historic
romance, it may be well, perhaps, to review the
modern associations of the locality, before reverting to those to which fiction has added a
new charm.   Sir John Whitefoord, of Whitefoord
and Ballochmyle, belonged by descent and inheritance to the land of Burns.   But his father,
who is said to have been the prototype of Sir
Arthur Wardour, resembled the Antiquary's neighbour in this at least, that he showed equally little
worldly wisdom in the management of his estates.
The beautiful glen through which the Ayr winds,
on the estate of Ballochmyle, near Mauchline, was
a favourite resort of Burns; and the misfortunes
which compelled its owner to part with his
paternal inheritance awoke the keenest sympathy
in the poet's breast.   His " Bonnie lass o' Ballochmyle," there is no doubt, was the sister of Mr.
Claud Alexander, an East Indian nabob, by whom
the estate was acquired.   But the lady resented
the freedom of the peasant bard, and left unan-
swered the letter in which he enclosed the beautiful
song inspired by her presence " Amang the braes

o' Ballochmyle." He had already sung a similar refrain as the farewell of Miss Maria Whitefoord to "the bonnie banks of Ayr;" but it was not till a later date that her brother, Sir John, learned to appreciate at his true worth the old tenant of Mossgiel. In Edinburgh the Ayrshire laird and the Ayrshire peasant met on a footing of equality, while the poet was not slow to revive associations with the favourite scenes of his home. In 1757 he addresses Sir John as "the first gentleman in the country whose benevolence and goodness of heart had interested himself for me, unsolicited and unknown." With tears of gratitude he thanks him for interposing on his behalf, when falsely traduced ; and closes with "the honest warm wishes of a grateful heart for your happiness, and every one of that lovely flock who stand to you in a filial relation." To Sir John he sent his touching "Lament for James Earl of Glencairn," accompanied with a special dedication in verse, in which he says :

"The friend thou valued'st ; I the patron loved."

In this is clearly shown the revival of old associations with scenes which he had spoken of in his slighted letter to the sister of the new laird of Ballochmyle as "the favourite haunts of my muse, on the banks of the Ayr." He chose for the new beauty an evening when nature presented

VOL. I.

CLARINDA'S LODGING, GENERAL'S ENTRY.

I. 168.

herself "in all the gaiety of the vernal year." With like apt allusion to the feelings of her who was bidding a last farewell to the home of her fathers and the scenes of her childhood, he pictured the parting of Maria Whitefoord, the sister of Sir John, among the withering flowers of Ballochmyle, when autumn fades into winter, and "nature sickens on the e'e :"—

> The Catrine woods were yellow seen,
>   The flowers decayed in Catrine lea,
> Nae lavrock sang on hillock green,
>   But nature sicken'd on the e'e.
> Through faded groves Maria sang,
>   Hersel' in beauty's bloom the while,
> And aye the wild wood echoes rang :
>   Farewell the Braes o' Ballochmyle !
>
> Low in your wintry beds, ye flowers,
>   Again ye'll flourish fresh and fair ;
> Ye birdies dumb, in withering bowers,
>   Again ye'll charm the vocal air.
> But here, alas ! for me, nae mair
>   Shall birdies charm or flow'ret smile ;
> Fareweel the bonnie banks of Ayr,
>   Fareweel, fareweel ! sweet Ballochmyle !

Sir John had a sort of hereditary right to play the poet's patron. His uncle, Caleb Whitefoord, excited the envy of Oliver Goldsmith by the popularity of his humorous sallies, published under the signature of *Papyrius Cursor*, at a time when the poet had still to look to the future for adequate appreciation. They, too, became friends in later years. Caleb Whitefoord formed one in the famous gatherings at the St. James's Coffee House ; where the invitation might well be expressed in Goldsmith's line :—

" Let each guest bring himself, and he brings the best dish ; "

for the guests included Johnson, Burke, Garrick, Reynolds, Whitefoord, and Goldsmith himself. Of those Garrick, Richard Burke, and Whitefoord. are named as the aggressors in the famous satirical epitaphs which provoked the latest flash of genius in Goldsmith's *Retaliation.* Its choicest epitaphs on Garrick, Burke, and Reynolds, are familiar to all, with their pleasant, kindly satire, so character- istic of the poet and the man. The epitaph of Caleb Whitefoord, prince of punsters, though in- ferior to them, has an interest of its own, with the bantering compliment of its close :—

" Merry Whitefoord, farewell ! for thy sake I admit
  That a Scot may have humour, I had almost said wit.
  This debt to thy memory I cannot refuse,
  Thou best-humour'd man with the worst-humour'd muse."

Whitefoord House has its memories, accordingly, in association with the poet Burns. The son and name- sake of Sir John appears to have been much in the poet's society while in Edinburgh, and even to have admitted him to his most sacred confidences, as appears from one of the poet's letters. "This," he writes to an Ayrshire correspondent, " is the great day,—the assembly and ball of the Caledonian Hunt,—and John has had the good luck to pre-engage the hand of the beauty-famed and wealth-celebrated Miss M'Adam, our countrywoman. Between friends, John is desperately in for it there."

But Whitefoord House is the parvenu occupant of a site famous in olden times as that of the lodging of the Earls Wyntoun, where one of the Queen's Marys dwelt, famed no less in romance than in song and veracious history. It was the court residence of one of the most powerful leaders of the Catholic party, when the widowed Queen of Francis II. returned from France, accompanied by a fair daughter of that house, to enter on her own independent sovereignty. All we know definitely of the building is derived from the extensive area laid down in Edgar's map of 1742, designated the "ruins of late Earl of Wintoun's house." It stood not far from the Girth Cross, directly opposite Queensberry House. Here, in its actual associations with history, we learn from the contemporary "Diurnal of Occurrents," that when, in February 1565, Henry Lord Darnley followed his father, the Earl of Lennox, to Edinburgh, he "wes lugeit in my Lord Seytoun's lugeing in the Cannongait besyid Edinburgh." From thence he followed the royal widow to Wemyss Castle, beyond the Forth ;

and—fool though he was,—outwitted the intrigues of practised diplomatists. He was of the royal blood of Scotland ; and, though direct from the court of Queen Elizabeth, was a Catholic. His marriage to Mary Stuart seemed therefore to augur well for the triumph of the party to which the Seytouns adhered ; and great, doubtless, was the rejoicing in their old halls.

We have to put ourselves under the guidance of romance, and acknowledge our obligations to the fertile fancy of Scott for a restoration of the Seytouns' lodging as it stood of old on the ruined site of 1742. For this purpose it is only needful to follow Roland Græme under the vaulted archway through which he vanished from Adam Woodcock's sight, to find ourselves in a paved court decorated with stone vases, and enclosed by a sombre quadrangle, with its windows surmounted with heavy architraves sculptured with religious devices and the armorial bearings of the Seytouns. Over the main doorway, boldly sculptured in stone, were their three crescents within the double tressure, on a shield supported by two mertrixes, or heraldic foxes, underneath which Roland found his way into the hall, dimly lighted by its latticed casements of painted glass. Here, too, the sculptor had wrought in stone scutcheons bearing double-tressures fleured and counter-fleured, crescents, wheat-sheaves, and other heraldic devices of the Seytouns, relieved by the arms and suits of mail which hung on the walls, with here and there their terse motto, *Semper*, or the punning slogan, "St. Bennet and set on."

With fancy ready to play the architect and do the work of the restorer, there is no need for a niggard hand in the decorations. But after all Roland Græme takes us no farther than the outer court. When Gordon of Rothiemay executed his famous bird's-eye view of Edinburgh in 1647, the Seyton lodging stood entire, with its open pleasure-grounds to the north, its close, and outer and inner courts. The latter is there shown as a large enclosed quadrangle, on a scale only equalled by one or two others among the civic mansions of the time.

Tracing its history chronologically, as we return to genuine chronicles, the Seyton lodging received in 1582 the French emissary Manzeville, when he visited the court of Holyrood as the special agent of the house of Guise, while La Mothe Fénélon was the accredited representative of Henry III., with secret permission from the captive queen, to address her son, James VI., by his royal title. There accordingly it is not mere fancy to picture to ourselves the emissary of the Guises plotting and intriguing with the leaders of the Catholic party; and filling the mind of Queen Elizabeth's agent with the keenest apprehensions by sending to the young king " a present of French apples, almond, and other fruit," which he interpreted as some preconcerted signal for action, and wrote accordingly in all haste to give his royal mistress warning.   But the Guises and Seytons were playing a losing game.   The final catastrophe to the latter came in 1715, when George, the fifth Earl of Winton, was attainted for his share in that ill-concerted rebellion ; and the old lodging in the Canongate was abandoned to desolation, and so fell into ruin.

The rest of the Queen's Marys followed the example of Mary Livingstone.   But so long as a queen resided at Holyrood, she must needs have her maids of honour ; and hence the name of the Queen's Marys appears to have passed into the general designation not only for such, but for the lady's bower-maid generally ; as in the couplet which Scott quotes from an old ballad :

> " Now bear a hand, my Maries a',
>   And busk me brave and make me fine."

Burns was familiar with snatches of more than one old song embodying traditional memories of the frail beauties of Mary's court.   " The bonnie lass o' Livingston " has the license as well as the humour of the older muse ; and "The Queen's Marie" is evidently a version of one of the ballads referred to by Knox, with its " bruit about the dancers of Holyrood," which it is a pity the old reformer was so fastidious about quoting; since he is tolerably plain-spoken in his own prose about matters " committed. in the courte, yea not far from the quenis awin lap." The ballad of " The Queen's Marie," preserved in the "Minstrelsy of the Scottish Border," was communicated by Mr. C. K. Sharpe. In his first letter to Scott he says—" From my earliest infancy I have been fond of old ballads, and have sat for days listening to the ' spinsters and the knitters in the sun' singing many of the songs published in your collection. Of course I learnt to repeat a great number, and I still retain in my memory a few entire, with an immense hoard of scraps. The Douglas Tragedy was taught me by a nursery-maid, and was so great a favourite that I committed it to paper the moment I was able to write. I have this copy still in ' beau spelling,' together with a song of ' Mary Hamilton,' whom I take to be the Queen's Marie in the ' Minstrelsy,' and the ditty of ' Fair Dysmal,' *alias* Ghismonda, taken from Boccaccio, with a strange debasement of Guiscard into a kitchen-boy. There is a variation from history in my ballad of ' Mary Hamilton,' the king himself being her gallant. He attempts to destroy her child before birth with the leaves of the abbey-tree, and she finally drowns it." The old ballad evidently lived in the memories of the peasantry of Annandale,

Nith, and Ayr.   Burns quotes one of its finest stanzas when writing to Mrs. Dunlop in 1795, in reference to the fate of one of the most gifted of Edinburgh's minor poets, William Falconer.   .

The variations between the Ayrshire version and that of Annandale, as preserved by Mr. Sharpe, illustrate the modifications which our old songs and ballads have undergone in their transmission from one generation to another.   They serve to show how little we are justified in assigning a modern origin to such because of some modern phrases interspersed, like rude darnings marring the genuine needlework of some fine old tapestry. The ballad of "The Queen's Marie," though gleaned from the traditions of various localities, and chiefly from Annandale, nevertheless has the scene laid in Edinburgh.   It extends in various versions to nearly forty stanzas ; but a much briefer specimen will suffice to illustrate the local flavour of this fine ballad-epic.

THE QUEEN'S MARIE.

There lived a lord into the south,
  And he had dochters three ;
And the youngest has gane to Holyrood
  To be the Queen's Marie.

She hadna been about the King's Court
  A twelvemonth and a day
Till frae the king's sight late or air,
  Marie Hamilton durstna be.

The king has gaen to the Abbey garden,
  To pu' the savin tree,
To scale the babe frae Marie's waim,
  But the thing it wadna be.

She has row'd it in her apron,
  An' drapt it in the sea ;
Now sink ye, or swim ye, bonnie babe,
  Ye'se get nae mair o' me.

Ride hooly, ride hooly now, gentlemen,
  Ride hooly now wi' me !
For never, I'm sure, a wearier burd
  Rade in your companie.

As she rade in by Holyrood
  She laughed loud laughters three ;
But ere she wan through the Netherbow
  The tear blinded her ee.

When she gaed up the Tolbooth stairs
  The corks frae her heels did flee ;
But lang ere she cam down again,
  She was condemned to dee.

Yestreen the Queen had four Maries,
  The night she'll have but three ;
There was Marie Seaton, and Marie Beaton,
  And Marie Carmichael, and me.

I charge you all, ye mariners,
  When ye sail o'er the faem,
Let neither my father or mither ken
  But that I'm coming hame !

O little did my mither think,
  That day she cradled me,
The lands I was to travel in,
  Or the death I was to dee !

Amid the revolutionary furor of civic reformers, time has spared a fine old mansion at the foot of Byres' Close, in the High Street, and with it some curious associations with song and history. In 1611 Sir John Byres of Coates,—a fine estate, on which the western skirts of the new town are fast encroaching,—built here his town residence, and inscribed on its lintel the date, and the initials of himself and his lady, with this pious legend :

J.B. BLISSIT . BE . GOD . IN . AL . HIS . GIFTIS. M.B.

But the family died out, the house fell into ruin, and at length Sir Patrick Walker, who had succeeded to part of the old estate, removed the lintel to the antique mansion of Coates House, which is destined to survive as the Deanery, or See House attached to the Cathedral of St. Mary now in process of erection, in fulfilment of his daughter's will. But another mansion at the foot of Byres' Close, which has escaped the fate of that of the old lairds of Coates, is still attractive as a specimen of good civic architecture of the sixteenth century, and still more so on accout of associations which connect it with a remarkable period of Scottish history, and a romance of Scottish song. Unless it is changed since I visited it last, a doorway on the east side of the close affords access by a flight of stone steps, guarded by its neatly carved balustrade, to a garden-terrace, on which stands the mansion of Adam, Bishop of Orkney, who on the 15th of May 1567, performed the ominous marriage service between his kinsman, the Earl of Bothwell, and Mary Stuart. In its title-deeds the old lodging is described as "that tenement of land, of old belonging to Adam, Bishop of Orkney, commendator of Holyrood-house; thereafter to John, commendator of Holy-rood-house," his son, who in 1603 accompanied James VI. to England, and as they reached the confines of his ancient dominions, received the keys of the town of Berwick, in his Majesty's name. Three years thereafter "the temporalities and spiritualitie" of Holyrood, were erected into a barony on his behalf, and he was created a peer, with the title of Lord Holyroodhouse.

The character of Adam Bothwell, Bishop of Orkney, is not specially calculated to win our admiration. He married Queen Mary in the Chapel of Holyrood Palace, according to the new forms of the Protestant Church, in despite of the protest of their framers; and then deserted the cause of the poor Queen, as soon as it appeared to be the losing side. Only two months after celebrating the marriage between her and Bothwell, he placed the crown on the head of her infant son. The following year he humbled himself to the kirk, and engaged " to make a sermoun in the Kirk of Halierudehous, and in the end therof to confesse the offence in marieng the Queine with the Erle of Bothwell." It is obvious that the time-serving old bishop had in him none of the elements which beget the martyrs either for truth or liberty. But the part he played in the memorable events of that stirring time makes both him and his city mansion objects of interest to the modern explorer. The building presents a semi-hexagonal front to the north, surmounted by elaborately sculptured dormer windows, decorated with appropriate inscriptions, now partly defaced by time. Over the north window is the motto: NIHIL . EST . EX . OMNI . PARTE . BEATUM ; another is inscribed: LAUS . UBIQUE . DEO ; and a third: FELICITER . INFELIX . The interior has long been modernised, yet amid all the changes which have robbed it of the traces of ancient grandeur, its chambers still retain a melancholy interest, from their association with events marking the fatal turning-point in the career of Queen Mary, which cost her her crown. The name of Adam, Bishop of Orkney, appears at the bond granted by the. nobility to the Earl of Bothwell, immediately before he put in practice his scheme of daring ambition. Here, therefore, in all probability, in the house of his pliant kinsman, the Earl and many of the nobles who played fast and loose in his unscrupulous plottings, met to mature the designs which ended fatally for so many ; and above all for the chief actors in the ill-omened match. On the night of the royal marriage, there was affixed to the palace gate this distich from Ovid's *Fasti*, B. v.—

"Mense malas Maio nubere vulgus ait."

May was of old an unlucky month to wed in. From that day it acquired a more ominous title ; and popular prejudice still perpetuates in Scotland the fatality which overhangs the luckless pair who choose their bridal-day in that month in which Bothwell and the Scottish Queen were wedded to misery and ruin. On the eve of the wedding of Sir Walter Scott's daughter, he writes from London, amid "a bustle and pell-mell of old and new friends which makes my very brain turn round :—I hope to be down in the end of April to witness that ceremony which cannot with good luck be performed in May."

But an old Scottish rhyme runs : " Better marry in May than rue for aye ;" and a tradition has been current, certainly for two centuries at least, relative to one member of the Bothwell family, in the episcopal lodging in Byres' Close, who would have had better luck even with a May wedding. For at least one hundred and sixty-six years the current local tradition concerning Lady Anne Bothwell has been definitely associated with the beautiful old song which Watson then inserted among the *Comic and Serious Scots Poems*, printed at

Edinburgh between 1711 and 1713, under the title of " Lady Anne Bothwell's Balow." It received its later designation of her " Lament " on the appearance of another version in 1724, in Allan Ramsay's *Tea-Table Miscellany*. It has passed through many phases before and since : and probably enough, like other songs and ballads, had been appropriated to diverse heroines ; but its most tender stanzas can be traced to the beginning of the seventeenth century ; and the tune is preserved in a MS. Lute Book of the Elizabethan age, now in the library of Trinity College, Dublin, the first tune in which is styled " Queen Marie's Dump." Mr. Chappell, in the comments appended to " Bishop Percy's Folio Manuscript," says " *Baloo* is a sixteenth century ballad, not a seventeenth. It is alluded to by several of our early dramatists ;" and on the faith of this and the clumsy patchings of later editors, including Bishop Percy, he would reject the old Edinburgh tradition, though with no better to offer in its place. But there is no conflict in the dates. Two fine stanzas of a different version of the exquisite old lyric occur in Brome's comedy of " The Northern Lass," printed in 1632. They may be traced half a century earlier, and yet have owed their origin to the wrongs of Lady Anne Bothwell, whose father died in 1593, in his seventy-third year.

In the *Memorials of Edinburgh* Lady Anne is styled the daughter of the first Lord Holyroodhouse, and it is added, " is said to have possessed great personal beauty ; " as had already been remarked in Mr. Robert Chambers' note to the ballad. But, according to Mr. C. K. Sharpe, she was not the daughter, but the sister of Lord Holyroodhouse ; and he drily adds in one of his marginal notes, " I never heard anything of her beauty. Her deluder was her own cousin ; for Bishop Bothwell married a daughter of John Murray of Touchadam, by Janet, a daughter of Lord Erskine ;—and so was my great-grandfather's grandmother's son : "—a kind of traditional authority which may recall to readers familiar with old chronicles the authentication by Ethelwerd to his relative Matilda, daughter of Otho of Germany, of his veracious chronicle of King Alfred, the brother of Ethelbert, King of Kent, who, he says, " was also my grandfather's grandfather !" As for the time-serving bishop whom Queen Mary preferred to the see of Orkney in 1562, and the Reformers rewarded for his desertion of her cause by winking at his excambing of the lands of his bishopric for the abbacy afterwards converted into a temporal barony for his son : he seems to have been a sort of compound of Eli and Simon Magus, whose iniquities were only too likely to be visited on his children.

His daughter's disgrace is noted by Father Hay, in his *Diplomatum Collectio*, where he thus records the family genealogy : " This Adam was a younger brother to Sir Richard Bothwell, Provost of Edinburgh in Queen Maries time, and was begotten upon Anna Livingstoun, daughter to the Lord Livingstoun." He then names his four sons ; and adds of their sister,—who, it will be seen, was cousin to one of the Queen's Marys,—he had also " a daughter, Anna, who, by her nurse's deceit, fell with child to a son of the Earle of Mar."

A portrait of Sir Alexander Erskine has been assigned as that of the cozening earl's son. The features, though handsome, have a sinister look. The face tapers to a point at the chin ; and a long pair of moustaches combine with the blue eyes to give a singularly sly and cat-like expression ; such as would well comport with the reputed betrayer of poor Anna Bothwell, while still of so tender an' age as the allusion of Father Hay implies. He was blown up, along with his brother-in-law, the Earl of Haddington, in the Castle of Douglas, in the Merse, in the year 1640 ; and the tradition which associated his name with the daughter of Bishop Bothwell ascribed his death to the special vengeance of heaven on her betrayer. But the date indicates some confusion among the reputed actors in this double tragedy. As for Adam Bothwell, he lies buried in the ruined nave of Holyrood Abbey; and we might be tempted to borrow for his epitaph Voltaire's play on the name of Père Adam, the fat friar at Ferney; "Here lies Father Adam, but not the first of men!" But not so; the bishop's monument, still attached to the second pillar east from the great window, records in the most encomiastic style of mortuary eulogy his services to "the staggering state," and to "the troubled church." Himself a Senator of the College of Justice, his sons are lauded for worthily following in his steps; but of the daughter who probably lies interred in the same roofless aisle, the epitaph of this "nobilissimus vir" makes no note.

The allusion in Father Hay's Manuscript History of the Holyroodhouse Family seems to leave no doubt that Bishop Bothwell had a daughter named Anna, of whom neither genealogists nor writers of encomiastic epitaphs were likely to make note. Accordingly, after all the cavillings and doubts which have been suggested, few traditions of so old a date are sustained by more confirmatory probabilities than that which associates the exquisite old ballad with the ancient lodging in Byres' Close. This at least is indisputable, that for the greater portion of the last two centuries the name of Anne Bothwell, the daughter of the Bishop of

Orkney, has been traditionally connected with its plaintive lines.   Here, accordingly, is the old Ballow, recovered from some of the earliest versions, in genuine antique form ; though there are variations of diverse dates, with abundant traces of the tampering of editors known and unknown :—

LADY ANNE BOTHWELL'S LAMENT.

Ballow, my babe, lie still and sleep,
It grieves me sore to see thee weep.
Wouldst thou be quiet I'se be glad,
Thy mourning makes my heart full sad ;
Ballow, my boy, thy mother's joy,
Thy father breeds me great anoy.

Ballow, my babe, lie still awhile ;
And when thou wakest thou'l sweetly smile ;
But smile not as thy father did
To cozen maids : nay, God forbid !
But yet I fear thou wilt go near
Thy father's flattering face to bear.

When he began to court my love,
And with his sugar'd words me move,
His feignings false and flattering cheer
To me that time did not appear ;
But now I see that cruel he
Cares neither for my boy nor me.

I cannot chose, but ever will
Be loving to thy father still,
His cunning hath purloin'd my heart
That I can no ways from him part ;
In weal or woe, where'er he go,
My heart shall ne'er depart him fro.

But do not, do not, pretty mine,
To faynings false thy heart incline.
Be loyal to thy lover true,
And never change her for a new ;
If good or fair, of her have care,
For woman's banning is wondrous sare.

Bairn, by thy face I will be ware,
Like siren's words I'll not come near ;
My babe an' I'll together live ;
He'll comfort me when cares do grieve ;
My babe and I right soft will lie,
And ne'er respect man's cruelty.

Farewell, farewell, the falsest youth
That ever kiss'd a woman's mouth !
Let never maid ere after me
Once trust unto man's courtesy ;
For if she do but chance to bow,
They'l use her then they care not how.
    Ballow, my babe, lie still and sleep,
    It grieves me sore to see thee weep.

CHAPTER VII.

At the Sign of the Mercury.

THE version of the exquisite old " Balowe " which is given in Allan Ramsay's *Tea-Table Miscellany*, under the title of "Lady Anne Bothwell's Lament," is a fair specimen alike of the virtues and the failings of the Scottish poet as a gleaner among the reliques of ancient poetry. Ramsay, it must be remembered, preceded Bishop Percy in the recovery, correcting, retouching, and giving a grace beyond the reach of any old minstrel art, to the simple songs and ballads of the olden time. It is easy to censure their irreverent presumption now. But let us not forget how much we owe to those who thus beguiled that polished, over-fastidious, artificial age, even by such questionable means, into a reception of the songs " old and plain," such as

> " The spinsters and the knitters in the sun,
>   And the free maids that weave their threads with bones,
>   Did use to chaunt " in Shakespeare's days.

Of this work, to which later English poetry owes

so much, Allan Ramsay has received greatly less than his due share of credit.   Bishop Percy merely followed in his steps, and freely turned his labours to account.   Nearly half a century after Allan Ramsay began the work with his collection of Scottish songs, in 1719, the courtly church dignitary is found introducing his *Reliques of Ancient English Poetry* to polite society, in much the same apologetic fashion as a modern fine gentleman of musical taste might venture into the drawing-room with some exquisite voiced, but tattered ballad-singer he had picked up in the gutter !   He is evidently by no means sure of the reception his protegé will meet with ; and half inclines to disown her at the first rebuff.   In his dedication to the Countess of Northumberland he apologises for " having nothing better to offer her Grace than the rude songs of ancient minstrels ; " " hopes that the barbarous productions of un-polished ages," in spite of the " impropriety " of their intrusion into so august a presence, may obtain, if not the approbation, at least " the notice of her who adorns courts by her presence, and diffuses elegance by her example."   But they are mere " first efforts of ancient genius ; " and are introduced to her ladyship, " not as labours of art, but as effusions of nature," which in the days of Pope and his school by no means implied a compliment.   All this sounds oddly enough now as the introduction to a collection embracing some of the choicest gems of antique poetry: "Chevy Chace" and "Otterburn," The Robin Hood ballads, "The Nut-brown Maid," "The Child of Elle," "Lady Anne Bothwell's Lament," and the like, marred though they were, according to the severer standard of our day, by interpolations and retouchings adapted to the wants of the time. Compared with all this, Ramsay's tone is manly and hearty. He tells the Duke of Hamilton, in his dedication of his *Evergreen*, "The following old bards present you with an intertainment that can never be disagreeable to any Scotsman;"— "they now make a demand for that immortal fame that tuned their souls some hundred years ago. They do not address you with an indigent face and a thousand pitiful apologies to bribe the goodwill of the critics. No! 'tis long since they were superior to the spleen of these sour gentlemen."

At the sign of the Mercury, in the old timber-fronted land still standing at the head of Kinloch's Close, in the High Street of Edinburgh, Allan Ramsay commenced his career as poet, publisher, and bookseller, about the year 1717. By birth he was well descended; for he came of the old lairds of Cockpen, before the Baroness Nairn gave them a niche, "sae proud and sae great," in Scottish song. But the younger line of

ALLAN RAMSAY'S SHOP,
AT THE SIGN OF THE MERCURY, OPPOSITE NIDDRY'S WYND.

P. 190.

the Ramsays of Cockpen had fallen on evil days. The poet lost his father in infancy; owed his later training to the goodwill of his stepfather, a small landholder with more children of his own then he well knew how to provide for; and so Allan, whose ambition was to be an artist, was brought into Edinburgh, and in 1700 apprenticed to a periwig-maker. But periwigs were works of art in that eighteenth century; and Allan showed himself through life a " pawkie chield," who never dropped the substance to go in pursuit of the shadow. So he stuck to his craft, made periwigs such as only an embryo artist and poet could accomplish; and tended his neighbours' heads without concerning himself about their brains, till he had achieved sufficient independence to venture safely on a change.

The eighteenth century was an age of clubs, and Ramsay was the founder of one styled the Easy Club. Its numbers were limited to twelve, and the ease which it cultivated was such as consorted with literary tastes. Each member was required to assume the name, if not also to affect the characteristics, of some Scottish author; and so Ramsay became *Gawin Douglas*. In his " Gentleman's Qualifications," addressed to the fellows of the Easy Club in April 1715, he refers to himself as " a poet sprung from a Douglas loin," in double reference to his assumed name, and to his actual descent through a grandmother, from Douglas of Muthil. *Buchanan, Hector Boece*, and others of the ancients, figure "'mongst the easiest men beneath the skies." The club is said to have been Jacobite in its secret leanings. But Stuart plottings were then least of all compatible with the aims of a fellowship seeking to "live at home at ease;" and Ramsay's address of that memorable year, 1715, clearly refers to intellectual schemings and recreations, such as better accorded with a poet's wishes :—

> " Since in our social friendship nought's design'd
> But what may raise and brighten up the mind."

Here, accordingly, among congenial wits, the poet produced his earliest verses. " Being," he says, " but an indifferent sort of an orator, my friends would merrily alledge that I was not so happy in prose as in rhime ; it was carried in a vote, against which there is no opposition, and the night appointed for some lessons on wit, I was ordered to give my thoughts in verse." These poetical lucubrations appear to have been printed under the patronage of the club ; and their success probably first suggested to him his later vocation of author and publisher.

At the sign of the Mercury, opposite Niddry's Wynd, Allan Ramsay's early poems were first published as broadsides, in the form of " Familiar Epistles," satires, songs, and elegies, and most frequently dealt with local celebrities or popular current events. Some of those appear in his collected works, pruned and polished to suit a severer taste ; but so popular were the original broadsides that their advent was anticipated like the new numbers of a sensational novel. The price, moreover, placed them within reach of all, and the citizens were in the habit of sending a penny to "the sign of the Mercury," with an order for Allan's last piece. The old house may still be visited at the head of Kinloch's Close, though shorn in recent years of the picturesque gabled attics beneath which the winged Mercury presided to such good purpose over Ramsay's muse. His "Elegy on Lucky Wood," and "Lucky Spence's last Advice," are specimens of a style of verse more graphic than poetical. But Mr. Sharpe, to whom some of the old broadsides were familiar, notes that they dealt with a freedom of allusion and satirical innuendo, much of which was happily deemed unfit for the elegant quarto volume of 1721, in which Ramsay's collected poems first appeared, dedicated "to the most beautiful, the Scots ladies," for their "innocent diversion." Let us do full justice to the author of "The Gentle Shepherd." He was competing with the ribbald muse of a rude age ; and no less as a collector and editor, than as an original poet, contributed to the refinement of later generations. If he pruned

at times where we incline to regraft, and grafted
where we unhesitatingly use the pruning-knife,
let us remember that he uprooted and replaced
more that was wholly noxious. At a much later
date, young Lady Anne Lindsay wrote her exquisite " Auld Robin Gray," because its fine air
had still nought but ribbald verse matched to it.
In his " Scribblers Lash'd," Ramsay thus refers to
the popular street ballads of his day :—

> " Another set with ballads waste
>   Our paper, and debauch our taste,
>   With endless larums on the street,
>   Where crowds of circling rabble meet.
>   The vulgar judge of poetry
>   By what these hawkers sing and cry ;
>   Yea, some who claim to wit amiss,
>   Cannot distinguish that from this."

His own volume included the ancient canto of
"Christ's Kirk on the Green," ascribed by him to
James I., which he supplemented with two additional
cantos. It also contained his "Lass of Peattie's
Mill," " Bessy Bell and Mary Gray," "The Yellow-
haired Laddie," "My Mither's aye glowrin' o'er me,"
an early version of "Auld Lang Syne," and other
songs that had, no doubt, already been sung into
popular favour on the High Street and the Canongate. But a piece of higher promise bore the title
of "Patie and Roger," and embodied the germ of
what he ultimately expanded into the fine pastoral

of "The Gentle Shepherd."   He takes his motto
from Prior's version of "Anacreon " :—

> "Let them censure, what care I ?
> The herd of critics I defy.
> No, no, the fair, the gay, the young,
> Govern the numbers of my song :
> All that they approve is sweet,
> And all is sense that they repeat."

The poet himself figures in a well-engraved frontispiece, with jewelled cap and slashed doublet.
The J. S. P. attached to it are, no doubt, designed
for *John Smibert pinxit*.   The painter and poet
were special friends, and Smibert's name appears
in the list of patrons attached to the volume.
The lucky poet realised four hundred guineas
from this first publication ; and, encouraged by
such good fortune, he produced, in succession, his
Fables and Tales, his *Fair Assembly*, and, in a
series of volumes between 1724 and 1736, his
famous *Miscellany of Scottish and English Songs*.
In his *Evergreen* he reproduced pieces of Dunbar,
Kennedy, Henryson, Lindsay, Montgomery, Alexander Scot, Sempill, and others of the elder poets ;
and along with them, Lady Wardlaw's spurious
"Hardyknute" as a genuine antique.   But Ramsay
had much more of the poet than the antiquary in
his composition ; and had, moreover, a poet's idea
of valuing verse less on account of its age than its
merit.   He lived in an era of literary masquerading

and spurious antiques, and had little compunction in patching and ekeing an old poem to suit the taste of his Edinburgh customers ; or palming off on them a "Hardyknute" or a "Vision" of his own day, or even of his own pen, as *Scots Poems wrote by the Ingenious before* 1600." In the former poem it is possible enough that Ramsay had, at the first, some faith as "a fragment of an old heroic ballad." But it is not until its insertion in his *Tea-Table Miscellany* that he so designates it, though there is good reason for suspecting that by that time he was no stranger to the secret of its authorship. As to "The Vision,"—though professedly "composit in Latin be a maist lernit clerk in tyme of our hairship and oppression,"—it was undoubtedly his own production. With an anachronism very characteristic of eighteenth century antiques, the gods of Olympus appear in his "Vision" carousing, till

> "Pan forgets to tune his reed,
>   And slings it cairless bye ;
> And Hermes, wingd at heils and heid,
>   Can nowther stand nor lye ;
>   Quhen staggirand and swaggirand,
>   They stoyter hame to sleip,
>   Quhyle centeries at enteries
>   Imortal watches keip."

The poet has here his own Mercury in view, stoitering home, as we may fancy, from the Easy

Club, while the centuries look out on the swagger-
ing god from every old close-head of the High
Street.   Among the genuine poets of *The Evergreen* is Alexander Scot, "the Anacreon of old
Scottish Poetry," as Pinkerton styles him ; and
to his pieces is affixed the authentication "Quod
Alex. Scot."   But to "The Vision," professedly
"translatit in 1524," is the ingenious variation
"Quod Ar. Scot," which was probably meant to
imply " quoth another Scot."

To such an experienced manufacturer of antiques
after the fashion in vogue in that eighteenth
century, the patching up of an old song, or wholly
inventing a new one to fit a favourite air, was a
very ordinary piece of business.   After enlarging
in his preface on the simple charms of the native
Scottish melodies, he says :—"My being assured
how acceptable new words to known tunes would
prove, engaged me to the making verses for above
sixty of them.   About thirty more were done by
some ingenious young gentlemen," who are indicated by initials, no doubt recognisable enough at
the time.   "The rest are such old verses as have
been done time out of mind, and only wanted to
be cleared from the dross of blundering transcribers
and printers ;" and so we have "old songs" marked
Z., and "old songs with additions" marked Q.
He then adds: "In my compositions and collections
I have kept out all smut and ribaldry, that the

modest voice and ear of the fair singers might meet with no affront." Such was the honest aim of poet and editor, for which he deserves all praise. Among his other gleanings and patchings, he no doubt added a finishing grace to the verses of the "ingenious young gentlemen," to whom, he politely says, "the lovers of sense and music are obliged for some of the best songs in the collection "—so numerous were poets in Edinburgh before Burns or Fergusson were heard of. In this way Ramsay catered for the taste of an approving public, while he undoubtedly contributed to its elevation and refinement ; and left to a more critical age to adjudicate as it best could on the genuineness of the antiques, whether with or without the attesting Z.

Who wrote our old songs and ballads it would have been hard to tell in Ramsay's day ; and, as we have seen, it is still less easy now. It is truer of a good many of them, than of Topsy, that they "grow'd." William Tytler, of Woodhouselee, drew the attention of Burns to the interest attaching to our ballad lore. Thereupon he recalled sundry snatches of old traditionary ballads, wrote them down, and sent them to his correspondent, as "a sample of the old pieces that are still to be found among our peasantry in the west. I once had a great many of these fragments, and some of those here entire ; but as I had no idea that anybody cared for them, I have forgotten them. I invariably hold it sacrilege to add anything of my own to help out with the shattered wrecks of these venerable old compositions ; but they have many readings." This is inevitable in all popular verse transmitted by oral tradition. The emendations of an imperfect recitation, and the interminglings of diverse half-forgotten stanzas—sometimes of different ballads,—must have led to numerous variations, and adaptations to changing manners and new localities. The makers of the romantic Scottish ballads were a joint-stock company, unlimited, till the printing-press found its way into the remotest nooks ; and tradition vanished with the brownies and the elves. But it is amusing to find Burns telling his correspondent that he held it sacrilege to make the slightest addition to the fragments of traditionary verse ; for at that very time he was supplying Johnson with songs, marked Z, like those of Ramsay, as genuine antiques. Yet he says elsewhere : " The songs marked Z in the *Museum* I have given to the world as old verses of their respective times ; but, in fact, of a good many of them little more than the chorus is ancient, though there is no need of telling everybody this piece of intelligence." Probably Burns could have truly said of some of the songs, as Scott does of his mottoes and fragments of " Old Plays," etc., in one of his letters to Constable :—" It is odd to say, but nevertheless it is quite certain, that I do not know whether some of the things are original or not."

This is no doubt the history of a good many of our romantic Scottish ballads. They are not altogether old, yet not wholly new. Dr. Robert Chambers played his part in earlier years as a collector of genuine songs and ballads. In 1829 his *Scottish Ballads Collected and Illustrated* made its appearance. The editor had condensed, compiled, and eked out the old materials on a bolder scale, and with a more openly avowed purpose than his predecessors, though in reality with an honesty of adherence to his originals as compared with Percy. But he makes the avowal, which Allan Ramsay might have made with even greater truth, of a " mode of editing ballads, deprecated by the antiquary as being little better than the deliberate vitiation of these revered compositions." In truth some of them may be fairly compared to the old Greek's boat, which had been patched until scarcely a morsel of the original wood remained. Yet it remains an open question : was it the old boat or a new one ?

Curiously enough, the very first among Dr. Robert Chambers's antique historical ballads is the " Sir Patrick Spens," which he was by and by to ascribe to a modern lady's pen. Great changes, he doubts not, have taken place in the form and language of this and other historical ballads, such as "The Gude Wallace," "Otterbourne," "The Douglas Tragedy," etc., before their fleeting traditional forms were arrested and fixed down by the types of the eighteenth century. "Yet, after all, there is evidence to prove that this change cannot have been very great during at least the last two centuries." When Dr. Chambers indicates a belief, as he does in this preface, that some of the ballads he undertakes to edit are but modified, and in some cases vulgarised versions of popular poems as old even as the twelfth and thirteenth centuries, he credits them with an antiquity sufficiently great to satisfy the most credulous defenders of their genuineness. But in later years a change came over the spirit of his dream. He took to science as his favourite pastime. Geology, or at least such "vestiges of creation" as pertained to the men and times of the drift, superseded literary antiquities. He even had, according to current belief, his own special mystery and literary masquerading ; and so the strata of Arthur's Seat, and the raised beaches and ancient sea-margins of the Lothians displaced his first love ; and he became incredulous about the age of younger antiquities. When he did at length spare a thought for the objects of his youthful study, it was embodied in the ingenious essay, published in 1859, entitled *The Romantic Scottish Ballads: their epoch and authorship*. The interval

between his first and last study of the ballads had
sufficed for a marvellous revolution since the
period when the fourteenth and fifteenth centuries
were among the later dates assigned by him to
what he then believed to be modernised versions of contemporary poems referring to real
incidents.   His new disquisition startled all lovers
of ballad literature with the novel theory that,
instead of belonging to any such ancient eras, or
being in any sense traditionary relics of our old
native minstrelsy, the romantic Scottish ballads are
forgeries of the eighteenth century ; and that the
author of the choicest and most popular of them
was Lady Wardlaw, the " begetter " of Hardyknute.

Elizabeth, Lady Wardlaw, of Pitreavie, the
inaugurator of the ingenious literary masquerading
of the eighteenth century, claims a very special rank
among those Scots ladies to whom, in 1721,
Allan Ramsay dedicated his first volume of
poems.   She must have been a belle in the Edinburgh Assemblies when the century began.   She
was described by one of her descendants as a
woman of elegant accomplishments, who not only
wrote verse, but also practised drawing and skilful
artistic cuttings with her scissors ; and was noted
for her wit and humour.   She had, moreover, as we
have now reason to believe, a certain turn for
such ingenious mystifications as are familiar to all
students of the literature of that eighteenth century.

But along with this she had great modesty and sweetness of temper ; confined her poetical pastimes and literary masqueradings to her own family circle ; and lived in such unassuming retirement, that it was left for Dr. Robert Chambers, more than a century and a quarter after her death, to assert for her claims to the authorship of some of the most beautiful romantic Scottish ballads which still retain their hold on popular favour.

According to the account which satisfied that uncritical age : in a vault of the ancient Abbey of Dunfermline—famous for its associations with royalty, from the days when Malcolm Canmore welcomed there the Saxon exile who first became his queen and then the patron saint of Scotland, to those of James VI. and his son Charles, who was born at Dunfermline in the year 1600,—there was found an ancient manuscript containing the greater part of the heroic ballad of Hardyknute. This was the notable initiation of such discoveries. By and by Macpherson's world-famous " Fingal," " Temora," and other epics of the Gaelic Homer followed. Then came Percy with his genuine ancient folio MS., which was made the guarantee for his half-spurious collection of patched and modernised antiques. To him succeeded the marvellous charity-boy of Bristol, with his *Rowley Poems* recovered from an ancient oaken chest in the Church of St. Mary Redcliffe, the work of an imaginary priest of the reign of Edward IV.

Horace Walpole produced his *Castle of Otranto*, an Italian MS. found in the library of an ancient Catholic family in the North of England ; Charles Julius Bertram duped the historians and antiquaries of Europe with his Itinerary of Richard of Cirencester, a monk of the fourteenth century ; and so the masquerading proceeded, with more or less ingenuity, poetical genius, and sheer mendacity, till it culminated in the impudent Shakespearean forgeries of Ireland.

The " Hardyknute " of Lady Wardlaw is to be classed with the maskings of Chatterton, and not with the forgeries of Bertram and Ireland.   The former are works of genuine worth, whatever be their true date or authorship ; the latter owed all their imaginary value to successful fraud.   On a copy of Allan Ramsay's *Tea-Table Miscellany*, in the Abbotsford library, is this marginal note, by Sir Walter Scott : " This book belonged to my grandfather, Robert Scott, and out of it I was taught Hardyknute by heart before I could read the ballad myself.   It was the first poem I ever learnt—the last I shall ever forget."   Giving free scope to his speculations as to the extent of Lady Wardlaw's share in the creation of the *Romantic Ballads of Scotland*, Dr. Robert Chambers claims to " be permitted to indulge in the idea that a person lived a hundred years before Scott, who, with his feeling for Scottish history, and the

features of the past generally, constructed out of
these materials a similar romantic literature ;" and
tracing the gradual development of Scott's literary
genius, from his collections for the *Minstrelsy*,
to his *Eve of St. John*, his *Lay of the Last Minstrel*, and *Marmion*, and so to his *Waverley* and
all the prose romances that followed, he adds :
" Much significance there is in his statement that
Hardyknute was the first poem he ever learned, and
the last he should forget.   Its author—if my suspicion be correct,—was his literary foster-mother,
and we probably owe the direction of his genius,
and all its fascinating results, principally to her."

No wonder that Lord President Forbes and Sir
Gilbert Elliot of Minto had the " Hardyknute "
printed ; or that the learned historical antiquary,
Lord Hailes, maintained to the last his belief that
parts of it were genuine.   In a better educated
and more critical age, Scott himself pronounced it
to be a noble imitation of the best style of the
old ballad.   Its greatest fault is its prolixity.   It
was protracted by its authoress, in an aim at com-
pleteness, when the genuine afflatus which had
inspired the opening stanzas was exhausted.   It
received additions in subsequent reprints, without seemingly exciting suspicion ; and when it was
admitted by Percy into his *Reliques of Ancient
English Poetry*, it was as " a Scottish fragment, a
fine morsel of heroic poetry."   As first printed in

1719, by Watson of Edinburgh, in a folio sheet, it was in the style and affectedly antique spelling of "the fair Gothic character" in which—like Rowley's later parchments,—it had been engrossed. The age was indeed a credulous one which could be persuaded to believe that a vellum manuscript had lain uninjured in a damp and ruined vault for some four or five centuries! But tested solely by its literary merits, and the critical standards of that eighteenth century at a date when Shakespeare had as yet only his first textual critic, Nicholas Rowe, Allan Ramsay could incur little censure had he unwittingly admitted among his "*Scots Poems wrote by the Ingenious before* 1600," the ballad fragment which opens with this spirited touch of nationality :—

> " Stately stept he east the wa'
>   And stately stept he west ;
> Full seventy zeirs he now had sene,
>   With skerss seven zeirs of rest.
> He livit quhen Britons breach of faith
>   Wroucht Scotland meikle wae ;
> And aye his sword tauld to their cost
>   He was their deidly fae."

As we have the ballad now, it runs to forty-two stanzas, and then ends abruptly.   But it has shared in the fortunes common to such antiques.   In 1781, John Nichols produced some supplementary stanzas ; and in 1783 Pinkerton published his *Select*

Scottish Ballads, in which it was, for the first time "given in its original perfection:" for, according to that veracious collector, the common people in Lanarkshire continued to "repeat scraps of both parts," so that he was able on such authority to make wonderful amendments on the earlier version ; while he was "indebted for the most of the stanzas now recovered to the memory of a lady in Lanarkshire." The additions are the laboured production of a black-letter antiquary. The poetry, as Scott said, "smells of the lamp," and could never have been preserved by oral tradition. It was worthy of that unscrupulous tamperer with old texts, of whom Ritson said, "If he had used the same freedom in a private business, which he has in poetry, he would have been set on the pillory;" but, as the Border Minstrel remarks, "he understood in an extensive sense Horace's Maxim, *Quidlibet audendi !*" But antiquity fought hard for a share in the fine ballad ; and James Oswald's "Caledonian Pocket Companion" is produced in proof that a musician, who was born about the beginning of the eighteenth century, had noted down the tune of *Hardie Knute* in this fashion :—

But the spirit of invention was not wholly exhausted in the literary masqueradings of that eighteenth century, which at their best somewhat puzzle our moral sense with their ingenious mendacities. Bishop Percy tells that "an ingenious friend" thought the author of Hardyknute had borrowed from other Scottish ballads in his collection ; and other critics have since taken up the hint, not always in very friendly fashion ; until at length Dr. Robert Chambers conceived the idea that Lady Wardlaw was sole creator of nearly the whole budget of Romantic Scottish Ballads ; and so when she patched " Gilderoy," and repeated " Hardyknute " in " Sir Patrick Spens," she was only dealing as she pleased with her own literary offspring. When Coleridge took to penning an Ode to Dejection, he started with this allusion to the last-named ballad :—

> " Well ! if the Bard was weather-wise, who made
> THE GRAND OLD BALLAD OF SIR PATRICK SPENCE,
> This night, so tranquil now, will not go hence
> Unroused by winds, that ply a busier trade
> Than those which mould yon cloud in lazy flakes,
> Or the dull sobbing draft that moans and rakes
> Upon the strings of this Eolian lute,
> Which better far were mute."

There is no reason to suppose that the author of " Sibylline Leaves " meant to be ironical ; and yet a better motto could scarcely be devised for " these same metre ballad-mongers," who throughout the eighteenth century plied their busy trade, harping on strings that better far were mute! But nobody could desire to stay the vibrating chords of the lute to which we owe " Sir Patrick Spens," whether that ballad be indeed old as the nuptials of the maid of Norway, or no older than those of Elizabeth Halket and Sir Henry Wardlaw of Pitreavie. That the writer of Hardyknute had borrowed from that and other Scottish songs was early assumed. Finlay, in the preface to his *Scottish Historical and Romantic Ballads*, published in 1808, while " inclined to think that the ballad of Sir Patrick Spens is the most ancient of which we are in possession," not only conceives the current version to have no claim to high antiquity, but he characterises some of its stanzas as modern interpolations. If so the agreements between Hardyknute and the old ballad might be easily accounted for. But it was reserved for one of the acutest and most painstaking of Scottish black-letter scholars, David Laing, to suggest in his notes to " Johnson's Musical Museum," that possibly " *Sir Patrick Spens* and *Hardyknute* were the production of the same author." This appears to have been the hint which begot in Dr. Robert Chambers such a fit of scepticism as ended in his renouncing his old faith, and making a wholesale transfer of Scottish ballad literature to Lady

Wardlaw, with the possible help of another Fife-shire poetess, or collector, Mrs. Brown of Falkland. From this it would follow that Lady Wardlaw in some mysterious way put in circulation a set of fugitive poems of rare beauty, of which she had succeeded in concealing the authorship from her most intimate friends ; while she allowed them to credit her with a piece of such inferior merit as to reveal only " the 'prentice hand " of an imitator. The date of production of the latter is well known. At the time of its issue from the Edinburgh press she was in her forty-third year ; and on the theory of her assumed authorship it must have been sub-sequent to this that her prolific muse suddenly bloomed, matured its fruits, and, unknown to all, scattered broadcast a " Sir Patrick Spens," " Gil Morrice," " Edward," " Gilderoy," " Young Waters," " The Douglas Tragedy," and in short all the tender and romantic Scottish ballads recovered in that eighteenth century.

It need scarcely be wondered that a theory so startlingly comprehensive in its results, and yet so entirely based on mere inference or assumption, has met with no very hearty reception. That ballads and songs were current in popular tradition, no one can doubt. We have one beautiful little lyrical fragment quoted by Wyntoun, referring to the death of Alexander III. " Robin and Makyne," another of our early ballads, is probably the work of Henrysoun, whom Dunbar bemoans in his "Lament for the Makars." His "Bluidy Sark," is another of the ballads of the beginning of the sixteenth century, tinged with the allegorical character of the age. The Otterburne, Harlaw, Flodden, Corrichie, Frendraught, and many another fight, down to Prestonpans and Culloden, have left their records in traditional song and ballad.

Doubtless the form of words underwent many a modification as it passed from mouth to mouth ; and the commingling of very diverse events and times in the modern versions of some old ballads is one of the surest evidences of antiquity,—though also of corruption. But when the printing-press undertook, in that eighteenth century, to displace the older process of oral transmission, it dealt with verse which had been subjected to every vicissitude of vulgar tradition. When it was finally committed to writing, and so to the press, the form depended a good deal on the transcriber. An old dame could be prompted in her recitation when memory or invention failed, and when she had done her best it was the transcriber's turn to give the finishing touches. Then, too, modern taste was apt to be fastidious,—could by no means tolerate the old fashion of calling a spade a spade. If some editors of Shakespeare had had the sole control in the transmission of his text, we should find some very tame proprieties substituted for the rough homeliness which gave no offence to the ears of the maiden Queen, for whose special delectation "The Merry Wives of Windsor" was produced.

The collectors of that eighteenth century were rarely more than one, or at most two, for a whole district. Hence the uniformity of style in the hints to a treacherous memory, where a Lady Wardlaw, or other collector given to versification, eked out the imperfect fragments, or had an eye to the proprieties. The new piece put into the old garment so frequently betrays the totally diverse ideas of a modern age, as to justify faith in the discrepant fragments. That Lady Wardlaw was given to such recensions is no matter of surmise. The old ballad of Gilderoy, for example—ascribed to the leman of the *Gille Roy*, or red-haired Highland freebooter,—existed in a black-letter broadsheet before 1650. In 1668 Sir Charles Sedley introduced into his play of "The Mulberry Garden" the verses, afterwards inserted under the title of "Gilderoy" in Johnson's Museum with a romantic story of their authorship by Duncan Forbes of Culloden, in youthful days when he was courting Mary Rose, his future wife. Mr. Sharpe had another story, which he got from a connection of Sir Alexander Halket of Pitferran, and a near relation of his own, which ascribed the lines to a brother of Lady Wardlaw. A modified version of the ballad appeared in Playford's *Wit and Mirth* in 1703. But the original bard had intermingled characteristic indelicacies with stanzas of genuine poetic merit; and so Elizabeth Halket—the future Lady Wardlaw,—at last took them in hand, and produced the current version, in which she retained some of the original stanzas, retouched others, and added several of her own ; making it, as Stenhouse says, "excellent and unexceptionable."

The same process is even better illustrated in the more ancient ballad of "The Young Tamlane," as printed in *The Border Minstrelsy*, where Scott tells us he was "enabled to add several verses of beauty and interest, in consequence of a copy obtained from a gentleman residing near Langholm, which is said to be very ancient, though the language is somewhat of a modern cast." The stanzas so accredited are no less modern in cast than the words, as nobody better knew than their editor. But a version of Tamlane was undoubtedly current in the early half of the sixteenth century, as its name appears in "The Complaint of Scotland," printed in 1548. Repeated allusions to the air or the song of *Thom of Lynn*, *Thomalin*, or *Tom o' the Linn*, occur between the sixteenth and eighteenth centuries. At the very close of the last century a version of it was popular in Ettrick Forest. As printed by Scott, it runs to sixty-seven stanzas, some of them with the genuine air of antiquity; others of them clearly betraying their modern origin. Take, for example, three stanzas in which Young Tamlane describes how he and his fellows, who have been spirited away to fairyland, disport themselves there :—

> " Our shapes and size we can convert
>   To either large or small;
> An old nut-shell's the same to us
>   As is the lofty hall.
>
> We sleep in rose-buds soft and sweet,
>   We revel in the stream ;
> We wanton lightly on the wind,
>   Or glide on a sunbeam.
>
> And all our wants are well supplied,
>   From every rich man's store,
> Who thankless sins the gifts he gets,
>   And vainly grasps for more."

The first two stanzas betray the ideas which the sylphs and gnomes of Pope's " Rape of the Lock " introduced into fashionable drawing-rooms ; the third is a mere echo of Goldsmith's " Hermit." But to conclude therefore that the whole ballad was a product of the Pitreavie mint would be to ignore evidence of antiquity, no less than to confound styles as dissimilar as ever betrayed the admixture of new and old materials.

There are one or two additional points to be noted in reference to the authoress of " Hardyknute." Lady Wardlaw, according to the narrative of Percy, played the part of a coy poetess, as others before and since her time have done. "A suspicion arose that it was her own composition. Some able judges asserted it to be modern. The lady did in a manner acknowledge it to be so. Being desired to show an additional stanza, as a proof of this, she produced the two last, beginning with 'There's nae light,' etc., which were not in the copy that was first printed." This is very much of a counterpart to Lady Anne Lindsay's proceedings about her "Auld Robin Gray," a far superior production to "Hardyknute;" but though Lady Anne composed a good many other pieces, none of them approached her first happy hit. There is not the slightest proof that Lady Wardlaw exhibited more than the usual coyness of lady poets, in an age when to be a poetess seems to have been thought somewhat unbecoming, if not indeed vulgar. Mr. Hepburn of Keith stated he was in the house with her when she wrote her Norse poem. Several of her descendants knew well about it, as George Chalmers tells, on the authority of Sir Charles Halket, in his *Life of Allan Ramsay ;* and Dr. Chambers quotes and italicises the statement that "Sir Charles Halket and Miss Elizabeth Menzies concur in saying that Lady Wardlaw was a woman of elegant accomplishments, *who wrote other poems.*"

The mystery of "Hardyknute," therefore, was

from the first no mystery to the Pitreavie family circle, or to intimate friends outside of it. If the poetess discouraged greater publicity during her life, it is obvious that her descendants exerted themselves to establish her claims to the authorship of what Dr. Chambers himself designates as, " to modern taste, a stiff and poor composition ;" while it was left to an ingenious antiquary, some hundred and thirty years after her death, to accredit her for the first time with the authorship of twenty-two of the finest, most vigorous, and tender of all the romantic ballads of Scotland !

As to Allan Ramsay, he was undoubtedly made a confidant at an early date. The " Hardyknute " appears in his *Evergreen*, as in Watson's edition of 1719, with the sub-title of "a fragment," and all its affectation of archaic spelling. But Ramsay found access in some way to a dozen new stanzas, —nor is it difficult to guess how. Bishop Percy refers to "John Clerk, M.D., of Edinburgh, an intimate companion of Lord President Forbes," as the person who prepared for the press the revised and augmented copy of the poem inserted in the *Reliques ;* and Mr. Hepburn of Keith was, as we learn, in Pitreavie House at the time when Lady Wardlaw wrote the original draft. On turning to Ramsay's own list of patrons, appended to the first collection of his poems in 1721, there are the names of James Hepburn Riccard, of Keith, jun., and John Clerk, M.D.,—two, no doubt, of the thirty ingenious young gentlemen, who proved capable, with the poet's supervision, of writing "some of the very best songs" in his Miscellany; and who were little likely to withhold from him the Pitreavie "manufacture" so thoroughly in his own line.   There is little mystery, therefore, as to the channel through which the authoress transmitted her latest additions and emendations to the editor of the *Evergreen*, at a time when he had in hand some spurious antiques of his own.

In the year 1725 Ramsay's famous pastoral, "The Gentle Shepherd," was published, and speedily reached a second edition, still under protection of Mercury's caduceus, opposite Niddry's Wynd.   But, immediately thereafter, the poet removed to the tall stone land forming the eastern tenement of the Luckenbooths.   There he replaced his celestial patron with the heads of Ben Jonson and Drummond of Hawthornden ; and, under such fitting patronage, started the first circulating library known in Scotland.

CHAPTER VIII.

Gay, Smollett, and Burns.

WHEN Allan Ramsay removed from his old quarters at the sign of the Mercury, opposite Niddry's Wynd, to the tall land alongside of St. Giles's Cathedral, it was as great a change as in later times would be the removal from the Old to the New Town. To the stranger entering Edinburgh by the Netherbow Port, a comparatively narrow street led westward a little way, till on reaching John Knox's house it suddenly expanded into a wide thoroughfare. Here the Well still flows which is referred to by William Powrie, one of the Earl of Bothwell's accomplices in the murder of Darnley, as the Endmyleis Well ; and here also happily remains the picturesque dwelling, of rare historical interest, where George Durie Abbot of Dunfermline, was succeeded by John Knox ; and to which, in 1563, the latter brought home his wife, Margaret Stewart, daughter of the good Lord Ochiltree. The house where Knox received the messengers of Queen Mary, and deliberated with the Scottish nobles and leaders of the Congregation, is now more nearly in the condition in which it stood in Allan Ramsay's days than it was as we remember it, when the misdirected zeal of later admirers of the Reformer had converted the remarkable piece of sculpture on the angle of the building into an effigy of Knox occupying a pulpit, with sounding board and tasseled cushion, after the most orthodox Presbyterian model of the eighteenth century. The transformed effigy was in reality only the central figure in the ingenious symbolic decorations of the ancient edifice. Moses, the Hebrew lawgiver, is seen kneeling, as on Mount Sinai, and receiving from God the tables of the Law. The Divine Being is represented by a blazing disc, half veiled in cloud, inscribed : ΘΕΟΣ . DEUS . GOD ; while the legend, cut in large Roman characters on the entablature running round the two fronts of the building, thus embodies our Saviour's summary of the decalogue : LVFE . GOD . ABVFE . AL . AND . YI . NYCHTBOVR . AS . YI . SELF. The removal in recent years of some modern additions disclosed a fine sculptured tablet above this, which bears, within a wreath, a shield charged with three crowns on a chevron, between three holly branches, with the initials I . M : M . A., doubtless those of the old citizen and his wife, who built and occupied it before Abbot Durie and his mitred brethren dreamt of any ruder censor than the Abbot of Unreason.

From Knox's house to the Salt Tron and the Old Town Guardhouse was, in the days of Allàn Ramsay, and long afterwards, a distinct place, apart from the central civic area which extended from the Guardhouse to the Luckenbooths; and beyond the Tolbooth the thoroughfare widened once more into the Lawnmarket. Neither the civic reforms which have since opened up the wide thoroughfares of the Bridges, Cockburn, St. Giles's, and Bank Streets, nor the Great Fire of 1824, had yet wrought their revolutionary transformations. The broad avenue of the High Street uninterruptedly reared its lofty crow-stepped gables to the sky; while below, from under pillared piazzas, the open booths projected their wares into the street, displaying the whole of the trader's stock. Scott has described the scene, as presented to the wondering eyes of Roland Græme; yet not greatly different from what must have been familiar to himself; and indeed what we have often seen in our own younger days, when the Lawnmarket was crowded with its linen and woollen booths; and bakers', cutlers', and book-sellers' stalls protruded from the piazzas, or spread out their tempting wares on open stalls in the street. In Ramsay's days each of the three open spaces had its own special crafts and hawkers; while distinct from all of them lay the great Grassmarket square at the foot of the West Bow.

Allan Ramsay's new library and book-store, with the heads of Ben Jonson and Drummond of Hawthornden replacing the heathen Mercury of humbler days, was in the very centre of the city. Right in front of his door stood the City Cross, unchanged since its translation to that site, in 1617, in order to widen the passage-way for King James, when in that year he gladdened his ancient Kingdom of Scotland with the light of his countenance. Here daily, after the mid-day meal, the city beaux were wont to congregate, emerging from the neighbouring closes to display their finery, and enjoy the news and gossip of the day. Mr. Sharpe's notes furnish me with a racy incident, illustrative alike of the manners of a bygone age and of scenes at times enacted at the Cross.

On the west side of the old Stamp Office Close, opening on the High Street a little below the Cross, there still stands an antique mansion, where, considerably above a century ago, resided Alexander, ninth Earl of Eglinton, and his lovely countess, Susannah Kennedy. She was somewhat of a blue-stocking, devoted to music, and the most conspicuous patroness of the Scottish muses in her day. Allan Ramsay, accordingly, became an object of her attention, won her special favour, and dedicated to her his fine pastoral poem, " The Gentle Shepherd." At a later date he presented the original manuscript to her, with a letter of grateful compliment, both of which were afterwards given to James Boswell, and are still preserved in the library at Auchinleck. Lady Effie, a daughter of the earl by his first countess, was a characteristic specimen of the jovial female roysterers of that eighteenth century. Mr. Sharpe printed a small edition of a spirited song, which was a special favourite of his own, illustrative of the old spirit of feminine joviality so strangely at variance with all modern ideas of propriety. A single stanza will illustrate the fashions which it celebrates :—

> " There were four drunken maidens
> Together did convene,
> From twelve o'clock in a May morning
> Till ten rang out at e'en ;
> Till ten rung out at e'en,
> And then they gied it ower.
> And there's four drunken maidens
> Doun i' the Nether Bow."

Dr. Robert Chambers tells, I believe on the same authority, of three gentlewomen adjourning one night after a merry-meeting in a tavern near the Cross. On emerging into the High Street it was bright moonlight ; and they made their way with little difficulty till they reached the Tron Church, where the shadow of its steeple, thrown directly across the street, arrested their steps. Fully persuaded that a broad river interrupted their further progress, they with grave deliberation took off their shoes and stockings, kilted up their petticoats, and waded through to the moonshine beyond ; finding, no doubt, in the cold contact with the pavement abundant confirmation of their hallucination.   Strange indeed is it to conceive of such manners.   But we must not test them by the standards of our own days of formal propriety and decorum, any more than the pranks of more juvenile ladies ; when, as Mr. Sharpe said, the first time he saw Miss Jane Maxwell,—afterwards the Duchess of Gordon,—she had been despatched by Lady Maxwell to the fountain-well in front of John Knox's House for a kettle of water, and was mounted on the back of a sow, of which she and her sister Miss Betty had succeeded in making capture.

Lady Effie Montgomery, daughter of the Earl of Eglinton, afterwards became the wife of George Lockhart, a leading politician and Jacobite of the reign of Queen Anne. He was the eldest son of the Lord President, Sir George Lockhart of Lee, the great rival of Sir George Mackenzie, whom Oliver Cromwell selected as his advocate in 1658, and who was shot at his own door in the Old Bank Close,—where Melbourne Place now stands,—by Chiesly of Dalry, on Easter Sunday, 1689, in revenge for a decision awarding aliment out of his estate to his wife and children.   Mr.

Sharpe says, " Sir George was at his own door, on his way home from church. Lady Lockhart, who was ill in bed, ran into the close in her shift. The murderer was taken red-hand. It must have been a strange scene. She was aunt to the witty Duke of Wharton, and remarried with one Ramsay, whom she divorced for bigamy. Her son, the Union Lockhart, married my aunt, Lady Effy Montgomery, of whom I can tell you some odd things ; " and so accordingly he did. " Union Lockhart," as he was called, was a crafty astute politician, well fitted to manage successfully the dangerous intrigues in which he engaged. His " Memoirs concerning the Affairs of Scotland " went through three surreptitious editions in 1714, and the Lockhart Papers, published in 1817, disclosed much curious matter relating to the Scottish Rebellion. Though resolutely opposed to the principles of the Revolution, he was named by Queen Anne one of the commissioners for the treaty of union. But he held a more important, though informal and secret commission, as the agent of the Scottish Jacobites ; and always maintained that had it not been for the fatal quarrel between the Duke of Hamilton—Queen Anne's ambassador at Paris,—and Lord Mohun, when both perished in a duel, plans were arranged which must have secured the succession to the queen's brother. His wife, Lady Effie, proved an able auxiliary to him in his secret intrigues on behalf of the Pretender. He resided chiefly at his country seat of Dryden, while Lady Effie paid frequent visits to Edinburgh. Her habit was to frequent the places of public resort, disguised in male attire, and joining freely in conversation with the Whig partizans, she was able to obtain important information for her husband. It chanced on one occasion that Mr. Forbes, a Whig notorious for his profligate habits, had got hold of some important private papers implicating Lockhart, which he was about to forward to the Government. According to the narrative communicated to me by her nephew, Lady Euphemia Lockhart dressed her sons—two fair and somewhat effeminate-looking, though handsome youths,—in negligee, fardingale, and masks, with patches, jewels, and all the finery of accomplished courtesans. Thus equipped, they sallied out to the Cross, and watching for the Whig gallant, they soon won his favour, and inducing him to accompany them to a neighbouring tavern—John's Coffee-house as we may presume, at the north-east corner of the Parliament Close, where, as Defoe tells us, the opponents of the Union were wont to meet,—the pseudo fair ones fairly drank him below the table, and then rifled his pockets of the dangerous papers.

Mr. Sharpe preserved the original manuscript of a very free lampoon, styled *The Ridotto*, written,

now nearly a century ago, conjointly by Christian
Bruce, the wife of James Riccart Hepburn, of
Keith and Riccarton, her sister-in-law, Lady Bruce
of Kinross, and Miss Jenny Denoon, their niece.
"This," he adds, "I know from Mrs. Hepburn's
granddaughter.   Miss Jenny was hump-backed
and breasted, but sang with much taste, was clever
as a composer of music, and counted a great wit."
The song was written in celebration of a ridotto,
or entertainment of music and dancing, held after
the fashion of Italian lenten relaxations, in the
long picture gallery of Holyrood House.   The
"welcome" refrain is repeated after each couplet.
Some of the lines are too free for modern ears,
but a stanza or two, with the accompanying notes,
may illustrate the manners of byegone times.

" I sing the Ridotto at Holyrood House,
  Where Cochrane and Squire Eccles the lieges did souce ;
      And welcome all of you, all of you, all of you,
      Welcome all of you to Holyrood House.

  There was Duke Hamilton with his turned coat ;
  Why wore you 't, my lord, ere the ribbon you got ?

  And there was Beau Seton made Lady Di' stare ;
  When he shines at the cross, must go there in a chair ;

  And Dirleton so spruce and so jaunty, God bless us !
  With his nose and his posey, a perfect Narcissus ;

  And then Fanny Gairdner, wi' braws in full sail,
  Slinking sly Gibbie Elliot close at her tail ;

And there was Bob Murray, though married, alas !
Yet still rivalling Johnstone in beauty and grace.

And there was my lady, well known by her airs,
Who ne'er goes to revel but after her prayers."

To this jeu d'esprit of that lively generation of beaux and belles Mr. Sharpe added these annotations: " Lady Di is Lady Diana Scott of Harden ; Dirleton is young Nisbet of Dirleton ; and Gibbie Elliot is Sir Gilbert, who celebrated his flirtations with Miss Fanny in a song which I remember to have heard. Bob Murray is my uncle, Sir Robert Murray of Clermont. He was very handsome, and married my mother's sister, Miss Renton. As for 'My Lady, well known for her airs,' this is the old Countess of Galway, a daughter of the Earl of Dundonald, and reputed a beauty in her youth. In her old age she put on great airs of piety and other virtues,—not including humility. She lived in the Horse Wynd, where her coach with six horses would drive up to carry my lady to a ceremonious visit to Lady Minto at the head of the Vennel. When she got into her chariot, her fore-horses' noses were already at Lady Minto's door." Of Beau Seton, who went in a sedan chair to display himself and his finery at the Cross, Mr. Sharpe says nothing ; but the habit of congregating there was common to all classes. There the lawyer met his clients ; the citizen made of it his Rialto, to talk with his brother traders over

business and civic gossip ; and. there the beau,
dressed for the Assembly in scarlet waistcoat,
lace ruffles and scarf, knee and shoe buckles, bag-
wig, and three-cocked hat, showed off to an admiring or envious crowd.

Thither it was that Allan Ramsay removed in
1725, and established his lending library, and the
mart for his own poetical productions, in the
eastern land of the Luckenbooths Row, with its
forestair fronting the city cross. His "Gentle
Shepherd," recently issued from the press, had
already reached a second edition before he deserted the old sign of the winged Mercury. His
reputation was no longer local. Editions followed
both in London and Dublin, and he took his
recognised place among British poets. Grow-
ing fame secured the sale of successive editions of
his collected works ; and so the poet flourished
alike in reputation and in fortune. The site of
his new library combined with the fame of its
originator to make of it a favourite resort of the
leading wits and men of letters, as well as of all
strangers who visited Edinburgh. When the Duke
of Grafton, as Lord Chamberlain, refused to sanc-
tion the representation of Gay's " Polly," written
by him as a continuation of his " Beggar's Opera,"
Lady Catherine Hyde, Duchess of Queensberry,
the eccentric beauty and wit of the court of
George I., espoused the poet's cause, and she and

the Duke withdrew from court in high dudgeon,
carrying him with them. Gay, accordingly, accompanied them to Edinburgh, became an inmate
of Queensberry House, Canongate, and, ere long,
an associate of the congenial wits of the Scottish
capital.

Queensberry House, the haunt of the witty
Duchess and the poet Gay, has since gone through
nearly every conceivable vicissitude ; and after
being a barrack, is now an Asylum and House of
Refuge for the Destitute. But its historical
associations go back to earlier times. It was
built in 1681 by Lord Halton, better known as
the Earl of Lauderdale, the unscrupulous agent
of the Stuarts in the attempt to convert his
countrymen to the court creed by the use of the
boot and thumbkins. When in 1686 James II.
had succeeded to Charles II., and the court creed
had undergone a change, the Earl of Perth con-
formed with courtierly compliance ; fitted up a
private chapel in his house in the Canongate ; had
it gutted by the Edinburgh mob ; and he and
his Duchess were pelted with mud. The Lord
Treasurer, William Duke of Queensberry, interposed on behalf of the city, when the renegade
chancellor was bent on wreaking on it an indiscriminate vengeance ; and for this and other
defections, as Lord Fountainhall records, " by a
letter from his Majesty, Queensberry is laid aside

from all his places and offices, as his place in the Treasury, Privy Council, Session, etc., and desired not to go out of town till he cleared his accounts. So he bought Lauderdale's house in the Canongate." William Douglas, first Duke of Queensberry, had a passion for building. Drumlanrig Castle is the most extensive of his works; but he also expended much labour and cost in completing the ducal lodging in the Canongate. "This Duke," writes Mr. Sharpe, "who was my great-grandmother's uncle, and of whom consequently I know much, was a strange original. He boggled at nothing in his courtly advances but popery. That split him with King James. He was a miser of the first water, yet magnificent in building and pleasure-grounds; totally illiterate, yet a collector of books; and commanding a style in his letters (which he always dictated to a secretary) that is admirable. I have much of his correspondence, that would make a curious volume. He died in the Canongate." The correspondence no doubt survives, and must be of value; for the duke exercised nearly absolute power in Scotland during the later years of Charles II., presided .as High Commissioner in the first Parliament of James II., and was curiously involved in the complication of affairs by which that king alienated such allies as the duke, and brought the Stuart dynasty to an ignominious end.

It was to the same Canongate mansion that Duke Charles and his Duchess carried off their aggrieved poet: and there that celebrated and most eccentric of beauties entertained him ; and with him such of the society of Edinburgh as it pleased her Grace to smile upon.   She was equally eccentric and capricious in dress and speech ; and is referred to in Horace Walpole's correspondence by such titles as " her mad Grace of Queensberry." She was the great-granddaughter of Lord Chancellor Clarendon ; and, while still "in maiden meditation fancy free," was celebrated by Prior, as

> " Kitty, beautiful and young,
> And wild as colt untamed."

Claiming as free a license as Lady Jenny, the denouement is thus presented in the close :—

> " ' I'll soon with Jenny's pride quit score,
> Make all her lovers fall ;
> They'l grieve I was not loosed before,
> She, I was loosed at all.'
> Fondness prevailed ; mamma gave way ;
> Kitty, at heart's desire,
> Obtained the chariot for a day,
> And set the world on fire ! "

A lady celebrated for sprightliness, wit, and beauty, by Prior, Pope, and Swift, as well as by lesser poets, can have been no ordinary woman. As to her sprightliness, it outran all bounds, and set every rule of conventional decorum at defiance.

She was a grief to Lord Chamberlains in other matters besides the plays of poets.   Horace Walpole describes her appearance at court on Sunday in a gown and petticoat of red flannel! and when he hints at less eccentric courses, it is in this fashion: "The Duchess of Queensberry is grown as tame as her neighbours."   But of her rare beauty, even in extreme old age, there is no question.   More than half a century after the death of the poet who had celebrated "Kitty beautiful and young," Walpole writes to the Countess of Ossory: "I saw the Duchess of Queensberry last night.   She was in a new pink lutestring, and looked more blooming than the Maccaronesses.   One should sooner take her for a young beauty of an old-fashioned century, than for an antiquated goddess of this age;" and so she bloomed on to her seventy-eighth year.

Under so rare a patroness the author of the "Beggar's Opera" was introduced to Edinburgh Society in those palmy days when duchesses still reigned in the Canongate and poets dwelt at the Cross.   Gay was not long of joining the congenial wits of the Scottish capital.   He had already manifested certain predilections calculated to win favour there, by selecting a number of Scottish airs for the songs in his new opera.   He speedily found his way to the haunt of the muses at the sign of Ben Jonson's and Drummond of Hawthornden's Heads, and joined the circle which was accustomed to meet at Allan Ramsay's. The scene had greater attractions for the English poet than he would have found in the romantic linn of Habbie's Howe or the wooded groves of Hawthornden ; for there the city gallants were wont to assemble daily—weather permitting,—in all the fashionable finery of the period, to interchange wit and gossip, admire and be admired.   The late William Tytler of Woodhouselee could carry back his memory to that olden time ; and had specially noted Gay's presence at those gatherings. He described him as a pleasant-looking little man in a tie-wig. Ramsay's humorous descriptions of the leading citizens met for business or pleasure at the Cross amused him. Mr. Tytler also recalled his questioning the Scottish poet as to the language, and allusions to national customs, in his " Gentle Shepherd ;" and his promising to communicate the results of his inquiries to Pope, who had already condescended to admire the fine pastoral poem.

The same central spot became the favourite lounge of Smollett when he visited Edinburgh in 1776, by which time the cross had disappeared. In the lively account of his visits, given in *Humphrey Clinker*, Smollett says : " All the people of business at Edinburgh, and even the genteel company, may be seen standing in crowds every day, from one to two in the afternoon, in the open street, at a place where formerly stood a market cross, which by the by was a curious piece of Gothic architecture, still to be seen in Lord Somerville's garden in this neighbourhood." For though the Luckenbooths continued long after this date to obstruct the thoroughfare, and Provost Kincaid succeeded to Ramsay in its eastern land: "Dun Edin's Cross" had already been swept away as a cumberer of the street.

Smollett's lodging was at the head of St. John Street, in the Canongate, then a most fashionable quarter, and now rich in associations of a literary kind. Here at a little later date was the residence of the distinguished lawyer, James Burnet, better known by his judicial title of Lord Monboddo. His works as an author, though characterised by much acuteness and great learning, are perversely one-sided, and now wholly out of date. Nevertheless, in his *Origin and Progress of Language*, he promulgated a system of anthropology which anticipated by nearly a century the assumed relation of man to the anthropoid apes. In accordance with the common practice of Scottish lawyers at that period, he repaired to the Low Countries, and for three years pursued his legal studies at the University of Groningen. Returning to Edinburgh, it chanced that he took up his quarters in the Lawnmarket on the very night of the Porteous Mob; and sallying out to witness the scene, he had some trouble afterwards in clearing himself from complicity in the popular revolt. In later days when he had risen to eminence at the bar, he had the reputation of giving the most attractive entertainments in old Edinburgh. Choice company was set off with "flowers of all hues and wines of all qualities; odours as well as light were diffused by the lamps;" and to all this the charm of music was added. Lord Cockburn, repeating the traditions of a younger generation, says, "The suppers of Lord Monboddo were the most Attic in his day."

When Burns came to Edinburgh, Lord Monboddo was in the enjoyment of his highest reputation alike as an author and a dispenser of attractive hospitalities; and the poet refers to his repeated entertainment at St. John Street. There the rare beauty of the Judge's younger daughter, Elizabeth, made a strong impression on his mind. In one of his private letters he speaks of her as unequalled "in all the combinations of beauty, grace, and goodness, since Milton's Eve on the first day of her existence." Nor did he confine his expressions of admiration to confidential letters. Mrs. Cockburn, the poetess, in writing of his visit to Edinburgh, says, "The ploughman poet has seen the Duchess of Gordon and all the gay world. His favourite for looks and manners is Bess Burnet,—no bad judge either." But the beauty which so charmed the susceptible poet was evanescent, and she to whom he refers in his " Address to Edinburgh," as fairest among all its daughters, bloomed with the hectic flush of consumption. When next he referred to her, it was in the passionate tenderness of his Elegy :—

> "Life ne'er exulted in so rich a prize
> As Burnet lovely from her native skies ;
> Nor envious death so triumph'd in a blow,
> As that which laid the accomplish'd Burnet low."

The year before the poet's visit to Edinburgh Lord Monboddo rode to London, travelling, as his custom was, on horseback, attended by his servant. While visiting the Court of King's Bench part of the court fittings gave way. Judges and barristers made in undignified haste for the door, while Lord Monboddo kept his seat with unruffled composure. On the panic subsiding, he was asked why he had not bestirred himself when everybody else was in such affright. He composedly replied, " He thought it was a ceremony of the court, with which, as an onlooker, he had nothing to do."

Within a few doors of the learned but eccentric judge lived Lord Eskgrove, the Earl of Aboyne, and the old Countess of Hyndford, whom Mr. Sharpe likened to the bearded countess of Don Quixote. To her, in later years, succeeded James

Ballantyne, the partner and confidant of *The Great Unknown* in all the Waverley mysteries.   Thither accordingly Scott frequently resorted ; and there to select and favoured guests the hospitable printer read snatches of the forthcoming novels, and hinted, with many a shrewd wink, at the literary riddle of that day.

St. John Street is approached through a broad archway piercing the line of houses in the Canongate, and immediately within this is the turnpike stair which gives access to the lodging where, in 1766, the Scottish novelist and poet of that elder generation—Tobias Smollett,—took up his residence with his sister Mrs. Telfer.   The northern windows of the house looked into the Canongate ; and, although, in accordance with the simple habits of that older time, Mrs. Telfer occupied only a flat of the tall land or pile of dwellings, it had sufficed, not long before, as the town residence of the Earl of Hopetoun.   Mr. Sharpe had gleaned some interesting reminiscences both of Smollett and his sister from the recollections of an elder generation. Mrs. Telfer, though then a widow, with somewhat straitened means, moved in good society, and had select parties in her Canongate flat.   She was described to Mr. Sharpe, by his mother, as a tall, sharp-visaged lady, with a hooked nose, a devotee to whist.   Her brother had then returned from that prolonged continental tour, the results of which, as set forth in his *Travels through France and Italy*, abundantly illustrate the distempered mind of an invalid. It was this manifestation of morbid irritability which provoked the sarcastic allusion of Sterne to the journey of "the learned Smellfungus" from Boulogne to Paris,—from Paris to Rome. "He wrote an account of them, but it was nothing but an account of his miserable feelings. I met Smellfungus in the grand portico of the Pantheon : he was just coming out of it. 'It is nothing but a huge cockpit,' said he. 'I wish you had said nothing worse of the Venus Medicis,' I replied ; for, in passing through Florence, I had heard he had fallen foul upon the goddess, and used her worse than a common strumpet."

Mrs. Sharpe repeatedly saw the novelist, and indeed figures among the characters incidentally referred to in his *Humphrey Clinker*. She described him to her son as a tall, handsome man, very pale. His conversation was exceedingly attractive, when he was not in ill humour ; but he was prone to satirical innuendo, full of venom at times, and was provoked to peevish irritability at the very sight of some of his visitors. He was suffering acutely from a boil on his arm, but this did not prevent his showing the attractive side of his character in congenial society. Dr. Carlyle, who is also referred to in *Humphrey Clinker*, met

him frequently, and speaks of him unreservedly as
"a man of very agreeable conversation and of much
genuine humour."   A rich flow of conversation on
literary subjects was enlivened with apt stories,
which he told with peculiar grace.   The Doctor
dwells on his polished manners and great urbanity,
and refers to an occasion when Smollett supped
in a tavern with himself, Commissioner Cardonnel,
Mr. Hepburn of Keith, John Home, and one or
two others ; and they spent so charming an evening, that he selects it from among all his frequent
meetings with "Roderick Random" as specially
worthy of remembrance.   "He was one," he says,
"of the many very pleasant men with whom it was
my good fortune to be intimately acquainted.
Mr. Cardonnel was another who excelled, like
Smollett, in a great variety of pleasant stories."

With such attractive manners, and great conversational powers, it is not surprising to learn
that Smollett mixed in the choicest of Edinburgh
society ; and, as we know, treasured up the
graphic pictures of men and manners which he
afterwards embodied in his last and best novel.
The Mathew Bramble who figures there is undoubtedly meant for himself ; and Jerry Milford
for his nephew Major Telfer, a son of the widow
in St. John Street.   The charming Miss R———n,
with whom the latter had the honour to dance
at the Hunters' Ball, and from whose bright eyes

he sustained some damage, is the source of these reminiscences of elder times. She was a granddaughter of Susannah, the beautiful and witty Countess of Eglinton; and inherited from her own mother the charms which Hamilton of Bangor celebrated as specially fitted "in the dance to shine." Lady Susan, the daughter of the countess, became the wife of John Renton, Esq., of Lammerton; and their daughter—whose bright eyes still flash out on us from the pages of *Humphrey Clinker*,—wedded Charles Sharpe, Esq., of Hoddam; and communicated to her favourite son recollections of her own youthful times, some of which are here gleaned for a still younger generation. But Smollett had more substantial reasons than the mere glances of bright young eyes for remembering the Rentons of Lammerton. A sister of Mrs. Sharpe married Mr. Telfer, another nephew of the novelist, who assumed the name of Smollett on succeeding to the family estate. Mr. Sharpe has left this memorandum, quoted in his memoir: "My grandfather Renton was educated at Christ Church, Oxford, and afterwards travelled in France. While at college he was a contemporary of the great Lord Mansfield; Trevor, Bishop of Durham; and Stone, Primate of Ireland. When the Bishop of Durham, in a progress through his diocese, came to Berwick, my grandfather went to wait upon him there, and carried my two aunts, Lady Murray and Mrs. Smollett, with him. When the bishop came out of the church (having his train borne up according to the fashion of that day), my aunts knelt down in the churchyard and he blessed them with an imposition of hands. My grandfather said, pointing to Lady Murray,—'My lord, this young lady is my daughter; pray give her a double portion;' on which the bishop again touched her head."

Mr. Charles Sharpe of Hoddam was a friend of Burns. He was a skilled performer on the violin, and a composer both of music and song. The poet, in one of his letters to him, says: "You are a feather in the cap of society, and I am a very hobnail in his shoes. . . . I am a fiddler and a poet; and you, I am told, play an exquisite violin and have a standard taste in the *belles lettres*. The other day, a brother catgut gave me a charming Scots air of your composition. If I was pleased with the tune, I was in raptures with the title you have given it; and taking up the idea, I have spun it into the three stanzas enclosed." The letter is an amusing specimen in Burns's best style, written and signed in the character of Johnnie Faa, the vagrant gipsy. A fine masonic apron, inscribed " Charles Sharpe of Hoddam to Rabbie Burns," is preserved as a memorial of this friendship between " cloth of frieze and cloth of gold."

When Burns visited Edinburgh in 1786, the tall narrow land of Allan Ramsay still continued to be a favourite haunt of the muses.   Mr. William Creech, who had then succeeded to it, was a man of good education, and had been in early life the tutor of the Earl of Glencairn.   The earl commended the Ayrshire poet to his notice; and they became great friends.   The gatherings at the Luckenbooths in Creech's day assumed a new aspect.   He was the publisher of Lord Kames and Lord Woodhouselee, of Dr. Blair, and Dr. Campbell the antagonist of Hume, of Cullen, Gregory, Adam Smith, and Dugald Stewart; of Henry Mackenzie "the Man of Feeling," Beattie, and Burns himself, besides many others of less note. From among this brilliant circle, the publisher was wont to invite select parties to his breakfast table; and these gatherings, designated by the wits *Creech's levees*, are alluded to in Burns's humorous poem "Willie's awa," forwarded by him to the bibliopole during his absence on a lengthened visit which he paid to London in 1787.

> " Nae mair we see his levee door
> Philosophers and poets pour,
> And toothy critics by the score
> In bloody raw;
> The Adjutant of a' the core
> Willie's awa'."

Creech was himself the author of a volume, entitled *Edinburgh Fugitive Pieces.*   The Mirror Club, of which Henry Mackenzie and Lord Craig were leading spirits, and which included other able men, such as Lord Cullen, Lord Bannatyne, and George Home of Wedderburn, among its members, was formed of the principal writers in *The Mirror,* a periodical issued every Wednesday and Saturday, from Creech's shop.   To this *The Lounger* succeeded.   The contributors' box stood at Mr. Creech's door, and the evening meetings of the club derived part of their entertainment from a critical examination of its contents.   Creech, like his predecessor in the famous Luckenbooths Land, bore his share of civic honours, and twice filled the office of Lord Provost.   He was a Fellow of the Royal Society, and one whose company was sought for his wit and humour.   But though Burns styles him "a birkie weel worth gowd," and evidently enjoyed his society, the witty book-seller was more complaisant in manner than liberal in his dealings as a publisher.   He was greedy alike of praise and of money, and after many delays in accounts, and some illiberality in their settlement, the irate poet took his revenge in this satirical sketch, which brings before the reader's mind the neat, dapper, little consequential figure of William Creech, Esq., in a less flattering aspect than he is presented by the pencil of Sir Henry Raeburn, in the portrait attached to his *Fugitive Pieces :—*

" A little, upright, pert, tart, tripping wight,
  And still his precious self his dear delight ;
  Who loves his own smart shadow in the streets
  Better than e'er the fairest she he meets ;
  A man of fashion too, he made his tour,
  Learned *vive la bagatelle, et vive l'amour ;*
  So travelled monkeys their grimace improve,
  Polish their grin, nay sigh for ladies' love.
  Much specious lore, but little understood :
  Veneering oft outshines the solid wood ;
  His solid sense by inches you must tell,
  But mete his cunning by the old Scotch ell ;
  His meddling vanity, a busy fiend,
  Still making work his selfish craft must mend."

The memoir of Creech attached to his published essays has for its appropriate tailpiece a carefully engraved view of the old building at the Cross, which for three generations had been the favourite haunt of the muses, and was known in its last days by the name of Creech's Land. Alongside of it is seen the narrow passage known of old as " Our Lady's Steps," and on the north-east corner of St. Giles' Church the niche in which once stood the statue of " our Lady, the Blessed Virgin Mary," which gave name to the adjoining thoroughfare. The site of the old tenement was a singularly commanding one. It was not only in the very throng of the busy city, " where merchants most do congregate," but, standing as it did on the lofty ridge of the old town, with the High Street and Canongate sloping away from before

 THE ADVOCATES' CLOSE.

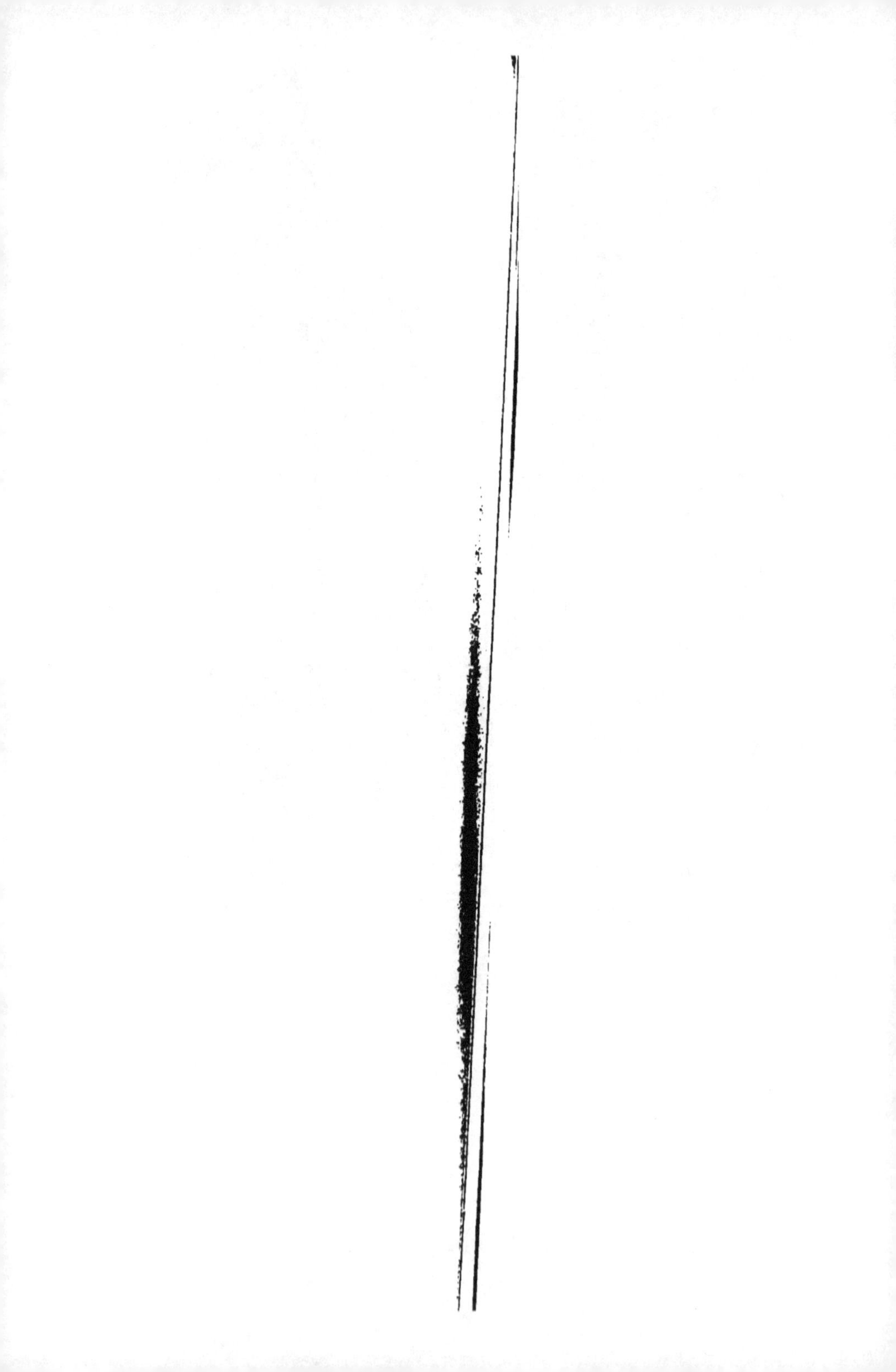

it into the sheltered valley of the Holyrood, it commanded a view across Preston Bay to the fertile landscape of East Lothian and the heights which skirt the German Ocean. On this fine landscape the poet Gay looked forth, while questioning the author of "The Gentle Shepherd" on the language and allusions of that fine Scottish pastoral poem. The wit and humour of his companion pleased him; as to the landscape, Mr. Sharpe remarks: "I don't think Gay could care for such things; his poetry and plays bear me out." But if Gay was indifferent to a noble Scottish landscape, rich with associations of Pinkie Cleuch, Carbery Hill, and Prestonpans; and with the ancient abbey and palace of Holyrood sheltering under Arthur's Seat: we need not doubt that both Smollett and Burns had an eye for all its charms; and that, to the latter especially, thoughts of other years were awakened by the scene such as he gives utterance to in his "Address to Edinburgh." Creech, the most enterprising of Scottish publishers anterior to Constable, died in 1815, and within two years thereafter the interesting old land, so rich in literary associations, was levelled with the ground. Looking now at the not too ample thoroughfare which extends between St. Giles's and the north side of the High Street, it is a marvel to think that from the days of the poet Dunbar, till those of Burns and of

Scott, the "Booth Raw" was allowed to cumber the main street of the city, and "hald the licht fra its Parish Kirk." It stood there before the Flodden wall was built; and peace had just followed the victory of Waterloo when at length its doom was pronounced, and the curious relic of ancient times and obsolete manners was swept away.

CHAPTER IX.

Ursa Major.

AN interval of seven years elapsed between the
stay of Smollett in Edinburgh, in 1766, and the
appearance of another literary star of the first
magnitude ; but that interval, slight as it seems,
is sufficient to bring the era a generation nearer
to my own.　For there died in Edinburgh, in the
year 1851, Mr. Robert Jackson, a kindly old
gentleman, far advanced in years, the venerable
representative of a past generation which now
seems so remote from us.　He took a lively
interest in local antiquities, and in all the curious
events and characters belonging to his native city.
In the article " Edinburgh," of *Chambers's Gazetteer
of Scotland*, are some interesting reminiscences
about the early history of the New Town, and the
origin of the names of its streets and squares,
which Dr. Robert Chambers informed me he
derived chiefly from Mr. Jackson.　But though I
also obtained some curious gleanings from his
retentive memory, the interest now attaching to

the remembrance of my intercourse with him is that he claimed in his own early days to have seen and conversed with Dr. Samuel Johnson.

The Lawnmarket, to which the chief local associations with the great moralist still pertain, is rich in other literary memories of last century. Here dwelt George Paton, bibliographer, and correspondent of all the venerable fellowship of antiquaries of that eighteenth century : the genuine counterpart of Davy Wilson, celebrated in Jonathan Oldbuck's panygyric as " the very prince of scouts for searching blind alleys, cellars, and stalls, for rare volumes. He had the scent of a slow-hound, and the snap of a bull-dog. He would detect you an old black-letter ballad among the leaves of a law paper, and find an *editio princeps* under the mask of a school Corderius." He was a custom-house clerk with a salary only at the last rising to £80 a year ; nevertheless he gathered together a wondrous collection of rare books in his rooms in Lady Stair's Close ; communicated their recondite contents to Lord Hailes, Gough, Bishop Percy, George Chalmers, Pennant, Herd, and all the literary explorers of the day ; was welcomed as a choice spirit in the select gatherings at Johnnie Dowie's tavern ; and died as he had lived, a frugal, contented, and happy old bachelor. It was to a house on the opposite side of the close, but with its entrance from the adjoining alley, that Robert Burns found his way when he came to Edinburgh in 1786, and took up his lodging with his friend Richmond there.

One of the most romantic traditions of Edinburgh, which Scott embodied in his *Aunt Margaret's Mirror*, has its associations with Lady Stair's Close, where may still be seen the dwelling of Elizabeth, dowager Countess of Stair, who, as the wife of the Viscount Primrose, was the heroine of the tale.   Here too the author of *Juventus Mundi* and much else of literary and historical worth, finds appropriate localisation ; for the town-mansion of his ancestor, Thomas Gladstone, merchant burgess, at the head of the close, is still one of the most striking features of the Lawnmarket. It is a tall structure of wrought ashlar, with corbelled angle and ornamental gables to the street, as shown in the accompanying sketch.   On shields cut below the corbels of each gable are the initials T. G. and B. G., with the merchant mark of the old burgess.   The house was acquired by him in 1631, and is mentioned in an injunction of Charles I. relative to the armed train-bands of the city in 1634, under the name of " Thomas Gladstone's Land." But the *genius loci* among all the native celebrities of the Lawnmarket must be regarded as he whom the admirers of Johnson would have thought it no extravagant antithesis to style the Great Immoralist.

In the year 1751 David Hume removed from Ninewells to Edinburgh, and soon after, writing to his friend Adam Smith, he says, " Direct to me in Riddal's Land, Lawnmarket."   He had assumed the responsibilities of an independent householder, and he thus facetiously describes to the great political economist his own first attempts at domestic economy :—" I have now, at last,—being turned of forty, to my own honour, to that of learning, and to that of the present age,—arrived at the dignity of being a householder. About seven months ago I got a house of my own, and completed a regular family, consisting of a head, viz. myself, and two inferior members—a maid and a cat.   My sister has since joined me, and keeps me company.   With frugality I can reach, I find, cleanliness, warmth, light, plenty, and contentment. What would you have more ?   Independence ?—I have it in a supreme degree.   Honour ?—That is not altogether wanting.   Grace ?—That will come in time.   A wife ?—That is none of the indispensable requisites of life.   Books ?—That *is* one of them, and I have more than I can use :"—and so the philosopher proceeds.   Nevertheless, some of the aforesaid requisites must have failed him in Riddle's Close.   Directly to the south of him, and right under his window, was the house of the famous old wizard of the West Bow ; and the titles of the property include " an express servitude upon the tenement of land called Major Weir's Land, that the same shall not be built higher than it is at present, lest it may anywise hurt or prejudice the said subject." With this look-out, Hume commenced his *History of England* in Riddle's Land. with books of his own, more than he could use, and the Advocates' Library within a stone cast of him. But if cleanliness, warmth, light, and plenty all held out, contentment must have failed ; for, although he writes to Dr. Robertson in 1759, " I have the strangest reluctance to change places," the *History* was finished in Jack's Land, Canongate ; and then, in 1762, back he came to the Lawn-market, finding for himself fitting and airy lodgings in the once fashionable and aristocratic quarter of James's Court, of which he became proprietor.

Entering by a narrow alley which pierces the line of houses on the north side of the Lawn-market, the visitor finds himself in a large quad-rangle surrounded by lofty, substantial buildings, which have evidently fallen to the lot of humbler occupants than those for whom they were erected. These courts, walled off by the intervening houses from the main street, were, in the Scottish metro-polis—like the similar edifices of the French nobility,—frequently designed for the protection of those within from the unwelcome intrusion of either legal or illegal force. But James's Court was a civic improvement scarcely dating back to times so lawless ; though it is of an older date than the deed of wild justice when Captain Porteous was dragged past its entry to the dyer's tree in the neighbouring Grassmarket. Built on the north declivity of the ridge on which the Old Town of Edinburgh stands, the windows of its chief range of buildings command a magnificent view of the modern city, the Firth of Forth, and the Fifeshire and Highland hills beyond ; while the outlook into the quadrangle is airy and spacious in comparison with the ancient courts and alleys of the old town. Thither, accordingly, the gentry, Lords of Session, and other dignitaries of note in their day, removed, as to a new, aristocratic quarter of the city ; and most memorable among them, the celebrated lawyer and statesman, Sir John Lauder, the author of *Fountainhall's Decisions*, and of *Chronological Notes of Scottish Affairs*. He acted as counsel at the trial of the Earl of Argyle, in 1681, at that of the Duke of Monmouth, in 1686 ; and appeared on behalf of the Duchess, vainly attempting to protect her estates from forfeiture for her husband's treason. He was a zealous friend to the Protestant cause at a time when few in Scotland ventured openly to oppose the Court ; so, when the Revolution came, he was among the first selected for preferment, and took his seat on the bench under the title of Lord Fountainhall.

To this same fashionable quarter of old Edinburgh David Hume removed, and continued to reside there till he built for himself a house in the new town, when he was succeeded by Boswell, the son of old Lord Auchinleck, another zealous supporter of the Revolution settlement. The father was bent on making him a lawyer, his own ambition was for the Guards. In the compromise between the two, he started for Utrecht, in the summer of 1763, professedly to study civil law; and, on his way through London had the good fortune to be introduced by Davis, the bookseller, to Dr. Samuel Johnson, as "a young gentleman fresh from Scotland." After studying a winter at Utrecht, he set out on the grand tour, in company with the Earl Marischal — visited Voltaire at Ferney,—Rousseau by the waters of Neufchatel; and, supplied by the latter with a letter of introduction, set off next for the island of Corsica, and so became a guest of the famous patriot chief, Pasquale de Paoli. When, a few years later, Paoli was driven into exile by the French invaders, Boswell welcomed the noble Corsican; in London introduced him to Johnson; and in Edinburgh entertained him in James's Court, and introduced him to Lord Kames, Robertson, Hume, and others, who, though greatly Boswell's seniors, had already admitted him to their circle.

It was as David Hume's tenant that Boswell

occupied his last old-town lodging ; and thither, in August 1773, he conducted Dr. Johnson from the White Horse Inn, in Boyd's Close, Canongate, where he had found him in a violent passion with the waiter for having sweetened his lemonade without the ceremony of a pair of sugar-tongs. The Doctor, in his indignation, threw the lemonade out of the window, and seemed inclined to send the waiter after it. Miss Eleonora Renton, the beauty to whom Smollett had given the pre-eminence in the gay circles of Edinburgh, in 1766, was, at this later date, the wife of Charles Sharpe of Hoddam, and in subsequent years communicated to her son her recollections of Johnson as a visitant to Edinburgh society. She was present at a tea-party given in St. James's Court on the occasion of the Doctor's arrival, and the notes of Mr. Sharpe's reminiscences, as derived from his mother, are now before me. The huge uncouth figure of Johnson rises once more before the mind's eye—ungainly still, in spite of some outward polish of his later years ; and the rough exterior, but the fitting garniture of the sturdy, defiant dogmatism with which he stormed the social strongholds of conventional decorum. It was a wondrous triumph for Boswell to get so distinguished a lion under his roof ; but, judging by what transpired on that occasion, one can understand the retort to his admiring host when he pronounced him to be a constellation of learning: "Then he must be the *Ursa Major!*" He appears to have treated the company much in the fashion he was wont to conduct himself towards their host, and the impression left on Mrs. Sharpe's mind was summed up in the laconic verdict of Mrs. Boswell: "He was a great brute!" Mrs. Boswell was a woman of admirable sense and an uncommon share of wit and humour, and won from Johnson the commendation that she had the mien and manner of a gentlewoman. She had, also, the very needful virtues of discretion and frugality, in both of which her husband was pre-eminently deficient. But, while fully alive to his weaknesses, she resented the bearing of Johnson towards him; and Boswell records with wonted *naïveté* her retort to himself: "I have seen many a bear led by a man; but I never before saw a man led by a bear!" Margaret, Duchess of Douglas, was one of the party, as Mr. Sharpe notes "with all her diamonds!" She was, according to him, notable among those of her own rank for her ostentation and her illiteracy. Dr. Johnson describes her as "an old lady, who talks broad Scotch with a paralytic voice, and is scarce understood by her own countrymen." Nevertheless he reserved his attentions during the whole evening almost exclusively for the Duchess. Mr. Sharpe adds, "The pity was that they did not fall out. The Doctor missed the rebuff of Lady

Margaret, who could be uncommonly vulgar ; and my mother's most humorous recollections of the scene were the efforts of Boswell, as their go-between, to translate the unintelligible gaucherie of her ladyship into palatable commonplaces for his guest's ear."

By the time Charles Kirkpatrick Sharpe was old enough to take an interest in his mother's re-collections of an elder generation, the details of that memorable tea-party in James's Court must have faded from her memory.   But a general impression of an unsocial self-assertion, and of blunt ponderous dogmatism, served to realise the bearing of Johnson in his first introduction to a select Edinburgh circle.   " Doctor," said Goldsmith in one of his happiest repartees, " if you were to write a fable about little fishes, you would make them all talk like whales ! "   But the digital sugar-tongs of the White Horse Inn waiter were probably by no means the only novelties of northern manners which helped to sour his lemonade, and make him more inclined to talk to the little fishes like a great bear.   A young fellow present—Mr. Sharpe thought, Andrew Nairne, a lawyer,—retorted on some remark suggestive of the Doctor's idolisation of a duchess, by commending Pope as a poet possessed of sufficient self-respect to

" Bare the mean heart that lurks beneath a star."

The duchess was deaf, and so the allusion was

less reprehensible.   But a Johnsonian duel followed, in which the most Mrs. Sharpe remembered was that the young lawyer stood his ground in spite of the doctor's most emphatic "No, sir!" His overbearing manner—not improbably stimulated by the very deference he met with, manifested as it was in unfamiliar fashions,—was not likely to be under great restraint at Boswell's tea-table; and the impressions conveyed by Mrs. Sharpe's recollections are confirmed by the lively letters of Captain Topham, who visited Edinburgh the following year.   He describes the reception of the doctor, by all classes, as having been of the most flattering kind; and he adds: "From all I have been able to learn, he repaid all their attention to him with ill-breeding; and when in company of the ablest men in this country, his whole design was to show them how little he thought of them." Lord Stowell, who was Johnson's travelling companion, related that the doctor was treated by the Scottish literati with a degree of deference bordering on pusillanimity.   But he notes as an exception the celebrated advocate, Mr. Crosby,—the original of Mr. Counsellor Pleydell, in *Guy Mannering*,—whom he characterised as an intrepid talker, and the only man who was prepared to "stand up" to Dr. Johnson.   But to this Mr. Sharpe adds his comment: "Your intrepid talkers are always noisy bullies; and 'tis like enough

Crosby was among the number.   He was a coarse man—married a woman who had been a street-walker.   He may have been an ingenious lawyer, but he was a dull man—many letters of his writing I have which prove this."

Among the little incidents of this stray reminiscence of olden times, the coincidence is noteworthy which thus placed the reception of Johnson in the mansion of David Hume, and furnished as Boswell's guest-chamber for the great moralist the very room which had recently had for its occupant the author of *The Essay on Miracles*.   It is told that being on one occasion at a party where Hume was present, a mutual friend proposed to introduce Johnson to him, when the intolerant moralist roared out, "No, sir!" It is not without reason, therefore, that the biographer of Hume questions if Johnson would have been able to "sleep o' nights" had he learned that he had been entrapped into the arch-infidel's very mansion.   But, in happy unconsciousness of their evil associations, Dr. Johnson writes, "Boswell has very handsome and spacious rooms, level with the ground on one side of the house, and on the other four stories high."   This curious but by no means uncommon feature of Edinburgh old-town dwellings, has a singular aspect to a stranger. Dr. Burton in describing it, while still the dwelling of David Hume, thus writes: "Entering one of the doors opposite the main entrance [into James's Court], the stranger is sometimes led by a friend, wishing to afford him an agreeable surprise, down flight after flight of the steps of a stone staircase, and when he imagines he is descending so far into the bowels of the earth, he emerges on the edge of a cheerful, crowded thoroughfare, connecting together the old and new town, the latter of which lies spread before him—a contrast to the gloom from which he has emerged. When he looks up to the building containing the upright street through which he has descended, he sees that vast pile of tall houses standing at the head of the Mound, which creates astonishment in every visitor to Edinburgh." The western half of this huge pile was destroyed by fire in 1858, and while its ruins remained, it seemed as if an eye-tooth had been knocked out of Auld Reekie, to the sore blemishment of her charms ; but it has been re-erected in the old Scottish style ; and adds a varied and striking feature to the general view.

In near vicinity to St. James's Court was Webster's Close, on the Castle Hill. In more modern days, when known as Brown's Court, it was the scene of the deliberations of the Society of Antiquaries, when it had the Earl of Bute for president ; and its enthusiastic founder and first vice-president, the Earl of Buchan, drew together an enthusiastic coterie of Scottish noblemen and gentlemen, for the purpose of "investigating antiquities, as well as natural and civil history in general, with a view to the improvement of the minds of mankind;" and, as he was able to report in 1782, "The success of their endeavours had already succeeded far beyond their most sanguine expectations." But in Johnson's day it was still Webster's Close, the residence of Dr. Webster, minister of the Old Tolbooth Kirk, and a man of mark in his day. His father had shared in the sufferings of the persecuted Presbyterians under the later Stuarts, and closed his career in better times as minister of the church to which his son succeeded. The younger Webster, while minister of Culross, was asked to press the suit of a gentleman who had in vain sought the hand of Miss Mary Erskine, a lady of fortune nearly related to the Dundonald family. His solicitations failed; but the fair lady hinted that, had he pleaded as well for himself, he might have been more successful. The hint was taken; and when, in 1737, the Tolbooth congregation invited him to succeed to his father's vacant charge, he removed to Edinburgh, and ere long made Miss Erskine his wife. He was a man of pleasing manners and a fine commanding figure; and with a lady of birth and fortune presiding at his table, his house became noted for its genial hospitality. Dr. Webster combined what would now seem the incongruous elements of a highly popular evangelical divine with the manners and accomplishments of a man of the world, and a wit of rare convivial powers.   In an age when hard drinking was habitual with all classes, his powers of endurance enabled him to enjoy society with impunity.   Dr. Carlyle, who belonged to the clerical party most opposed to him, speaks of him as best known by the designation of *Dr. Bonum Magnum*.   But though he is at little pains to conceal his prejudice against him, the stories he tells about the convivial excesses of his own friends abundantly prove his recognition of the maxim that "a love of claret to any degree was not reckoned in those days a sin in Scotland." The story is told of a belated acquaintance overtaking Dr. Webster on his way homeward towards dawn, not without symptoms of recent conviviality. "Eh! Doctor, what would the auld wives o' the Tolbooth say if they saw you now?" was the salutation of his friend.   "Tut, man!" retorted the divine, "they wadna believe their e'en."   Dr. Webster enjoyed great popularity and influence in his day; and is still gratefully remembered as the originator of the Widows' and Orphans' scheme of the Church of Scotland.   At his table Dr. Johnson was introduced to some of the wits and men of letters who then gave a charm to Edinburgh society; and on him the Doctor relied, as his letters show, for information relative to the Scottish Highlands, when he was preparing the narrative of his *Journey to the Western Islands of Scotland.*

To the east of James's Court stands " Thomas Gladstone's land," with its associations with the train-bands of 1634, in that *juventus mundi*, or youth of the civic world, while Charles I. was still king ; and with the added charm which the genius of a later generation has revived in connection with the old merchant burgess of the Lawnmarket. Adjoining this is Lady Stair's Close, which of old formed the chief thorough- fare to the New Town, when the embryo earthen mound was in process of formation, and Bank Street was still among the undeveloped improve- ments of the coming time. Half-way down the close, on its western side, a picturesque old mansion bears on its lintel this pious legend : FEARE THE LORD, AND DEPART FROM EVILL, with the date 1622, and the arms and monogram of Sir William Gray of Pittendrum,—the ancestor of the present Baroness Gray. Sir William Gray was a man of rare energy, and of much influence. By virtue of a patent granted by Charles I., the ancient title of Lord Gray reverted to his family ; nevertheless he devoted himself to commerce, and became one of the most prosperous merchants of his day, greatly extending the foreign trade of

I.

GLADSTONE'S LAND

P. 262.

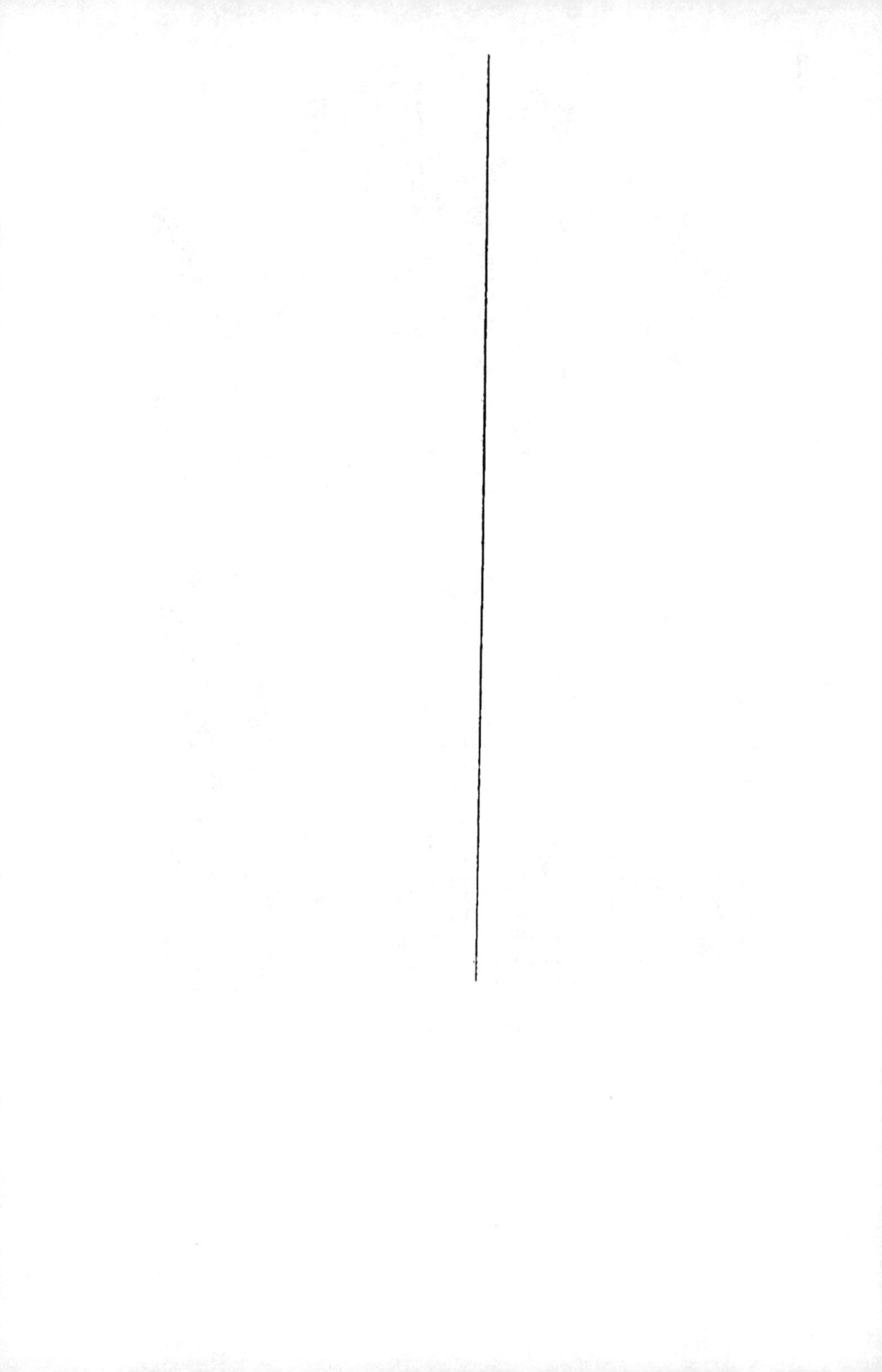

Scotland, and acquiring for himself much wealth. But on the breaking out of the civil war he adhered to the royal party, and shared in its misfortunes. The Scottish Parliament imposed on him a fine of 100,000 merks for corresponding with Montrose ; and after imprisonment, first in the Castle of Edinburgh, and then in the Tolbooth, he obtained release on paying a commuted penalty of 35,000 merks. We learn from Sir Thomas Hope's diary, that, on the 12th May 1645, "a daughter of Sir William Grayis departit off the plaig, quhilk put us all in greit fear." This was the last terrible visitation of the pestilence to Edinburgh ; when grass grew thickly about the cross, the inhabitants fled in dismay ; and at a time when an immediate attack on the city by the victorious army of Montrose was anticipated, Maitland tells us "scarce sixty men were left capable of assisting in its defence."

A romantic legend of the Canongate connects itself with the persons and events of this memorable time. During one of the tumultuous civic outbreaks of the Edinburgh mob, soon after the accession of Charles I., the house of the Provost was fired, and a reign of terror prevailed for a time. On the restoration of order, one Andrew Gray, a younger son of the Master of Gray, was convicted as the ringleader of the mob ; and, notwithstanding the interposition of powerful friends, he was condemned to the halter.   But on the very eve of his execution, when the scaffold was already in preparation, he effected his escape from the Tolbooth, by means of a rope and file conveyed to him by a faithful vassal.   A boat lay at the foot of a neighbouring close, by which he was ferried over the Nor' Loch; and long before the Netherbow Port was opened, a lessening sail near the mouth of the Firth told to the eye of his faithful vassal that Andrew Gray was safe beyond pursuit.

Years passed away; the sack of the Provost's house, and the escape of the ringleader had faded from men's memories, and now all thought was absorbed on the terrible outbreak of the plague, in that year 1645, the year of the pestilence. The train-bands had been summoned in vain, in dread of the approach of Montrose, when a new danger called for action.   A strange vessel, of curious form and rigging, which was pronounced by old seamen to be a Barbary rover, sailed up the Forth, and cast anchor in Leith Roads.   An armed detachment landed, and, making its way unopposed through the Water Gate, and up the Canongate, demanded admission at the Netherbow Port.   The magistrates entered into parley with the leader; warned him of the danger within the walls of the plague-stricken city, and offered exorbitant terms of ransom : but all in vain.   The city could only be ransomed by the delivery to the pirates of the chief magistrate's son.   But, as it proved, the only child of Sir John Smith, the Provost, was a daughter, who then lay stricken of the plague, of which her cousin Egidia, the daughter of Sir William Gray, had recently died.   This information wrought an immediate change on the rover.   He intimated his possession of an elixir of wondrous potency; and demanded that the Provost's daughter should be entrusted to his care, engaging either to restore her cured, or to depart without putting the city to ransom.   No offers, however, could induce him to enter the city; and at length yielding in this dreadful alternative to the urgency of his friends, the Provost had his daughter borne in a litter to the house in the Canongate, outside the Netherbow Port, where the rover had fixed his quarters.   There he tended on the fair invalid, and, ere long, to the delight of her father, restored her to him safe and well.

The dénoûment of the story bears that the strange physician proved to be Andrew Gray, who, after being captured by pirates, and sold as a slave, had won the favour of the Emperor of Morocco, and risen to rank in his service.   He had returned to his native land, bent on revenging his wrongs on the magistrates of Edinburgh, when, to his surprise, the Provost proved to be a connection of his own.   The remainder of the tale is soon told.   Provided with a free pardon, he settled down a wealthy citizen of the Burgh of Canongate, bringing home to his house his fair patient as his bride : in proof of which the house stands to this day on the north side of the Canongate, adorned with an effigy of his royal patron, the Emperor of Morocco, and is still known to all as the Morocco Land.   When, in earlier years, I was busy hunting up the picturesque nooks and romantic legends of old Edinburgh, I had the curiosity to obtain access to the title-deeds of this property.   The earliest dates no farther back than 1731 ; but it is a disposition of the property to one John Gray, a merchant, and, it may be, a descendant of the Barbary rover and the Provost's daughter.   To complete the tale, it is added that he had vowed never to enter the city but sword in hand ; and having abandoned all thought of revenge, he kept the vow till his death, and never again passed the threshold of the Netherbow Port.

The later name of " Lady Stair's Close " is derived from the heroine of a still more romantic legend than that of the Barbary rover.   Elizabeth, daughter of the second Earl of Loudoun, was married, while a mere girl, to James, first Viscount Primrose, a man of ungovernable passion and dissolute habits.   One morning, as she was dressing herself in her chamber, she saw in her mirror the door opened steathily and her husband enter with a drawn sword in his hand. His face betrayed the malignant passions which influenced him; and the cruelty she had already been subjected to had repeatedly led her to believe that her life was in danger. Fortunately her bedroom window was open, and sufficiently near the ground to admit of her leaping out, half dressed as she was. She sought protection from Lord Primrose's mother; and secured deliverance from a yoke which had become intolerable.

The actual sight of her husband thus reflected in her mirror may have had its share in shaping the romantic story on which Scott founded his *Aunt Margaret's Mirror*. Lord Primrose went abroad. Some time afterwards a foreign conjuror visited Edinburgh; Lady Primrose was induced to consult him; and proceeding in disguise to his rooms in the Canongate, in company with a female friend, they were instructed to look into a large mirror. As they continued to gaze, its surface shaped itself into definite forms, until they could perceive the interior of a church, with a bridal party at the altar; and, to her astonishment, she discerned her husband in the bridegroom. The ceremony was about to proceed, when another person entered, sword in hand; and advancing with an angry look, Lady Primrose recognised in him her own brother. But as she eagerly gazed into the mirror the whole became once more obscure, till only the blank surface remained. On the return of her brother from a foreign tour Lady Primrose learned that, while travelling in the Low Countries, he had actually so interposed at the very crisis, when Lord Primrose was about to be united in marriage to the daughter of a wealthy Dutch merchant.

After a lengthened widowhood, Lady Primrose married the celebrated Earl of Stair ; and, as the dowager Countess, was long looked up to as the leader of fashion.   In accordance with the simple manners of Edinburgh society in the last century, the countess occupied a single floor on the stair of Sir William Gray's former mansion ; and an admission to her select circle was courted as one of the highest objects of ambition among the smaller gentry of the period.   " My mother's sister, Lady Murray of Clermont," writes Mr. Sharpe, " told me that when she went to visit the dowager, her stair was so narrow that she had to tilt her hoop.   But that was a common occurrence in the old-town closes ; and ladies' hoops were constructed like the graith of Milton's devils, when the crowd of them swarmed and got jammed in Mulciber's Close.   The giants shrank and collapsed, like my lady's hoop and fardingale." The marvel, however, remains as to what became of this magnificent amplitude of hoop when it had safely passed the ordeal of the narrow stair, and expanded to its due proportions in the chamber of dais.   The description calls up an amusing picture of high life in the days of our great-grandmothers, with the leader of ton in the Scottish capital—the widow of an earl and field-marshal, who held high command under Marlborough, at Ramillies, Oudenarde, and Malplaquet ; was the representative of George I. at the Court of Versailles, and the companion of George II. at Dettingen,—condescendingly receiving the *élite* of fashionable society in the second flat of a common stair down one of the closes of the old town.   Yet such were the habits of Edinburgh society at a period when the distinctions of rank were guarded with a degree of jealousy of which we have little conception now.

CHAPTER X.

The Flowers of the Forest.

SMOLLETT, in his *Humphrey Clinker*, specially indicates the old civic resort of Edinburgh's men of business, as well as of her literary coteries, and her poets, as the place "where formerly stood a market cross, a curious piece of Gothic architecture ;" for already in his day it had been transferred to Lord Somerville's estate of Drum. In a characteristic etching of Charles Kirkpatrick Sharpe, executed as a frontispiece for some old poems printed under the supervision of his friend David Laing, he represents a female ballad-singer, with a sheaf of broadsides in her hand, and a boy-dwarf seated on a creepy by her side. One of his slighter pencil sketches on my own "Memorials" proofs, which forms the frontispiece of the present volume, furnishes a tragi-comic travesty of a somewhat similar scene. The crow-stepped gables of the old High Street, with the city cross surmounted by the Scottish unicorn, form the background. The latter was associated with so many choice local incidents that it might well have been deemed safe from desecration.   Above all, it was the romantic memorial of the Flowers of Ettrick Forest, and the gallant host that perished on Flodden Hill.

Had the bard of "Marmion" only come a little earlier to revive such associations, the old cross would have stood unscathed, as on that night of doom when a cry was heard from it at the midnight hour; and Platcock—the Megæra of medieval super-stition,—summoned nobles, knights, and burgesses of Scotland "to compeir before his maister within fourtie dayes."   The circumstantial details with which Lindsay of Pitscottie authenticates the supernatural doings of that stirring time read oddly enough as a counterpart to other doings of the century in which the printing-press of Walter Chepman had just been set up near by the same market cross ; and influences had thus been intro-duced which were to work strange revolutions before long.   It was a time when light was breaking along those rugged northern hills in many golden gleams, and when Europe at large was casting off her medieval swaddling bands.

Ere the Flowers of the Forest had been weeded away on Flodden Hill, the poets and philosophers of Scotland had learned in some vague way of a new world recently discovered beyond their old engirdling ocean.   When Dunbar wrote to the king "of this warldis instabilitie," where "sugared words and figured speeches" are no true index of

mind or heart, and purposes are fickle as wind or
rain, he thus comes to the point :—

> " I knaw nocht how the kirk is guided,
> But benefices are nocht leal divided ;
> Some men have seven, and I nocht ane :
> Quhilk to consider is ane pain."

He then reflects that the king's long-promised
benefice might have reached him in shorter time,
had it come from farthest India, the isles of Africa,
or even from the new-found isle that lies beyond
"the great sea-ocean :"—

> " It might have comen in shorter while
> Fra Calicut and the new-found isle,
> The partis of Transmeridiane :
> Quhilk to consider is ane pain."

But the new-found isle beyond the ocean was a
very vague world of insubstantiality to the men
of that time. The *Novus Orbis* had no clear relation to their own ; and when, so late as 1528, Sir
David Lindsay wrote his *Dreme*, Dame Remembrance, who there plays the part of Virgil to Dante,
and becomes the poet's guide to purgatory, situated
in the centre of the earth ; and to the crystalline
and the empyreal heavens ; also, as he says,

> " Gart me clearly understand
> How that the earth tripartite was in three ;
> In Afric, Europe, and Asie. . . .
>
> .   .   .   .   .   .
>
> First Asia contained is in the orient,

> And is well more than both the other twain ;
> Afric and Europe in the occident :

that is in the west.   For though, under the guidance
of Dame Remembrance, he

> Saw famous isles, many a one,
> Which in the ocean-sea was situate,

and proceeds to declare their names, there is no
special one yet known to him indicative of a
western continent beyond the deep sea main.   It
was, indeed, no new world which Columbus sought ;
but only an ocean highway westward to Cathay
and the Orient ; and so, thirty-six years after his
great discovery, Lindsay still writes undoubtingly
of the three old continents as the sole divisions of
the tripartite earth.

Old-world memories come back strangely amid
the unhistoric wilds of a continent which has thus
so recently established relations with the past ; yet
nothing so promptly revives such associations as
the notes of some well-known air.   Rarely has this
been more vividly presented to my mind than when
the familiar tune of " Castles in the Air," dear to
me as one which I have heard sung by the author
of the song in old times, caught my ear in the notes
of an Indian guide paddling me in his birch-bark
canoe among the bears and musk-rats of the Muskoka river.   He did not know the words, nor indeed
the language.   But notes and words seemed one ;

and recalled the homely philosophy of my old friend :—

" For a' sae sage he looks, what can the laddie ken?
He's thinking upon naething, like mony mighty men :
A wee thing mak's us think, a sma' thing mak's us stare ;
There's mair folk than him building castles in the air.

The day was one of rare beauty ; the little party of holiday-makers constituted the whole world to one another in that sylvan solitude ; and memories of olden times came back on us like dreams of another life. "This is the very poetry of existence," exclaimed my friend Judge Galt, a son of the famed "Sir Andrew Wylie of that ilk ;" of "Lawrie Tod," and other scions of paternal literary genealogy. The judge sat in his canoe paddled by his Indian henchman ; while I glided along side in another, propelled by the paddle of my Chippewa gillie. The scene was a beautiful Canadian river in all the wildness of forest nature. The bear, the wolf, and the wild deer, the beaver and musk-rat, the porcupine, squirrel, and chipmunk, haunted its wooded banks ; and as lovely speckled trout as angler could desire lurked in the pools above its frequent rapids. We had escaped from the August heats of Toronto to this charming sylvan retreat ; and were *en route* for the Lake of Bays, where choice sport, and life under canvas, were in store for us.

" Merry it is in the good greenwood,
    Where the mavis and merle are singing ;
  When the deer sweeps by, and the hounds are in cry,
    And the hunter's horn is ringing."

So chaunted my companion, in joyous harmony with the feelings of the hour, though we were a month too early for Canadian deer-hunting ; and lapsing into a critical vein at the thought of this, we questioned how far Scott was correct in timing the notes of the mavis and the merle with the sweep of the deer and the cry of the hounds. Then as we recalled the note of the blackbird—as heard again after long absence from my native land, like the welcome voice of an old friend,—how comes it, we asked, that this fine poetical name of the *merle* should be superseded by so poor a commonplace as the *blackbird?*   And so, in the wild greenwood, under its dark pines and drooping cedars, with the maple, the sumach, and the sweet-scented basswood of the Muskoka, where no mavis or merle ever sang we " recalled fair Scotland's hills again ;" and dallied with many a pleasant memory of song and scene. The memories of that day come back on me now in fitting association with " The Flowers of the Forest ;" for there, amid strange wild-flowers of the primeval forest, it was a rare chance to catch what seemed to be a fresh glint, presently to be referred to, from old Ettrick Forest and the minstrel memories of Flodden.

If the antiquity so long assigned to the Scottish traditionary ballads have any foundation in truth, it might well surprise us that they should include no echo of the Flodden wail. It is not, indeed, the custom of the national poet to celebrate defeats ; but as Burton says : " as a calamity, rather than a disgrace, Flodden has ever been spoken of with a mournful pride for the unavailing devotedness it called forth." The king, scorning all strategy and true generalship, fought in the fore-front of the battle. Earls and barons who should have been the leaders of their men, and churchmen whose duties lay far apart from that field of carnage, clustered around him in gallant rivalry, as though it had been a mere joust for honour and fair ladies' smiles ; and ere the field was lost and won, the flower of that generation of Scotsmen had been weeded away, like grass beneath the mower's scythe.

Did the poet who sang so tenderly his " Lament for the Makars," when his poetic rival, Walter Kennedy, lay at the point of death, spare no monody for his royal master and friend ? Among those who never returned from the fatal field, Alexander Stewart, Archbishop of St. Andrews, who had studied under Erasmus at Padua, was mourned by that great scholar as one of rare promise. With him perished George Hepburn, Bishop of the Isles ; and, according to the contemporary record, Andrew Stewart, Bishop of Caithness, and the Abbots of Inchaffray and Kilwinning. It is obvious, therefore, that ecclesiastics claimed no exemption from the general summons to arms. Among such the name of the poet Dunbar is traceable in the treasurer's accounts, by the payment of his pension up to May 1513. From the date of the fatal battle in which his sovereign perished, every reference to him disappears. It is not therefore without reason that the conjecture has been hazarded that he too accompanied the king to Flodden, and shared his fate ; and so the voice was silenced that should have sung the royal dirge. If he did survive, the events of that fatal day involved the overthrow of his most cherished hopes ; and might well inspire a lament still more plaintive than his wail over the graves of his brother-poets. To baron's castle, burgher's booth, and peasant's cot, the same tale of national disaster and personal loss was everywhere borne back. It could almost be said once more : "There was not a house where there was not one dead ;" and many a tragedy of widowed bride and orphaned heir inspired earlier songs than the Lay of the Last Minstrel.

But the traditional antiquity of the songs and ballads of Scotland has been subjected to most unromantic inquisition in recent years. An age of uncritical credulity has been followed by one too sceptical to give credit to any ordinary evidence ;

and the result is the discredit of many a cherished idol. The craftsmen of Selkirk sent their company of eighty stalwart "souters," under the leadership of its town-clerk, William Brydone, subsequently knighted for his gallant deeds ; but few of his followers returned to resume the sewing of the single-soled shoon. Selkirk itself seems to have been well-nigh razed. A charter granted to the burgh by James V. twenty-two years thereafter refers to its having been reduced to utter ruin by fire and pestilence. Two years latter its rebuilding is declared to be needful for "defence againes owre auld ennemyis of England," and for restoration of a royal burgh "continualie sen the field of Flodoune oppressit, heriit, and owrerun be thieves and traitors, whairthrow the haunt of merchandice has cessit amangis thame of lang tyme bygane."

A blazon of the burgh arms is traditionally referred to the local legend which tells that, on the return of the little remnant of the survivors to Ettrick Forest, the first object which greeted their sight was the dead wife of one of their fallen comrades, lying on the outskirts of Ladywood Edge, with her babe still suckling at her breast. The heraldic blazonry of the local legend is thus referred to in a letter of Sir Walter Scott to Charles Kirkpatrick Sharpe: "I want your assistance in planning a silver cup for the Souters of Selkirk, to be given to the knaves by the Duke. He wishes to have the *birss* (*a bonâ fide birss*) disposed some-how as an ornament on the top on't.   Now as the arms of the town are picturesque, being a female figure with a child in her arms seated on a sarco-phagus, I thought the *birss* might be put into her hand, but on trying it, it looks as if she was just going to flog the wean.   Then I thought of dis-posing it at the end of a sort of silver handle or sceptre.   But that looked like a broom, and showed as if the poor woman had undertaken to be house-maid and child's-maid at once.   Pray aid with your wit, for mine is pumped dry."   The difficulty was solved by converting the *birss*, or bunch of hog's bristles, the professional cognisance of the Selkirk Souters, into the top of a silver thistle sur-mounting the emblematic group.   The old For-esters' honours have been assailed in all ways. Ritson sneered at the idea that eighty souters could be found in a border burgh, or indeed in all Scotland, at the time; while Dr. Johnson records his opinion that there was never a shoemaker north of the Border till Cromwell's soldiers taught the art to the barefoot Redshanks of the Dee!   The sculptured stones of Scotland show, on the con-trary, that the souter's craft was in vogue before the Bruce or the Stuarts stepped into Macalpin's vacant brogues; and southern mosses have yielded curious antique specimens of the "single-soled shoon" of the Border craftsmen.   Scott describes those made by the Souters of Selkirk as a sort of brogues, with a single thin sole, to which the purchaser sewed on another of thick leather, as is done with the Indian moccasin of light deer-skin to adapt it to the rougher traffic of the clearings.

The popular local song of "The Souters of Selkirk" is no inapt illustration of the traditionary process of transmitting our ballad literature. Scott recovered a very modernised version, with the anachronism of "The Earl of Hume," a title of nearly a century later than Flodden. His predecessor in the sheriffdom of Selkirk noted the words as not very ancient; though local tradition universally referred their allusions "to the battle of Flodden, and to the different behaviour of the Souters and Lord Home upon that occasion." But he adds that "at election dinners, etc., when the Selkirk folks begin to get fou', they always call for that tune;" and doubtless the old refrain was readapted with many a variation, to the local contests of the hour, including even a famous football match between the families of Home and Philiphaugh which is said to be alluded to in one of the stanzas given by Scott. But the older *Musical Museum* of Johnson—famous for Burns's share in its production,—preserves a far more spirited version. Johnson was himself a native of Ettrick Forest, and gives both the air and words as he had heard them sung and played in his youth. The original melody he describes as "a bagpipe tune of eight diatonic intervals in its compass." The words have a genuine local flavour very different from the "modern antiques" of Ramsay, Percy, and other eighteenth-century collectors :—

> Up wi' the Souters o' Selkirk
> > And down wi' the fazard Lord Hume !
> But up wi' ilka braw callant
> > That sews the single-soled shoon ;
> And up wi' the lads o' the Forest
> > That ne'er to the Southron wad yield ;
> But deil scoup o' Hume and his menzie,
> > That stood sae abiegh on the field !
>
> Fye on the green and the yellow !
> > The craw-hearted loons o' the Merse ;
> But here's to the Souters o' Selkirk,
> > The elshin, the lingle, and birse.
> Then up wi' the Souters o' Selkirk,
> > For they are baith trusty and leal ;
> And up wi' the lads o' the Forest,
> > And down wi' the Merse to the deil !

Here doubtless is an echo of the Flodden wail over the desertion of the lads o' the Forest, by Lord Home and the men of the Merse ; though changed in its transmission through successive generations into a vague embodiment of local rivalries.

The " Flowers o' the Forest " illustrates still more distinctly the same process of an ancient lyric, with its popular refrain passed on from elder generations, and its echoes furnishing the hint for more than one song and ballad associated with events of later times.   Sir Walter Scott assigns the authorship of the singularly beautiful song, as printed in his *Border Minstrelsy*, to a lady of family in Roxburghshire.   The version there given was procured, as he tells us, through the intervention of the Rev. Dr. Somerville.   He had been tutor in the family of Sir Gilbert Elliot, by whom he was subsequently presented to the parish of Minto ; he had, therefore, good opportunities of knowing the literary secrets of Minto House.   In greatly more modern years the joint biographers of *The Songstresses of Scotland* have undertaken to give a circumstantial account of the origin of the song.   Considering indeed that they recall a little incident which happened nearly a century and a quarter ago, the narrative is only too minute.   Miss Jean Elliot when in her thirtieth year, was riding home, after nightfall in the family coach in company with her brother. Their conversation turned on Flodden, and its fatality to the men of the Forest, and he laid a wager of a pair of gloves, or a set of ribbons, that she could not write a ballad on the subject.   "Yielding," says her biographer, " to the influence of the moment, Jean accepted the challenge.   Leaning back in her corner, with all the most mournful stories of the countryside for her inspiration, and two lines of an old ballad which had often rung in her ears, and trembled on her lips, for a foundation, she planned and constructed the rude framework of her 'Flowers of the Forest.'" Afterwards the song was duly and correctly written down ;—and so, having won her ribbons by composing, as her first attempt in verse, one of the most simply plaintive and beautiful lyrics in the language, Miss Jean relapsed into sober prose for the rest of her days, prolonged though they were for nearly half a century thereafter. The circumstantiality of this story is all the more remarkable from its occurrence in a biographical sketch of the reputed authoress, otherwise so vague.

In his notes to Johnson's *Museum*, David Laing gives the same family tradition, on the authority of a gentleman who was acquainted with Miss Elliot during the latter period of her life. What such traditions are worth has been seen already in the case of Lady Wardlaw ; but it is not to be doubted that Miss Elliot had some share in the creation or revival of the beautiful song. Nor is its association with the land and the race of the Elliots in any way inapt. No fairer tract is to be found in the Lowlands than that which stretches through the vale of Teviotdale, famous in song and story for the deeds of the Scotts, the Kerrs, the Elliots, and other Border clans ; and, among them none had sent forth a gallanter array of men of mark, and women of true worth, than the house of Minto. They took their fair share in rough Border life, when that was their vocation; and dowered their daughters with "half a Michaelmas moon," or the fair moiety of a September night's foray, when a bride had to be portioned. When times changed they adapted themselves to a new world. Sir Gilbert, the elder, made his first hit as a young lawyer in rescuing William Veitch, a covenanting minister, from an arbitrary arrest by the Scottish Government, in the old persecuting days of the Stuarts. He had a hand, too, in the escape of the Earl of Argyle from his prison in Edinburgh Castle, and so, for a time at least, from the scaffold. No wonder that he found it needful, ere long, himself to escape beyond arbitrary arrests, and take refuge in Holland. But with the Revolution came the reversal of his attainder, and, ultimately, his elevation to the bench. As a judge, his duties took him to Dumfries, where his old client, William Veitch, was now parish minister. When they met, the latter, referring playfully to the good fortune that had rewarded the efforts of the young lawyer on his behalf, remarked to the judge: "Had it no been for me, you would be writing papers yet at a plack a page!" "Ah, Willie," retorted Lord Minto, if it hadna been for me, the pyets would have pyked your pow on the Netherbow Port." It is his son who ultimately rose to be Lord President of the Court of Session, that we have to picture to ourselves, in like homely Doric, challenging his daughter relative to her first and last song. He was a man of musical and literary tastes ; and it would be more in keeping to find Jeanie palming off on him a spurious antique, for he it was, in conjunction with Duncan Forbes of Culloden, who printed Lady Elizabeth Wardlaw's "Hardyknute" in a folio tract, as an ancient ballad found in the crypt of Dunfermline Abbey.

As to the brother Gilbert, to whom the prompting of the song has been assigned, he, too, had a literary turn ; was himself a song-writer ; and a specimen of one of his adaptations to an old tune will help us better than most other means to test the style of the " Forest " song by that of the age assigned to it. " My sheep I neglected "—his best production,—was written for the old Ettrick and Yarrow tune of " My apron dearie." Its pastoral affectations accord perfectly with the taste and style of his day, and may enable the reader to realise his probable reception of such a choice anachronism as that which is ascribed to the tête-a-tête with his sister Jean, as the two rode home in the Minto family coach in the gloaming of that year 1756. A single stanza will suffice:—

> "My sheep I neglected, I left my sheep-hook,
> And all the gay haunts of my youth I forsook ;
> No more for Amynta fresh garlands I wove ;
> For ambition, I said, would soon cure me of love.
> Oh, what had my youth with ambition to do ?
> Why left I Amynta ? why broke I my vow ?

> Oh, give me my sheep, and my sheep-hook restore,
> And I'll wander from love and Amynta no more."

The story of the authorship of Miss Jean's supposed lyric is evidently due to the family tutor, Dr. Somerville, who was minister of Jedburgh when he "furnished the version which Scott inserted in the *Border Minstrelsy*." As to the Doctor, he was the author of a *History of Political Transactions and Parties* in the times of the Restoration and Revolution; and made no pretence of discriminating between sixteenth and eighteenth century lyrics. Scott would certainly have favoured the idea of the song being a genuine antique; but what could he do with his sole version of it furnished by the old tutor of the Minto family as the product of one of its daughters? He had to take song and authorship together. Yet, as it turns out, it is but a slightly modified version of one that had been in print nearly thirty years before. It is to be found, as reproduced below, in the appendix to a volume entitled *An exact and circumstantial History of the Battle of Flodden, in verse, written about the time of Queen Elizabeth: published from a curious MS. in the possession of John Askew, of Palins-Burn, in Northumberland, Esq. With Notes, by Robert Lambe, Vicar of Norham-upon-Tweed.* This scarce volume, printed and sold by R. Taylor, Berwick-upon-Tweed, 1774, includes pieces relating to Flodden, from Fulwell, Skelton, and other early poets, and also sundry ballads intermingled among the copious prose notes of the appendix. Among the latter the "Flowers of the Forest" is introduced as "an old Scotch song on the Battle of Flodden, fought A.D. 1513." This acceptance of it as a genuine antique is the more noticeable, as another ballad which the editor quotes in confirmation of certain arguments on the date of his poem, is ascribed to "one Gifford, a servant to Edward Cope of Eadon, Esq.," about 200 years ago; and a version of "Sir James the Ross" is stated to be "written by a very ingenious young lady, Miss Christian Edwards, daughter of a gentleman in Stirlingshire, author also of several other poetical pieces." The metrical *History of the Battle of Flodden* is in four parts, with a further subdivision in seven fits, and extends in all to 577 stanzas. Of its English origin there can be no doubt. A stanza or two will suffice to illustrate its character. The Scottish nobles are described as responding to King James's summons, "well busked, and for battle bent."

> " And thus arrayed in armour bright,
> They met in Edinborough town ;
> There was many a lord, and many a knight,
> And baron brave of high renown.
>
> Of prelates proud, a populous lave,
> And abbots boldly there were known :

With Bishop of St. Andrew's brave
  Who was King James's bastard son.

Surely it was an unseemly sight
  And quite against our Christian laws,
To see a prelate press to fight
  And that too in a wicked cause."

The poem travels over the whole record of Scotland's evil deeds, and glances at sacred and classical history after the fashion of older chroniclers. Its opening stanza, indeed, seems to indicate that it is only a portion of a more ample metrical history. But at times it has the quaint vigour of the true Border ballad. Lord Hume, of whose defection the English chronicler has nothing to say, thus exhorts his liege lord :—

" For England's king, you understand,
  To France is past with all his peers ;
There is none at home, left in the land
  But joult-head monks, and bursten fryers ;

Or ragged rustics, without rules,
  Or priests prating for pudding-shives,
Or millners madder than their mules,
  . Or wanton clerks waking their wives.
  .   .   .   .   .   .
What lusty troop is yon I see?
  Sir Edward Stanley did enquire,
A yeoman said It is, I see,
  Bryan Tunstal, that bold esquire.

For in his banner I behold
  A curling cock, as though he would crow ;

> He brings with him his tenants bold,
>   A hundred men at least I know.
>
>   .   .   .   .   .
>
> All Staincliff hundred went with him,
>   With striplings strong from Worledale :
> And all that Haughton hills did climb,
>   With Langstroth too, and Littondale."

And so it goes on in prolix, yet vigorous ballad fashion, mustering the whole array of the northern counties to join the Earl of Surrey's banner.   It is a piece after Scott's own heart; and it seems marvellous that the volume never came under his notice. Here then, as fitting addition to the English record of the fight, is appended the old Scottish song, with a glossary, and this note : "The tune to this song, called the Flowers of the Forest, is a pretty melancholy one."   It will be seen that the following differs in various points from the current version of this beautiful song, and it is worthy of note that the more frequent refrain in this earlier printed text is some variation of the form :—

> "Since our braw foresters are a' wede away ;"

while that which takes its place in the *Border Minstrelsy*, occurs only once both in this and in the undisputedly modern version of Mrs. Cockburn.

> "I have heard of a lilting at our ewes milking,
>   Lasses a lilting, before the break of day ;
> But now there's a moaning on ilka green loaning,
>   That our braw foresters are a' wede away.

> At boughts, in the morning, nae blithe lads are scorning ;
>   The lasses are lonely, dowie, and wae ;
> Nae daffin, nae gabbin, but sighing, and sabbing ;
>   Ilka ane lifts her leglin, and hies her away.
>
> At e'en at the gloming, nae swankies are roaming,
>   'Mong stacks, with the lasses, at bogle to play ;
> But ilka ane sits dreary, lamenting her deary,
>   The Flowers of the Forest that are a' wede away.
>
> At harrest, at the shearing, nae youngsters are jeering,
>   The bansters are runkled, lyart, and grey.
> At a fair, or a preaching, nae wooing, nae fleeching,
>   Since our braw foresters are a' wede away.
>
> O dool for the order sent our lads to the border :
>   The English for anes by guile gat the day.
> The Flowers of the Forest, that aye shone the foremost,
>   The prime of our land lies cauld in the clay.
>
> We'll hear nae mair lilting at our ewes milking,
>   The women and bairns are dowie and wae ;
> Sighing and moaning on ilka green loaning,
>   Since our braw foresters are a' wede away."

Here then we see that an earlier generation than that for which Scott produced his song was already familiar with it, and entertained no doubt of its antiquity. That fragments of some much older version lingered in the popular memory has never been disputed. Not only the tune, but the main part of the first stanza, are acknowledged in the *Border Minstrelsy* to be ancient, and Scott subsequently gleaned another old fragment, presenting, as he says, "a simple and affecting image to the mind :"—

> " I ride single on my saddle,
>   For the flowers of the forest are a' wede away."

The beautiful ballad has already been alluded to in association with a choice holiday among Canadian wilds ; for my friend Judge Galt then communicated to me the information that his father used to repeat an old version differing considerably from that of Scott, but all that he could now recall was the solitary line :—

> " 'Twas peace and good order frae Spey to the border."

It was charming to snatch, amid Canadian wilds, even such a fragment of the beautiful old lyric ; though I fear it is but an echo of what can be guaranteed little more than a single century's antiquity. In 1776 Herd printed in his *Collection of Scottish Songs and Ballads* a long narrative ballad, evidently made up from the two familiar lyrics of Mrs. Cockburn and Miss Elliot, with this for an opening stanza. If it be the same that Mr. Galt used to repeat, it lacks the flavour of genuine antiquity :—

> " From Spey to the border was peace and good order,
>   The sway of our monarch was mild as the May ;
>   Peace he adored, which Soudrons abhorred,
>   Our marches they plunder, our wardens they slay."

As to the old air with which the Vicar of Norham was familiar upwards of a century ago, it was no

doubt the same which is preserved in the famous
Skene MS., the "Lute Book" of a lady of the
family of the Skenes of Hallyards, eminent as
lawyers in the times of James VI. and Charles I.;
but the tune could scarcely have survived along
the borders down to the eighteenth century without being sung to some current version of the words
of which the refrain survived in its name. No in-
justice, therefore, I believe, will be done to Miss
Jean Elliot, if we credit her with the service—and
that is not a slight one—of recovering the oral
versions current in her native district, and restoring
to life, possibly enough with considerable ekeings
and patchings of her own, one of the very finest of
all the genuine old Scottish songs. As to the
modern story of a wager of gloves or ribbons, Dr.
Somerville, it is manifest, had never heard of it;
nor had such a rumour reached the ear of Scott
or Sharpe.

It is now considerably more than a century
since that memorable riding home, after nightfall
by Miss Jean and her brother Gilbert. Nevertheless, my own information relative to the reputed
poetess is derived from one who was very familiar
with her when she dwelt on the first floor of a house,
shown in the accompanying sketch, and alongside
of it the arched passage which gave access from
Brown Square to the Candlemaker Row and the
neighbouring fashionable quarter of the Cowgate.

MISS JEANIE ELLIOT'S HOUSE.

Dr. Robert Chambers was the first to point out the locality in his *Traditions of Edinburgh;* but it is worthy of note that he supplemented his remarks on the authorship of the song with this correction in the appendix: "*N.B.*—It is only said that Miss Jeanie Elliot wrote some of the verses of this (supposed) ancient version." In a note to his *Scottish Songs* he had previously re-marked of her: "She spent the latter part of her life chiefly in Edinburgh, where she mingled a good deal in the better sort of society. I have been told by one who was admitted in youth to the privileges of her conversation, that she was 'a remarkably agreeable old maiden lady, with a prodigious fund of Scottish anecdote, but did not appear to have ever been handsome.'" She had, according to another account, a sensible face, and a slender well-shaped figure. "A family minia-ture," says Miss Tytler, "represents her in advanced years, apparently a little delicate old woman, in close cap, ruffle, and ample snowy neckerchief. She has the large nose and mouth which belong to an expressive rather than a beautiful face, but the mouth is kindly in its sagacity. Her eyebrows are well arched, and her eyes look lively under her sober head-dress."

The informant of Dr. Chambers, who in his youth was admitted to the privilege of conversation with Miss Jean Elliot, was Charles Kirkpatrick

Sharpe; but his private comments on "Miss Jeanie" as he styled her, unless when he banteringly spoke of her as "The Flower," by no means indicated his estimation of his ancient intercourse with her as a privilege. The following notes are thoroughly in unison with his caustic comments on contemporaries. His likings and dislikings were freely avowed; and his pen as well as his pencil was effective in its satirical touches. His description must therefore be taken *cum grano salis;* for he had a sharp tongue when he was in the censorious vein, and had reasons of his own, as will be seen, for bearing no special love to the reputed songstress. "I was civil to Miss Jeanie in the 'Traditions,' not wishing to hurt the feelings of her relations." So writes Mr. Sharpe on my later margins; and as nearly half a century has elapsed since he communicated his pleasant gossip to my valued friend Robert Chambers, and both narrator and annotator are gone, with all whose feelings could be affected by any comments on the old lady of Mr. Sharpe's boyhood, there can be no reason for withholding his sketch now, be it portrait or caricature. "There is no lingering testimony to her beauty in the family traditions," writes Miss Tytler. Mr. Sharpe, who spoke from memory of his own, says: "Miss Jeanie, like Muckle-mou'd Meg, had an open countenance!" Then, referring to her reputed fund of Scottish anecdote, he says: "In fact she had, I suppose, a good memory. She was ill-natured, always irritating my aunt Campbell against her family ; vulgarly ugly, yet dressing as if a beauty ; vulgar in speaking—she said ' I cane't,' in place of I can't. My mother said she spoke like all lawyers' daughters of her day. When Miss Jeanie's old sedan appeared at my aunt Campbell's door, in George Square, of a summer's evening *at tea-time*, we all became sad, knowing that a thunderstorm would ensue. My aunt and Jeanie retired after tea into the back drawing-room, and, after a long prate, off jolts Jeanie in her sedan, and my aunt falls foul on the whole company : her excellent daughters, a female cousin who resided with her, and your humble servant. We never knew exactly what evil we had done, for ' The Flower of the Forest ' was all hints and innuendos ! But we were all degenerate, wicked, etc. etc. etc. Of late years I have doubted much about Jeanie being the authoress of the song imputed to her, and wrote a letter to the cousin mentioned above on the sub-ject. She was the only survivor of a most pleasing coterie of sensible women, much older than the boy who *hated* Jeanie. Her answer was that tho' she never heard of any other verses the *Flower* had com-posed, Miss Elliot *never told lies*, and that she had heard her mention the song as her own invention."

So far, then, a not too partial critic, in spite of his own doubts, leaves the claim of authorship ·

undisturbed. Yet such a claim might be compatible enough with the actual credit which I am disposed to assign to her of having pieced together the fragments current in Teviotdale, in her younger days, in association with the old tune; introduced it in its revised form to her own generation; and so given permanency to the song in a form more or less due to her handiwork. This idea is confirmed on turning to the more modern song. Alison Rutherford of Fairnielee, better known as Mrs. Cockburn, was a true poetess, with an equal mastery of the humorous and the pathetic. The version of the "Flowers of the Forest," of which she is the undoubted authoress, is tender and beautiful; and adapts itself admirably to its plaintive air. But, though free from the pastoral affectations of Sir Gilbert Elliot's verse, it manifestly belongs in its mode of thought to the eighteenth century. But the associations with Alison Cockburn's muse connect themselves with other events and times than those of Flodden Field, and must be reserved for another chapter.

The following rude fragment, found in an interleaved copy of *Dalrymple's Remarks on the History of Scotland*, picked up by me some thirty years ago at an old book-stall, has already been printed. On trying to trace the book to its original owner, I was told that he was an advocate who had been beggared in a suit of some notoriety then promoted by a claimant to the earldom of Stirling. Two leaves were torn out, so that what remains are only the concluding stanzas. The following note is appended in the same hand :—"This I got from an old man, James Spence, gardener at Earlsha'; it had been on the fly-leaf of a psalm-book in the family as long as he remembered." On showing the original manuscript to Mr. C. K. Sharpe, he pounced on the "shrowd" of the third stanza as an anachronism betraying a modern hand, at least in the later transcription. This he would have replaced with *sark* or *sheet.* I had added a foot-note suggesting *said* as the last word in the first stanza, for the sake of rhyme. He pencilled below it his quaint comment thus :—

> " The worse the clink
> More true I think !   C. K. S."

At the same time he added the suggestion of *mouth* for *soth* in the second stanza. Imperfect and dis-connected as it is, the fragment is worth preserving as the remnant apparently of an old ballad, embodying the tradition, or myth, that James IV. made his escape from Flodden, and abandoning crown and country, made his way as a palmer to the Holy Land :—

*   *   *   *   *

> " An' about the mids o' the night
>   He crap to the field o' the bluid ;
>   Laigh he bowit, an' dour he lookit,
>   But never a worde he spak.

He turned the dead knight round about,
Till the moon shone on his bree ;
But his soth was tined with a bluidy gash,
Drumbelee grew his ee.

'Up and awa, my lither foot-page,
An' Scotland and I maun part ;
But sweere by the dead, in ilk bluidy shrowd,
That thou layn my lare i' thy hart.

'Giffe I were a king, as now I'm nane,
Ille battell wold I prove,—
My birdie ladie in Holyroode ;
Wae worth the wyt o' luve.'

Sanct Giles sall ring ilk larum belle,
Wauk up the craimes and bowse,
Earl Angus has taen him to Floudenne,
  *   *   *   *   *

He cut the crosse on his right shoulder
O' claith o' the bluidy redde,
An' he's taen his ways to the holy land
Whereas Christe was quick and dead."

CHAPTER XI.

The Jacobite Muse.

WHATEVER uncertainty may remain as to the actual antiquity, or the modern ekeings and patchings which are embodied in the "Flowers of the Forest" accredited to Miss Jean Elliot, there is no mystery about the other version of the song. If Miss Elliot did actually compose, or even make up in part from antique gleanings, the version which Scott inserts in his *Minstrelsy* as *Part First*, then the so-called *Part Second* is in reality the older of the two. It, too, is the work of a daleswoman, a true daughter of "The Forest," and owes its peculiar grace, as so much that is choicest and best not only in tender pathos but in hearty humour in song and ballad does, to one of Scotland's daughters.

Without raising anew the question of Lady Wardlaw of Pitreavie's contributions to the romantic ballads of Scotland, we owe to Lady Anne Barnard "Auld Robin Gray," to Lady Grisel Baillie "Werena my heart licht I wad die,"—a song to which so melancholy an interest has been added from the application by Burns of one of its verses to himself shortly before his death ;—Lady Nairne is the authoress alike of the most tender of Scottish lyrics, " The land of the Leal," and of the humorous and piquant songs, " The Laird of Cockpen," and " John Tod." Besides those, our list of Scottish songstresses includes such names as Miss Jenny Graham, Miss Christian Edwards, Miss Blamire, Miss Anne Home, Mrs. Grant of Carron, Miss Cranston, afterwards the wife of Professor Dugald Stewart, with others of every rank down to Burns's Jean Glover, the authoress of " Ower the muir amang the heather," and, according to the poet, a thief, and something worse. To those have to be added Alison Rutherford of Fairnielee, a flower of the forest of rare beauty, and one who proved her claim to rank with the old minstrels of Teviotdale alike by songs of genuine tenderness and raciest humour.

In her later years of widowhood, as Mrs. Cockburn, she resided in Crichton Street, in the then fashionable neighbourhood of George Square, and she now lies interred near by, in Buccleuch Churchyard. The tombstone of the poetess is in the north-east corner of the old burying-ground, not far from the graves of the poet Blacklock, and the scholar and antiquary Dr. Alexander Adam. Here too lies one of the strange oddities of that elder time, Suph Johnstone, who in her own way helped to an enrichment of Scottish song. She has already been alluded to among "the heartsome set" in the old assemblies over which the Hon. Miss Nicky Murray presided, and on which poor Oliver Goldsmith looked with envious eyes in his Edinburgh undergraduate days. Miss Suph must then have been about thirty. In her later years she was Mrs. Cockburn's near neighbour and frequent guest. She lived in a flat in Windmill Street, and was well known to another neighbour, young Walter Scott, who recalls her jockey-coat, masculine stride, strong voice, and occasional round oath, with certain memorable doings one night at Mrs. Cockburn's, where the Amazon kicked his poor sister's shins for moving her feet under the card-table at which both were seated. But also he says, "I remember many of her songs, for example :—

   ' Eh ! quo' the tod, it's a braw light night,
    The wind's i' the west, and the moon shines bright,' etc."

In earlier years she resided with the Lindsays at Balcarras in Fifeshire, played in rough kindly fashion with the children, sang her songs to them ; and among others, a beautiful old Scottish melody, to words of which only this couplet survives :—

   " But, oh ! quo' he, it's come o'er soon,
    The bridegroom grat when the sun gaed down."

Suph Johnstone was not troubled with much

delicacy about the words, so long as they suited the music, but happily others were more sensitive. The melody charmed Lady Anne, then only in her twenty-first year, and finding the song unfitted for refined ears, she set to work to redeem this air from such associations, and produced the exquisite ballad of "Auld Robin Gray." We have a portrait of the strange amazon sketched by the same pen. Miss Sophia Johnstone was the daughter of the Laird of Hilton, an eccentric, hard-drinking laird, who vowed he could see no good that ever came out of education or restraint, and so allowed a girl naturally of much ability to grow up untaught and uncontradicted. The opinion of Lady Anne Lindsay was that no education could have made her one of the fair sex. But that was a little too hard upon her. "Nature," she says, "seemed to have entered into the jest, and hesitated to the last whether to make her a boy or a girl. Her taste led her to hunt with her brothers, to wrestle with the stable boys, and to saw wood with the carpenter. She worked well in iron, could shoe a horse quicker than the smith, made excellent trunks, played well on the fiddle, sang a man's song in a bass voice, and was by many people suspected of being one. She learnt to write of the butler at her own request, and had a taste for reading which she greatly improved. She was a droll ingenious fellow; her talents for mimicry made her enemies," yet also she had warm friends, of whom Mrs. Cockburn was an appreciative one. Lord Cockburn, who knew her only in old age, retained a kindly recollection of her. He describes her as sitting in her singular half-masculine raiments in Edinburgh drawing-rooms, respected and liked. Her talk was intelligent and racy, rich both in old anecdote and in shrewd modern observation, but spiced with a good deal of plain sarcasm. She must have been a strange drawing-room figure, even among the simple social circles of that olden time, with her greatcoat and man's hat, "her dark wrinkled face, and firmly pursed mouth, the two feet set flat on the floor and close together, so that the public had a full view of the substantial shoes," and the prompt freedom of her rebuke when any lady or gentleman, of whatever rank or age uttered in her hearing what she forthwith pronounced to be "surely great nonsense!" She was undoubtedly an oddity and an original.

But Suph Johnstone's sole claim to a side niche among the songstresses of Scotland is the share due to her musical powers in inspiring the production of "Auld Robin Gray," and her friendly relations, in later years, with the authoress of the "Flowers of the Forest." She figures in the character of free, heart-easing mirth, in a song written by Mrs. Cockburn in honour of the Balcarras family; for she was one of its attachés—came on a visit to

the young Countess soon after her marriage, and
was still there thirteen years after. The song, the
preservation of which is due to Mr. Sharpe, begins
thus :—

> "All health be round Balcarras' board,
>   May mirth and joy still flow ;
> And may my Lady and my Lord
>   Ne'er taste of future woe.
>
> For here by brandyvine inspired
>   The frolic took its birth,
> While Horn and Suph, and all conspired,
>   To spread around the mirth."

Colonel Horn, who afterwards rose to the rank of
General, is the mirthful ally here associated with
Miss Suph.   For it must be remembered that Miss
Sophia Johnstone, on whom the cruel experiment
of dispensing with all education was thus tried,
was a lady of birth, and a connection of the Balcarras family.   Her sister Alicia became the wife
of Erskine of Dun, and the mother of Margaret,
Marchioness of Ailsa.

Of Mrs. Cockburn, her sister poetess Lady
Anne Barnard writes "as a woman of genius,
remembered by her song of the 'Flowers of the
Forest,' which can never wither." Dr. Robert
Chambers thus communicated to me reminiscences
of her, gleaned from an elder generation :—"She
must have been an unusually charming specimen
of the old Scottish lady. I have been told of her
that even when near eighty, her beautiful auburn

hair, which she wore on a toupee, retained its youthful tint, untouched by time. There actually was not a single grey hair; and, with this, she preserved not a little of her youthful vivacity, wit, and intelligence." She was born, in 1712, on the paternal estate of Fairnielee, within sound of the Tweed, and close to where Gala Water joins the Border river. Her earliest piece must have been written when she was still a girl. Her brother, the future Laird of Fairnielee, had been disappointed in a love-suit for the hand of one of the "quality ladies" of Edinburgh, and his sprightly sister laughed the love-sick swain out of his despondency by a parody of the old song—"Nancy's to the Greenwood gane," suggested probably by the name of the haughty fair one :—

> "Nancy's to the Assembly gane,
>   To hear the fops a' chattering ;
> And Willie, he has followed her,
>   To win her love by flattering."

But, as the sprightly satirist hints, the homely virtues of the Tweeddale youth were no charms wherewith to attract such a "bonny Nancy," who thus sets forth as among the indispensable requisites for him who can hope to please her fancy :—

> "Ane that can flatter, bow, and dance,
>   And make love to the ladies ;
> That kens how folk behave in France,
>   An's bauld amang the cadies."

VOL. I.   X

The said cadies were the servitors and jacks-of-all-work, who hung about the Assembly doors, ready to do an errand, or bandy a saucy jest with any of the quality who were so inclined. This serves, however, rather as an illustration of Mrs. Cockburn's youthful vivacity than of her poetic powers. But the humours of an assembly retained their charms for her when younger generations had stepped into her place. She says of herself in bantering comment on what the gossips are circulating about the gay doings of her old age : " You are mistaken, madam. I know that woman perfectly well. It is her humour to dance, and it's yours to talk. She will do as she pleases, and allow you the same freedom. . . . She has too great a regard for truth to pretend to youth. But for the same reason she will not affect the infirmities of age ; and, if her vigour continue, will dance as frankly with her grandson as with any man whatever." She freely owns that dancing is delightful to her ; describes in one of her letters how she contrived to give a ball in her own little drawing-room, at the " bespeak-. ing " of her favourite, Captain Bob Dalrymple. The festive scene must have been in the house in Blair's Close, Castle Hill, the birthplace of Sir David Baird ; from which she removed, at a later date, to Crichton Street, in the then fashionable neighbourhood of George Square. She laughingly comments on the devices necessary to make room

BLAIR'S CLOSE, CASTLEHILL,

     THE LODGING OF MRS. ALISON COCKBURN.

in her straitened lodging for twenty-two guests, and nine couple always on the floor. " I think," she says, " my house, like my purse, is just the widow's cruise. Our fiddler sat where the cupboard is, and they danced in both rooms ; the table was stuffed into the window, and we had plenty of room. It made the bairns all vastly happy." And now, to complete the picture, we have to fancy her as the bright young beauty, full of life and spirit, just wedded to Mr. Patrick Cockburn, a son of the Lord Justice-Clerk, then in extreme old age, to whose closing years she devoted herself as the daughter of his house. " I was married, properly speaking,"—so she writes long afterwards,—" to a man of seventy-five. I lived with him four years, and, as the ambition had seized me to make him fond of me—knowing also nothing could please his son so much,—I bestowed all my time and study to gain his approbation. He disapproved of plays and assemblies—I never went to one." No wonder that Robert Chambers speaks of her as " a woman of ten thousand."

When the modern version of " The Flowers of the Forest " was reproduced by Scott, in 1803, he wrote of her as an attached friend of his mother, and one who had been among the first to discern his own genius. Young Walter, indeed, was " not quite six " when she described him as " the most extraordinary genius of a boy I ever saw ;" and the appreciation was mutual. "When he was taken to bed he told his aunt he liked that lady, 'For I think she's a *virtuoso* like myself.' 'Dear Walter,' said his aunt, 'What is a *virtuoso?*' 'Don't you know? Why, it's one who will know everything!'" When Mrs. Cockburn removed to Crichton Street she was in the immediate vicinity of the Scotts; and Walter was old enough to enjoy and bear his share in the contests of gay wit and repartee of her *petits soupers*, to which her own powers of conversation gave the special charm. She had been dead only a few years, having survived to her eighty-third year, when Scott thus wrote of her: "Even at an age advanced beyond the usual bounds of humanity she retained a play of imagination, and an activity of intellect, which must have been attractive and delightful in youth, but were almost preternatural at her period of life. Her active benevolence, keeping pace with her genius, rendered her equally an object of love and admiration." At the time of her death the song by which she is specially remembered had been produced more than half a century. There is a hint in one of her letters, long afterwards, as if she meditated a companion piece. Burns, when in Edinburgh in 1786, won her prompt appreciation. She aptly describes him as "the ploughman poet, who receives adulation with native dignity, and is the very figure of his profession, strong and coarse, but has a most enthusiastic heart of love. . . . The man will be spoiled, if he can spoil; but he keeps his simple manners, and is quite sober. No doubt he will be at the Hunters' ball to-morrow, which has made all women and milliners mad." Again she writes: " Do you know Burns ? I am to get a very pretty little thing he calls 'The Rosebud.' I wish I could write a ballad called 'The Forest Restored.'" The lines she alludes to were probably those said to have been written on the death of his little daughter, but which the date of this notice would contradict. Allan Cunningham speaks of them as "these tender and affecting lines." They are, in truth, rather commonplace, and not at all suggestive of the intense grief of the poet, who "loved the child dearly, and mourned her loss with many tears," for it was in 1795, when he was himself fading before he had fully bloomed. But as an actual autograph presented by the ploughman poet himself at such a time, it was well calculated to impress the fair songstress :

> " Here lies a rose, a budding rose,
>   Blasted before its bloom ;
>   Whose innocence did sweets disclose
>   Beyond that flower's perfume.
>   To those who for her loss are grieved
>   This consolation's given—
>   She's from a world of woe relieved,
>   And blooms a rose in heaven."

It was charming to get such a "Rosebud" from the poet's own hand; and the association of ideas is obvious enough, which suggested a counterpart to the old song on the reblooming of "The Flowers of the Forest a' wede away." In 1793 Burns wrote to Thomson, urging that her song must be set to the notes. "It is charming as a poem. The three stanzas are worthy of a place, were it but to immortalise the author of them, who is an old lady of my acquaintance, and at this moment living in Edinburgh."

According to the traditions of her old circle, Alison Rutherfurd's song was written in her maiden days, which ended in 1731; and Dr. Robert Chambers quotes Sir Walter Scott as his authority for stating that a turret in the old house of Fairnielee was pointed out as the place where it had been written. Commercial disasters are said to have wrought the ruin of seven lairds of ancient family in Teviotdale in one year; and the youthful poetess, catching the echoes of the old lament which still lingered on the Border, wrote her tender and beautiful song. According to the date assigned to its production, Jean Elliot was scarcely out of her cradle at the time; yet the version ascribed to her pen, more than a quarter of a century nearer our day, is far more primitive and archaic in character than that of the young beauty of Fairnielee. Without the pastoral affectations of

Gilbert Elliot's song, Alison Rutherfurd's perfectly accords with the style of the age in which it was produced—though with a rare tenderness all its own,—and seems thereby to confirm the probability that the more antique-looking version is really composed in the main of genuine materials perpetuated by the dalesmen from elder times :—

" I've seen the forest adorn'd of the foremost,
    With flowers of the fairest, both pleasant and gay ;
Sae bonnie was their bloming, their scent the air perfuming,
    But now they are wither'd and a' wede away."

Mrs. Cockburn continued to employ her pen freely; though with no thought of publication ; and unfortunately only fragments have been preserved. She wrote a set of toasts descriptive of her friends, with a humour akin to Goldsmith's " Retaliation," of which the following was the impersonation of Scott's father, then a young and handsome man :—

" To a thing that's uncommon—
    A youth of discretion,
    Who, though vastly handsome,
    Despises flirtation :
    To the friend in affliction,
    The heart of affection,
    Who may hear the last trump
    Without dread of detection."

Sir Walter says of her : " She was one whose talents made a stronger impression on her contemporaries than her writings can be expected to produce.   In person and features she somewhat resembled Queen Elizabeth ; but the nose was rather more aquiline."   Whether designedly or not, she would seem to have helped still further to suggest a comparison with the Tudor queen by her style of dress.   A lady who had known her intimately thus described her to Charles Kirkpatrick Sharpe :—" She had a pleasing countenance, and piqued herself upon always dressing according to her own taste, and not according to the dictates of fashion.   Her brown hair never grew grey ; and she wore it combed up upon a toupee,—no cap,— a lace hood tied under her chin, and her sleeves puffed out in the fashion of Queen Elizabeth, which at that time was quite peculiar to herself."   But her highest charms pertained to her lively intellect and fine conversational powers.   " She maintained," says Scott, " the rank in the society of Edinburgh which French women of talent usually do in that of Paris ; and her little parlour used to assemble a very distinguished and accomplished circle, among whom David Hume, John Home, Lord Monboddo, and many other men of name, were frequently to be found."   She appears, indeed, to have fully mastered what I fear is one of the lost arts.   Her charming little supper parties included such well-chosen company, and such wise and witty converse, that nobody noted the frugal fare, which she was wont to describe as like that of Stella—

> " A supper like her mighty self,
>   Four nothings on four plates of delf."

Sharpe, though ever disposed to look askance on one whiggishly inclined, cherished the memory of Alison Cockburn, and rescued from oblivion some of her fugitive verse. I owe to him this fragment of one of her songs, possibly preserved in a more perfect form in some of her letters. He had possessed it complete, but could only recall a line or two of a second stanza :—

> " Where Tweed runs on to win the sea,
>   And 'hint her speeds braw Gala Water,
> There's ne'er a bush o' Fairnielee
>   But minds her of the words he taught her—
> But minds her o' the winsome time,
>   And all their kindly ploys thegither,
> He taught her ! was it no mysel'?
>   Mysel' in truth, and no another."

But Alison Cockburn belongs to the age which found other work for the muse than reviving long forgotten memories such as those of Flodden. The Baroness Nairne who could sport with the prosaic courtship of Mrs. Jean and the Laird of Cockpen, or awaken feelings of tenderest sorrow in her " Land of the Leal," threw the same genuine feeling into her Jacobite ballads. She wrote with fine humour, " Wi' a hundred pipers, an' a', an' a'," " The Women are a' gane wud," and " What do ye think o' Geordie noo ?" and with a loyalty which was genuine and heartfelt :

> " The Whigs may scoff, the Whigs may jeer,
>   But ah ! that love maun be sincere
>   Which still keeps true whate'er betide,
>   And for his sake leaves a' beside.
>   He's ower the hills that I lo'e weel
>   He's owre the hills we daurna name,
>   He's owre the hills ayont Dunblane
>   Wha soon will get his welcome hame."

It was natural that the muse should find her truest inspiration in a failing cause ; nor could the most enthusiastic of Hanoverians discover anything that was romantic in their "Wee wee German lairdie !"   It was hard indeed for the liveliest wit to make a butt of Prince Charlie, or a hero out of King George or the Duke of Cumberland.   But Mr. Patrick Cockburn came of a Revolution family. His father had filled the office of Lord Justice-Clerk under William of Orange ; and their ancestors, the Lairds of Ormistone, had been distinguished in the cause of the Reformation in earlier times of trial and suffering.   So Mr. Cockburn, like the father of Sir Walter Scott, discerned the real issues beneath the haze of superficial romance ; and Mrs. Cockburn was no less keen in the cause of the Protestant succession and constitutional liberty.   She took the opposite side to that which Lady Nairne espoused so well ; and when Prince Charles Edward, in the midst of his brief triumph, held court at Holyrood, and laid bootless siege to Edinburgh Castle, Mrs. Cockburn employed her pen on a sprightly parody of the proclamation he had just issued.   A popular old tinker's song, traditionally affirmed to commemorate an amour of one of the Kenmure family, when lurking in the disguise of a gipsy tinker in Cavalier times, supplied the air and the idea ; and at the very time that the Highlanders were masters of the town, the witty poetess wrote her parody to the tune of "Clout the Caldron."   Setting out on a visit to her Jacobite kinsfolks, the Keiths of Ravelston, the temptation was irresistible to take with her the mirthful effusion, and retaliate in their own coin some of the squibs that were current enough against the side she espoused.   But as she was riding home again, with the wicked parody in her pocket, the carriage was stopped at the West Port by the Highland guard, and a search proposed for Whig letters or missives.   Fortunately she had been sent back in the family coach ; the Ravelston arms on the panel were recognised, and so the witty poetess escaped a search which might have led to very unpleasant consequences.   No political differences could affect her estimation in the minds of those who knew her best.   By her will a lock of her hair was wrought into two rings for her " earliest and most constant and affectionate friends, Mrs. Keith of Ravelston, and her brother William Swinton."   But upwards of half a century intervenes between the perilous ride in the Ravelston

family coach and this memorial of enduring friendship.   The humorous pasquinade was recovered by
Dr. Robert Chambers from a MS. collection of songs
made by an Edinburgh lady before 1780 :—

> " Have you any laws to mend,
>   Or have you any grievance?
> I am a hero to my trade,
>   And truly a most leal prince.
> Would you have war, would you have peace,
>   Would you be free from taxes?
> Come chapping to my father's door,
>   You need not doubt of access.
>
> " Religion, law, and liberty,
>   Ye ken are bonnie words, sirs,
> They shall be a' made sure to you,
>   If you'll fecht wi' your swords, sirs.
> The nation's debt we soon shall pay,
>   If ye'll support our right, boys ;
> No sooner we are brought to play
>   Than all things shall be tight, boys.
>
> .   .   .   .   .
>
> " I'm sure for seven years and mair
>   Ye've heard o' sad oppression,
> And this is all the good ye got
>   By the Hanover succession.
> For absolute power and popery,
>   Ye ken its a' but nonsense ;
> I here swear to secure to you
>   Your liberty of conscience.
>
> " And for your mair encouragement,
>   Ye shall be pardoned byganes ;
> Nae mair fight on the Continent,
>   And leave behind your dry banes.

> Then come away, and dinna stay,
>   What gars ye look sae lundart?
> I'd have you run and not delay
>   To join my father's standard."

The version of the old gipsy song after which this was fashioned, as preserved by Ramsay in his *Tea-Table Miscellany* bears unmistakable traces of the patchwork of that artificial age, in its classical incongruities of Jupiter, Leda, Europa, and Argus, all thrust into the plea of the " gentle jinker." But Mrs. Cockburn had too much genuine wit and true genius to indulge in such affectations ; and in spite of the prosaic elements of the party she had espoused, it is obvious that the Whig poetess was no unequal match for her Jacobite rivals. But it was inevitable that the tragic incidents of a failing cause, sustained as it was with such devoted though mistaken loyalty, should furnish the tenderest inspiration for the muse ; and the wail over " the brave who sank to rest" upon Culloden Moor even now prolongs its echoes with as plaintive music as that which mourned the weeding away of the forest flowers on Flodden Hill.

Another of the Whig songstresses of that eighteenth century, of whose productions even less is known than of Mrs. Cockburn's, was Helen Cranstoun, a granddaughter of William, fifth Lord Cranstoun, who in 1790 became the wife of the distinguished philosopher Dugald Stewart. The ladies of that age excelled in lyrical verse; but they shrunk from its acknowledgment, as though it had been an indelicate, or vulgar art; and we owe to the intervention of the poet Burns, the only acknowledged song by which she is known: that tender and beautiful one, "The tears I shed must ever fall," which first appeared in Johnson's *Musical Museum* in 1792. To "this song of genius," as Burns calls it, he added the closing quatrain, to make the stanzas suit the music, according to his courtly fashion, to the fair muse. By means of the like friendly aid Clarinda's (Agnes Craig M'Lehose), song addressed to himself, of which he pronounced part of the first stanza "worthy of Sappho," was wedded to the old air of "The Banks of Spey," and honoured with a place in the same *Musical Museum.* The poetical relations of Clarinda and her Sylvander form, indeed, a curious episode in the Edinburgh life of the susceptible poet; and the scene of their romantic interviews at General's Entry, Bristo Street, is the most characteristic local memorial of the poet's visit to the Scottish capital. In the view of Clarinda's lodging, a bird's cage at the open window marks the scene of those interviews between the poet and her to whom he wrote the farewell song, also included in Johnson's *Museum :*—

> " Clarinda, mistress of my soul,
> The measured time is run;

> The wretch beneath the dreary pole
> So marks his latest sun."

The intercourse of the poet with Professor Dugald Stewart and his gifted wife began under very different circumstances. Professor Stewart was one of the smaller Ayrshire lairds, and the relations between him and the poet were early and interesting. He was in the habit of receiving into his house at Edinburgh a select number of his students as pupils; and in 1786, when the Ayrshire ploughman was just awaking to fame, one of those pupils, Basil, Lord Daer, son of the Earl of Selkirk, accompanied the professor to his country house at Catrine, on the Ayr. The farm of Mossgeil was only a few miles off; and on that " ne'er-to-be-forgotten day," the 23d of October of the same year, the memorable event in the young bard's career of his first actual meeting and dining with a lord occurred. The professor has left on record his impressions of that interview, in which he was struck with the manner of the rustic bard, " simple, manly, and independent; strongly expressive of conscious genius and worth, but without anything that indicated forwardness, arrogance, or vanity." But we have also the poet's own more graphic picture of the scene when " Rhymer Robin first dinner'd wi' a lord !" He had been to writers' feasts; indulged in the company of godly priests, and even joined at the gatherings of squires of the quorum :—

> " But wi' a lord ! stand out, my shin,
>   A lord, a peer, an Earl's son !
>   Up higher yet, my bonnet !
>   And sic a lord ! lang Scotch ells twa,
>   Our peerage he o'erlooks them a',
>   As I look o'er my sonnet.
>
> But oh for Hogarth's magic power !
> To show Sir Bardie's willyart glower,
>   And how he star'd and stammer'd,
> When goavan, as if led wi' branks,
> And stumpin' on his ploughman shanks,
>   He in the parlour hammer'd."

At a later date he visited Professor Stewart in Edinburgh, and rambled with him over the Braid Hills and other romantic environs of the city, charming him, as he says, "still more by his private conversation than he had ever done in company. In his political principles he was then a Jacobite ;" as was natural in a poet of the time. The town-house of the celebrated philosopher, a once fashion-able mansion of the Canongate, where many a distinguished guest besides the Ayrshire bard was entertained, no longer exists. On the site, now occupied by a brewery, a little to the east of Queensberry House, formerly stood Lothian Hut, as was named the small but beautifully finished mansion erected by William, third Marquis of Lothian, about 1750. It was occupied for twenty years after his death by the dowager Marchioness, and afterwards by the Lady Caroline d'Arcy, the widow of the fourth Marquis. To her succeeded Professor Dugald Stewart, with their son the Lord Powerscourt, and other young noblemen, as his pupils; and the poetess Helen Cranstoun as his wife. Their home became noted for its genial hospitalities. The poet Campbell, who had shared in them, describes the hostess as the habitual and confidential companion of her husband during his studies; and "when he had given a truth an intelligible shape, she helped him to illustrate it by a play of fancy and of feeling which could only come from a woman's mind." To others she was remarkable for intellectual vigour and a winning gentleness of manner, which combined to make her looked up to with a respect such as mere rank failed to command.

But here Mr. Sharpe's notes once more enable us to peep behind the scenes, and supply a glimpse of old times and manners, when noble dowagers and young marquises made themselves at home in the Canongate; though it must be borne in remembrance that the Whig proclivities of the Professor and Mrs. Stewart were certain to preclude any very flattering reminiscences by the annotator. "Lothian Hut," he remarks, "was a pretty, small house, the principal rooms on the ground-floor. When quite a boy, I was at a ball there, given by Mrs. Stewart, a clumsy-looking, clever woman—her husband ditto. Mrs. Stewart wrote songs. There is one of them in Johnson's

Museum, somewhat lackadaisical.   Another, meant
to be humorous, was a Whig version of:—

> ' As I came doun the Canongate
> I heard a crowder play,
> 'Twas never good for Holyrood
> Till Charlie gaed away.'

Or something of that sort.   But there was no
humour in her; though she was undoubtedly
clever."   He then gives some of his recollections
of the residenters in Lothian Hut, including a
narrative of the courtship of Lord Ashburton, one
of the professor's pupils, who married a niece of
Mrs. Stewart; but subsequent information, communicated to me from more reliable sources,
suffices to show that the caustic wit of the carica-
turist had in this, as in other cases, tempted him
to exaggerations, to which his political and social
prejudices gave additional extravagance.   For, as
is obvious enough, Mr. Sharpe reserved little of
his veneration for contemporaries, and none for
Whigs—real or suspected; though he made no
pretence to Jacobite leanings of more modern
date than the times of Montrose and Claverhouse.

But the satirical humour which Whig and
Jacobite songstresses indulged in, and which found
its readiest theme in the unheroic characteristics of
the first Georges, was no new feature of Scottish
song.   The occasion was an apt one; the age was
free-spoken; and wit and sarcasm combined to turn
it to the best account.   Since then Edinburgh has

made up for earlier slights on the new dynasty; not always hitting the humours of our cynical critic any better in its loyalty than its treason: for he thus described himself in his "Epitaph," appended to a rhyming will, written in 1802 :—

> "Here rests, forgetting and forgot,
>   No murderer, robber, thief, or sot ;
>   No Tory worshipper of kings,
>   No Whig, the most accursed of things !"

CHAPTER XII.

Antiquarian Crosses.

WHATEVER our politics may be, there is some
comfort in the fact that neither all the inspiration
nor all the humour of elder song pertained to the
Jacobite muse ; for the world is still divided into
Tories and Radicals, by whatever name they may
be known. Every generation has its heart-broken
Conservatives, mourning over the overthrow of
cherished idols ; but each new era is no less prolific
of its crop of Radicals, ready to hew out for it
fresh highways, careless of the overthrow of all
that is most venerable and hoary, if—as it is so apt
to do,—it stand right in the way of modern progress.
A century ago Edinburgh had her local poet and
satirist, James Wilson, better known by his *nom de
plume* of Claudero, whose verse, in alternate
lampoon and tragic wail, deals with the vandals of
the eighteenth century, and the ravages they
wrought. The Royal Porch of Holyrood, the
Netherbow Port, and the ancient City Cross, each
in turn excited his wrathful lament at their overthrow ; as, in more recent years, bereaved anti-

quaries clamoured in vain over the ruined church of the Holy Trinity.   There are crosses enough to be borne by all of us, and everyone fancies his own the hardest to bear ; but how can a busy generation be expected to sympathise with a set of grumblers, whose chief grievance is that their crosses are taken away ?

In the oddest and most unaccountable manner, moral as well as physical epidemics break out at times, and spread contagion far and wide.   Sometimes the fever takes a political form, and, ere its furor is abated, crowns and thrones topple over in direst fashion.   In a neighbouring nation, indeed, it has grown chronic ; and, as " my friend, the Tory member's elder son," says in " The Princess " :—

> "Yonder, whiff! there comes a sudden heat,
> The gravest citizen seems to lose his head,
> The king is scared, the soldier will not fight,
> The little boys begin to shoot and stab ;
> A kingdom topples over with a shriek
> Like an old woman, and down rolls the world
> In mock heroics."

In the eighteenth century the prevailing epidemic throughout the British Islands took the form of a mania for the demolition of city-gates, crosses, churches, and much else of historical and architectural value.   In its reaction in our own day, the epidemic furor for " restoration " has at times been little less destructive—as Edinburgh's collegiate church and cathedral of St. Giles too amply testifies.

The city of Bristol had, at the former era, a poet of true worth, with satirical powers no less keen than those of Claudero. "The Churchwarden and the Apparition: A Fable," is the satirical anathema of "the marvellous boy," penned when only eleven years of age, on the demolition, in 1763, of a beautiful cross of curious workmanship, which had stood for centuries in the churchyard of St. Mary Redcliffe; had been admiringly described by William of Worcester in the days of Edward IV.; and was removed at last for no better reason, apparently, than that it interfered with the straightening of a walk in the churchyard. But Joe Thomas, the delinquent churchwarden, was only following the example of his betters; for, that same year, the Dean and Chapter of Bristol, as Chatterton says,

> "Sold the ancient Cross to Hoare
> For one church dinner, nothing more!

Bristol High Cross, after more than one disaster, restoration, and change of site, had found a suitable resting-place in the College Green, under the protection of the Cathedral Chapter. There, if anywhere, it might have seemed safe, beyond reach of vandal hands. But, like that of St. Mary Redcliffe, it was found guilty of being an incumbrance to the fashionable promenade on the College Green, where, but for it, ladies and gentlemen in amplest hoops and skirts might walk eight or ten abreast. So the Dean and Chapter authorised its demolition ; and, but for the taste of a neighbouring proprietor, who secured the stones, and rebuilt it on his grounds, its beautiful carved masonry would have been carted away as mere rubbish.

A mania for such demolitions possessed that eighteenth century. Few cities of any note have not some desolated site—the naked witness to the revolutionary furor, which, under the name of modern taste, swept away the antique memorials of elder times. It is a curious subject for the study of the psychologist how far such moral epidemics may be traceable to some actual fever of the blood and brain, which communicates itself like any other infectious disease, and, ere it has run its course, leaves such evidence of the desolating track it has pursued.

It was in 1753 that the Edinburgh satirist bewailed the destruction of its Abbey gatehouse. Again, the very year after Chatterton's assault on the vandals of Bristol, who wrought the demolition both of the Redcliffe and the City Cross, the fate of the Netherbow Port—the Temple Bar of Edinburgh,—furnished the theme of Claudero's wittiest prose in " A Sermon preached by Claudero, on the Condemnation of the Netherbow Porch of Edinburgh,

9th July 1764." In its "Last speech, confession, and dying words," the old port tells of its honours in the days of "King James VI. of ever glorious memory ;" and of its slights in those of the usurper Cromwell. It grows penitential over its many crimes, of which, "alas! the greatest of all was the receiving the head of the brave Marquess of Montrose from the hands of dastardly miscreants." But its pride revives, and it recalls the time when "a patriot duke, the great Argyll, in the grand senate of our nation," successfully resisted its threatened doom. But "what was too hard for the great ones of the earth, yea even queens, to effect, is now, even now in our own day, accomplished." For—as every reader of *The Heart of Midlothian* knows,—the demolition of the Netherbow Port had been specially determined on in 1736, when Queen Caroline's wrath was roused by the slight put on her royal clemency by the famous deed of vengeance of the Porteous mob.

Again the innovations of civic vandals rouse the ire of the satirist. In the same fatal year in which the Abbey gateway was swept away, the foundation of the new Royal Exchange was laid, which ere long rose in all its glory, a massive though now somewhat antiquated pile, which then took the place of a host of time-worn ruinous buildings, and seemed, according to the fashionable standard of that day, a marvel of architectural grace. But right in front of this triumph of new-fangled taste stood the City Cross, with the same wrinkled visage which had witnessed the riding of the Parliament when the second James succeeded to the throne of the royal poet to whom we owe the "King's Quair." It had, indeed, undergone both local and architectural changes in later times, but the old pillar still remained, with its rich Gothic capital, as when the phantom heralds of another world proclaimed from it the doom of the fourth James :—

> "And thundered forth the roll of names
> Foredoomed to Flodden's carnage pile."

It was an eyesore to the "men of taste" of that eighteenth century. To us of this later century it is difficult to realise the idea that, with no special incitement to action, magistrates and citizens appear to have united in a common crusade against the fine old historic monument, rich in associations with every national rejoicing and every national tragedy during three of the most memorable centuries of Scottish history. It stood out of the way, in what was then a broad plaza of the High Street, midway between the straightened crames of the old Luckenbooths and the deformity of the Town-Guard House, which continued for more than a century later to encumber the street. Father Time had not yet beat his scythe into the new pruning-hook of the iron rail, before which so many memorials of the past have since given way. But Edinburgh, hemmed in for a couple of centuries within her old Flodden wall, became suddenly conscious of an intolerable sense of constraint, and so relieved the irritation by knocking down whatever obstruction yielded with least trouble to her fit of violence. The Luckenbooths had stood in the way for centuries, and were allowed to stand ; and, as for the citadel of the Town Guard,—which, according to the author of *The Heart of Midlothian*, might, "to a fanciful imagination, have suggested the idea of a long, black snail crawling up the middle of the High Street, and deforming its beautiful esplanade,"—it was placed by its ungainly utility wholly beyond the sphere of modern taste, and so stood secure in undisputed ugliness. But the ornate gateway at the Netherbow, the picturesque towers of the Flodden wall, and the ancient City Cross, whence, for centuries, royal edicts and "the voice of Scotland's law" had been proclaimed "in glorious trumpet clang," were all swept off the face of the street, and of the earth, as worthless nuisances.

Claudero's muse had work enough in hand. There issued from the press, in good octosyllabic rhymes, "The last speech and dying words of the Cross of Edinburgh, which was hanged, drawn, and quartered, on Monday the 15th of March 1756, for the horrid crime of being an incumbrance to the street." In homely fashion the Cross thus vainly asserts its claims on an unsympathising generation :—

> " I peace and war did oft declare,
>   And roused my country everywhere ;
>   Your ancestors around me walked,
>   Your kings and nobles 'side me talked ;
>   And lads and lasses, with delight,
>   Set tryst with me to meet at night."

Sporting with an oft-repeated play on the name of the ancient Scottish guillotine, it says—

> " On me great men have lost their lives,
>   And for a *Maiden* left their wives.
>   Low rogues likewise oft got a peg
>   With turnip, glaur, or rotten egg ;
>   And when the mob did miss their butt,
>   I was bedaubed like any slut.
>
>   .   .   .   .   .
>
>   I've seen a *Tory* party slain,
>   And *Whigs* exulting o'er the plain ;
>   I've seen again the *Tories* rise,
>   And with loud shouting pierce the skies ;
>   Then crown their king, and chace the Whig
>   From Pentland Hill to Bothwell Brig.
>   I've seen the covenants by all sworn,
>   And likewise seen them burnt and torn ;
>   I neutral stand, as peaceful *Quaker*,
>   With neither side was I partaker."

So the old Cross makes its moan, not without some touches of sly humour : as in its reminiscences of political tergiversations in ticklish times, and its équivoque on the quaint epithet of *The Maiden*, which had so often done its fatal work on that very site. From the day when its axe sheared off the heads of some of the miserable subordinates in the assassination of Rizzio, while the chief agents went scot free, the Maiden and the Cross had been associated in the execution of the Regent Morton, John, Lord Maxwell of Caerlaverock, Patrick, Earl of Orkney, Sir Michael Preston, Sir John Gordon of Haddo, George, second Marquis of Huntly, Archibald, first Marquis of Argyll, and his son, the ninth Earl of Argyll, who catching the spirit of Sir Thomas More, said "it was the sweetest Maiden he had ever kissed !"

> " Lightly for both the bosom's lord did sit
> Upon his throne, unsoftened, undismayed
> By aught that mingled with the tragic scene
> Of pity or fear ; and More's gay genius played
> With the inoffensive sword of native wit,
> Than the bare axe more luminous and keen."[1]

The accounts of the city treasurer and the records of the Privy Council abound with curious items in reference to the Maiden, from "the Compte of the Heding Aix," or cost of its original construction in 1565, onward through the next two centuries, in which from time to time occur such charges as that of June 9 1582, "The Lokman [or public executioner] for scharping the Maden

---

[1] Wordsworth's Ecclesiastical Sonnets, xxii.

vjs. viijd." and a little later a similar charge "for ule and saip to cresche the Madin with," *i.e.* oil and soap to grease the Maiden. The ancient guillotine survives as a prized historical relic among the treasures of the Society of Antiquaries of Scotland ; and, thanks to certain good brothers of that conservative fraternity, and especially to David Laing and James Drummond, R.S.A., the Cross is not even now wholly among the things that were. In its hour of doom, an appreciative friend, Lord Somerville, as has been already noted, rescued the broken pillar which formed its oldest and most characteristic feature, and had it erected on his estate of Drum, near Edinburgh. There, unheeded and well-nigh forgotten, another century passed over it, till, with the better taste of a more refined age, the mutilated fragment was replaced within the sheltering recess between the North Transept and the Albany Chapel of St. Giles' Church ; not without a hope that future restorers may yet rehabilitate the pillar with somewhat of its pristine character as the City Cross.

In spite of its many historical associations the old civic cross has become in a special manner the monument and memorial of Flodden field. Romance and poetry have peopled it with Marmion and Lindsay, De Wilton and Saint Hilda's abbess; while fiction and history contend as to which shall claim the phantom heralds, who, in vision passing nature's law, cited the Scottish king and nobles to appear before their Lord within forty days ; and, as the veritable chronicler of the time tells, "when the field was striken, there was no man escaped that was called in this summons, save one citizen, Mr. Richard Lawsoun, who, "being evil dispossed, ganging in his gallrie, strat fornent the croce, hearing this voyce, thought marvell quhat it should be : so he cryed for his servand to bring him his purs, and tuik ane croun and kest it over the stair, saying, 'I for my pairt appeallis from your summondis and judgement, and takis me to the mercie of God.'"

No record of any event in Scottish history reveals such evidence of universal grief as that of Flodden ; and well it might.   A period of rare intellectual brilliancy, and of widespread national prosperity and progress, was abruptly changed to one of disastrous ruin.   The little kingdom, in its outlying northern nook, had been for a brief period the cynosure of all eyes.   In every chivalrous and manly accomplishment its sovereign was a model to Europe ; while in letters, and above all in poetry, the mantle of Chaucer's genius had passed from the Occleves, Lydgates, and Skeltons of the. south, to become the inheritance of a galaxy of Scottish poets of rare worth.   James I., the poet-king, had dedicated his " Quair " to his " Maisteris, dear Gower and Chaucer," in rhythmical stanzas worthy of the royal pupil of such masters in the divine art. His son and grandson had both been distinguished by poetical and artistic tastes ; and now, under the patronage of James IV., Walter Chepman—the Scottish Caxton,—had set up his printing press ; and Edinburgh, at the time when such doom overshadowed it, was a very nest of nightingales. In the old lodging of the provost of St. Giles, near by the later Parliament House and Westminster Hall of Scotland, Gawin Douglas was busied with his fine vernacular translation of Virgil's Æneid ; or employed himself in elaborating in tuneful numbers his quaint allegories of "King Harte" and the "Palace of Honour." William Dunbar, the poet-laureate, and "Rhymer of Scotland,"—as he is styled in the treasurer's accounts of Henry VII.,—had already written his beautiful allegory of "The Thrissil and the Rois," as the epithalamion of the Princess Margaret, on her espousal to James IV. ; and was following it up with Boccaccian tale, lyric, and satire, according to the humour of his versatile muse. Edinburgh, its court, its lawyers, judges, and ecclesiastics, its merchants, craftsmen, and even its beggars, incite his satirical pen ; while in tenderest elegy he mourns the loss of poets, some of whose names survive to us only in his verse.

Walter Kennedy is known to us chiefly as Dunbar's rival in the characteristic literary duello styled "The Flyting of Dunbar and Kennedy ;"

while "Gentle Roull of Corstorphine," Broun of Dunfermline, Sir John Ross, Stobo, and Quintyne Schaw, are only remembered as objects of his grief in the "Lament for the Makaris." But while elder poets were thus passing away, and, with some, their works perishing with them ; there was already entering on his career the vigorous Scottish dramatist whose bold Interlude, the "Satire of the Three Estates" was, in the following reign, to exercise so marvellous an influence in developing and guiding popular opinion :

> " The flash of that satiric rage,
>   Which, bursting on the early stage,
>   Branded the vices of the age,
>   And broke the keys of Rome."

This famous satirical drama, ere long, so effectually aided the Reformers, that Pinkerton says, truly enough—"Sir David Lindsay was more the reformer of Scotland than John Knox, for he had prepared the ground : John Knox only sowed the seed." In the low valley on the north-west side of the Calton Hill may still be traced, in spite of the changes wrought by the encroaching town, the natural amphitheatre, where, as the old printer Henry Charteris tells us, he sat patiently for nine hours on the banks at Greenside, in the year 1544, to witness the play. But that date reminds us that a new generation had risen up to take the place of those who fell on Flodden Hill, and that

Lindsay is the poet of a later reign ; though, as the youthful page of the prince who succeeded to the vacant throne, he and Dunbar must have often met at Holyrood and Linlithgow.

But Dunbar is pre-eminently an Edinburgh poet. The minutest details of its city life are familiar to him, and its royal court is his highest ideal of all that is pleasant in life. Among the eccentricities of his versatile muse is his profane parody of the Mass for the Dead, in his "Dirige to the King at Stirling," when James IV., in one of his penitential moods, had retired to the Franciscan cloisters there. It serves, by its licentious freedom, to illustrate the excesses against which the bold satirist of the succeeding reign directed the lash of his keen wit with such effect. But its leading idea is the contrast which the festive halls of Holyrood present to Stirling, or any other royal resort :—

> "We that are here in Heaven's glory
> To you that are in Purgatory,
> Commend us in our hearty-wise,—
> I mean we folk in Paradise,
> In Edinburgh with all merryness,
> To you in Striviling in distress,
> Where neither pleasance nor delight is."

The poet contrasts the meagre fare, and the ale— "and that is thin and small,"—which alone graces their table at Stirling, with the invitation he proffers "in Edinburgh's joy" :—

> " To eat swan, crane, partridge, and plover,
>   And every fish that swims in river ;
>   To drink with us the new, fresh wine
>   That grew upon the river of Rhine ;
>   Fresh, fragrant clarets out of France,
>   Of Angiers, and of Orleans,
>   With many a course of great daintie :
>   Say ye Amen, for charitie."

Again and again, in his "Flyting," his "Tydingis fra the Sessioun," and others of his minor poems, Edinburgh is his theme ; but above all, in the satirical address above referred to, "To the Merchantis of Edinburgh," he has preserved a singularly graphic picture of the Scottish capital in the prosperous years immediately preceding the events which compelled the building of the Flodden wall. Here we see once more the High Street crowded with huxters and fishwives, redolent of haddock and skate, and clamorous with the flyting of carlins and pedlars, or the whine of sturdy beggars. The City Cross and Tron are cumbered with retailers of tripe, whelks, curds and milk ; ballad-singers harp on the same old tunes of " Now the day daws," or " Into June "; and so the satirist proceeds with his picturings of city life : minstrels and beggars jostling with tailors, souters, and itinerant vendors of all sorts, amid a babel of street cries, doggerel ballads, and the altercations of rival traders. To complete the picture of what was little less characteristic of Edinburgh three centuries later : we see once more the Luckenbooths clustered like a honeycomb round St. Giles's church, shutting out the light from its aisles ; and the lofty stone tenements, cumbered with fore-stairs, and dark with timber-fronted galleries, as they continued to be—to the delight of artist and antiquary,—when we ourselves were young. It is a stinging satire, designed to shame the merchants of Edinburgh into rescuing their "nobill toun" from abuses which threaten.

> " For laik of reformation
> The commone proffeitt to tyne and fame."

But so little did it avail, that the "buith raw," with its unsavoury alley which formed the approach in the poet's day, through hampering crames and luckenbooths, to the parish church, continued to merit its opprobrious designation, till it was swept away with the whole picturesque deformity in the present century. The poet thus assails the civic deformities, unparalleled elsewhere :—

> " Your stinkand style that standis dirk,
> Haldis the lycht frae your Parroche Kirk,
> Your foir-stairis makis your houses mirk,
> Lyk na countray bot heir at hame :
> Think ye nocht shame,
> So litill polesie to work
> In hurt and sklander of your name !
>
> At your hie Croce, quhair gold and silk
> Sould be, thair is bot crudis and milk ;

> And at your Trone but cokill and wilk,
>   Pansches, pudingis of Jok and Jame.
>   Think ye nocht schame,
>   Sen as the world sayis that ilk
>   In hurt and sclander of your name !
>
> Your common menstrallis has no tune,
> Bot " Now the day dawis," and " Into June,'
> Cuningar men maun serve Sanct Cloun,
>   And nevir to other craftis claim.
>   Think ye nocht schame
>   To hold sic mowaris on the moune
>   In hurt and sclander of your name !
>
> Tailyourris, souteris, and craftis vyle,
> The fairest of your streetis dois fyle ;
> And merchants at the stinkand style
>   Are hamperit in ane honey-came.
>   Think ye nocht schame
>   That ye have neither wit nor wyle
>   To win yourself ane better name ! "

So the poet proceeds with his satirical picturings, full of graphic detail and interesting allusion. But the old tunes of the street minstrels were too good to be hackneyed even by them. In the very year of Flodden, Douglas wrote, in the summer prologue of his Virgil, of the lark upspringing to salute the bright morrow with her song :—

> " Thereto thir birdis singis in their shaws
>   As menstrals play *The jolly day now daws.*"

The song itself, after being long supposed to be lost, was recovered from an ancient MS. in the library of Edinburgh University, and wedded anew to its original music—the "Hey tuttie tattie" of Burns' grand battle song; the plaintive melody of Lady Nairne's "Land o' the Leal." At the period when Dunbar penned the bold satire which recalls to us the Edinburgh of James IV., he appears to have enjoyed as friendly relations with his royal master and his court as Sir David Lindsay afterwards did with his son, James V. He was also in special favour with the Queen, and the popularity of his satires and other lighter pieces, contributed for the entertainment of the King, doubtless led to the multiplication of copies, and so to the preservation of many of those slight effusions; while his choicer works, and even the noble international allegory from his laureate pen, narrowly escaped destruction. "The Queen's reception at Aberdeen," which evidently gives the description of a progress of his royal mistress in which the poet himself bore a part, is another of his literary remains the preservation of which is due to the recovery of a single manuscript. Some of the inestimable waifs of Walter Chepman's printing-press are nearly as unique: for such poems as "The Goldyn Targe," Dunbar's most elaborate allegory, "The Flyting," and his "Lament for the Makaris," were issued by Chepman as mere broadsides, after the fashion perpetuated by Allan Ramsay; and we owe their preservation now to the same fortunate chance to which the recovery of many a prized old ballad is due. It need not therefore surprise us, if even now there were to be recovered in some neglected nook of public or private library, the dirge of the Flodden King, from the same pen to which we are indebted for the " Lament for the Makaris," written when his brother poet, Walter Kennedy, lay at the point of death: and he says of that reaper Death :—

> " Sen he has all my bretheren taen
> He will not let me leive alane ;
> On force I maun his next prey be :
> Timor mortis conturbat me."

The shadow which had passed over his life is abundantly manifested in his writings. The "Golden Targe" ranks with the fine allegory of "The Thrissil and the Rose," as poems of a high class in theme as well as in treatment. But the gay court of the chivalrous king is reflected in many a minor poem. With the freedom of Chaucer and the license of Boccaccio, he tells the tale of " The twa maryit Wemen and the Wedo ;" "The twa Cummeris ;" and, in fabled allegory, doubtless intelligible enough to the courtiers of Holyrood and Dunfermline, of "The Tod and the Lamb." In his "Fenyiet Freir of Tungland" he expatiates with caustic humour on the fortunes of a charlatan of the day. "Of a Dance in the Queen's Chalmer" illustrates in freest fashion the license permitted in the relaxations of the court, when " Dunbar the Makkar " took the floor ; and poet, physician, and lord and lady in waiting, joined with the court fool in the sports of the hour. All show the poet, in unrestrained gaiety, playing his part as court wit and rhymer, in the charmed circle of which James IV. and his English Princess were then the centre.

Again, " The Dance of the Seven Deadly Sins " is a marvellously witty but profane travesty of the services of the church, produced by Dunbar for the enlivenment of the Court of Holyrood, immediately preparatory to the austerities of Lent, which the king observed with such superstitious devoutness. On Fastern's Eve, or Shrove Tuesday, the poet in a dream sees heaven and hell displayed to him ; Mahoun, as the devil is styled, demands a dance on the occasion, and forthwith the seven deadly sins enter and play their part in the court masque or mumming. The impersonations are replete with graphic power. His Pride, Ire, Envy, Couvetyce, Sweirness, Lechery, and Gluttony, are pictured with a realistic aptitude of detail not unworthy of comparison with Spenser's treatment of the same allegorical materials in his " Duessa," or " Pride and her Counsellors," in book i. canto iv. of his *Faerie Queen;* though at times the rough, homely naturalness is no less provocative of comparison with Burns. Here, for example, is Envy:—

> " Next in the dance followed Envy,
> Fill'd full of feud and fellony,
>   Hid malice and despite ;
> For privy hatred that traitor trembléd ;
> Him followéd many freik dissembléd
>   With feigned wordés quite ;
> And flatterers into menis faces ;
> And back-biters in secret places,
>   To lie that had delight ;
> And rounders of false leasingis.
> Alas ! that courts of noble kingés
>   Of them can never be quite."

In the closing stanza Mahoun calls for a Highland pageant ; " Syne ran a fiend to fetch M'Fadyen, far northward in a neuk," and a piece of rough satire follows, equal to the freest humour of Burns ; or of some of the most sportive license of the Jacobite muse.

It seems inconceivable that one whose minor poems—his " Complaint to the King," his " Remonstrance," his " Petition," his humorous address "That he was John Thomsounis Man," etc.—abound with allusions to the kindly freedom and familiarity of intercourse which he enjoyed with his royal master, should have remained unmoved by the great sorrow, when the flower of Scotland's nobles were " a' wede away." His muse was not less responsive to tender than to humorous impulses. The world's instability, and its vanity, impress him deeply, in thoughtful hours ; and he writes with keenest feeling of the transitory nature of all earthly joys :

> " Sin' earthly joy abidis never,
>   Work for the joy that lastis ever ;
>   For other joy is all but vain :
>   All earthly joy returns in pain."

In his latest supplement to Dunbar's poems, printed after an interval of thirty-two years, David Laing remarks on the extraordinary fact that not even the slightest allusion to Dunbar has ever been recovered of a date subsequent to the partial payment of his pension in May 1513; and he accordingly hazards the conjecture that he accompanied the king to Flodden and shared in his fate. There were churchmen enough among the king's attendants, including his own natural son, Alexander Stewart, Archbishop of St. Andrews, to make the presence of the poet with his royal master possible enough. As to the minor poems ascribed to Dunbar, referring to incidents of a later date, Mr. Laing conceives they can have no weight in settling the question ; as it is possible enough they are erroneously assigned to him. But at the same time, it has to be borne in remembrance that in so far as policy guided his laureate pen there was little in the circumstances of the court, subsequent to the nominal accession of James V., to stimulate him to any public lament for his royal master. The tone of despondency with which his religious poems are imbued, accompanied as it is with an earnest devotional feeling so much in contrast to his lighter effusions purposely written for that king and his court, is far more suggestive of the poet having lived on into the troubled period which succeeded his death, and shared in the reverses by which his brother poet Douglas was driven into exile.

The only direct allusion to the death of the king to be found in the minor poems ascribed to Dunbar occurs in the address to the Queen Dowager. Unhappily, the loss sat all too lightly on the widowed queen. Her griefs—already wept in the solitude of Linlithgow's bower,—invited no tender elegy over that husband whose unburied remains she did not trouble herself to reclaim. On the 9th of September 1513 James IV. lay dead on Flodden Hill ; in the following August his widow wedded the young Earl of Angus, whose father's death on the same fatal field had thus opened up to him pride and fortune, in the midst of such unparalleled national disaster. We must therefore bear in remembrance who the widow is to whom Dunbar, or other courtly laureate, addresses the verses in which he thus ventures to allude to her dead lord :—

> " I me commend with all humility
>   Unto thy beauty, blissful and benign,
>   To whom I am, and shall aye servant be,
>   With steadfast heart and faithful ; true meneing

> Unto the Dead withouten departing ;
> For whois sake I shall my pen address
>   Songes to make for thy recomforting,
> That thou may live in joy and lustiness.
>
> O fair sweet blossom, now in beauty's flower,
>   Unfaded both of colour and virtúe,
> Thy noble Lord that dead has done devoir,
>   Fade not with weeping thy visage fair of hue.
>   O lovesome, lusty Lady, wise and true,
> Cast out all care, and comfort do increace ;
>   Exile all sighing, on thy servant rue ;
> Devoid langor, and live in lustiness."

The national calamity was borne by all with exemplary courage ; but its bitterness was reserved for others than the widowed queen, who only a few years before had been welcomed by Dunbar in his noblest verse, in which, in graceful allegory he pictured all nature joining in the wish, "Christ thee conserve from all adversity." The sceptre had passed to an infant's hand. A Parliament was summoned forthwith, but it, too, embodied the inexperience of a younger generation. Twelve earls, and thirteen lords of Parliament—the flower of the Scottish nobility,—had fought and fallen around their king ; among whom was Archibald Douglas, Earl of Angus, the Provost of Edinburgh, whose heir so speedily found a consort in the royal widow. The magistrates of the city had mostly shared the fate of their chief and king, but neither the manhood of Edinburgh nor of Scotland had perished. There is a fine courageous simplicity embodied in the proclamation which the temporary civic rulers issued on the first rumour of disaster. The magistrates, "in respect that they were to pass to the army," had appointed George of Touris and four others with full jurisdiction in their absence ; and on the very day after the battle they issued a proclamation, that "Forasmuch as there is a great rumour now lately rissen within the town, touching our Sovereign Lord and his army, of the which we understand there is come no verity as yet," they straightly command all citizens capable of bearing arms to have their weapons and armour ready, and to muster at the ringing of the common bell, for the defence of the town against the invader ; while the women are warned not to be seen on the street clamouring and crying, but to repair to the church, and offer up prayer for the national welfare.

The poet of the new reign is Sir David Lindsay, and he too admitted Edinburgh to a share of the humour of his caustic muse. But in this he had a graver purpose than either the pastimes of the court or the mirth of the citizens. With results which have not even now exhausted their influence, he directed his satiric shafts against "the great idolatry, and manifest abomination" of Edinburgh's special festival, when annually, upon St. Giles's day, the statue of their patron saint, and with it the veritable arm-bone of St. Giles, was borne in procession through the streets. John Knox by and by followed in like vigorous prose, in his assault on the same object of popular acclaim: till at length the fickle mob, in 1558, in a new fever-fit of reforming zeal, soused their patron saint in the foulest pool of the Nor' Loch; and only four years later the magistrates ordered St. Giles's silver-work, ring, and jewels, the reliquary for his arm-bone, and the vestments for his image, to be converted into money for the repair of the church.

Times had strangely changed since that so recent date when the penitential king, James IV. could be scared in the midst of his Lenten vigils by the apparitions of St. Andrew and St. John; or warned of his doom by phantom heralds from the spirit world. The beautiful ruins of Linlithgow palace overhang the little lake behind the burgh town, distant only fifteen miles from Edinburgh; and beside it still stands the fine collegiate church, the scene of one of the best authenticated ghost stories on record. There, in St. Katherine's aisle, on a fair June day, in the year 1515, while the king was engaged in penitential devotions on the anniversary of his father's assassination, the phantom apostle appeared before him, and warned him of his fate, and of that of all who followed him, if he went forth to war. "I heard say," says the contemporary chronicler, that "Sir David Lindsay,

Lyon Herald, and John Inglis, the Marshall, who were at that time young men, and special servants to the king's grace, thought to have taken this man, but they could not, for he vanished away betwixt them and was no more seen."

In olden times, when the poet Barbour described the favourite palace of the Scottish Jameses, it was but a "peel mikel and stark," a stronghold, and not a palace; as best suited such troubled times. But its site was attractive; its distance from the capital rendered it of easy access on horseback; and when James IV. made it his favourite resort, it became a palace worthy of its noblest royal occupants. There history and romance contend for their share in its old memories, and poetry lingers over the sculptured bower where "the Rose" of Dunbar's beautiful allegory "wept the weary day;" while her inconstant lord listened, in Holyrood or elsewhere, to the syren voice of Lady Heron. There, in the following reign, Lindsay played his lute, and penned some of his free-spoken wit and wisdom for behoof of their too early crowned son; and there at Epiphany, in the year 1539, his famous "Satire of the Three Estates" was enacted by royal command before the King and his Queen, Mary of Guise. There also their hapless daughter, Mary Stuart, was born; and in later times her son varied its palatial architecture with additions in the quaint ornate renaissance characteristic of himself and his age, in order to adapt it for the reception of his own Queen, Anne of Denmark. To him also was due the elaborately sculptured fountain, the ruins of which still adorn the centre of the quadrangle; and which in our own day Prince Albert reproduced in facsimile to adorn the courtyard in front of Holyrood Palace.

The fate of the ancient palace of Linlithgow came at last in inglorious fashion. On the night of the 17th of January 1745, General Hawley paused there in his retreat before the Highland forces of Prince Charles Edward, of whom only the day before he had expressed the utmost contempt. He quartered his demoralised troops in the chambers of the palace, where they forthwith proceeded to kindle blazing fires on the hearths. A lady of the Livingstone family, who occupied some of the royal apartments, expostulated with the General on their reckless proceedings; and receiving only a contemptuous rejoinder, she retorted with spirited irony that she could run away from fire as fast as himself! She took horse, accordingly, for Edinburgh, but ere she dismounted the palace was in flames, and by the following night there remained only a blackened ruin. Time has since done its work. The roofless walls, mellowed with the tints of another century, seem to harmonise with the historic associations which they awaken. It is a lovely spot for a summer's ramble ; and now that the railway has placed it within easy access, it seems but as a suburban appendage to Holyrood, as in the olden time when the court was wont to pass in royal cavalcade from one to the other.